Laura Marney was born and sometimes lives in Glasgow. She holds a part-time post at Glasgow University. Many of her short stories have been published in magazines and anthologies or broadcast on the radio and television. She is the author of three previous novels: *No Wonder I Take a Drink, Nobody Loves a Ginger Baby* and *Only Strange People go to Church*, all published by Black Swan. Although she has lived in Barcelona she insists all of the characters and situations described here, or at least nearly all, are fictional.

D1150781

www.rbooks.co.uk

Also by Laura Marney

NO WONDER I TAKE A DRINK
NOBODY LOVES A GINGER BABY
ONLY STRANGE PEOPLE GO TO CHURCH

and published by Black Swan

MY BEST FRIEND
HAS ISSUES

Laura Marney

BLACK SWAN

TRANSWORLD PUBLISHERS
61–63 Uxbridge Road, London W5 5SA
A Random House Group Company
www.rbooks.co.uk

MY BEST FRIEND HAS ISSUES
A BLACK SWAN BOOK: 9780552773195

First publication in Great Britain
Black Swan edition published 2008

A CIP catalogue record for this book
is available from the British Library.

Addresses for Random House Group Ltd companies outside the UK
can be found at: www.randomhouse.co.uk
The Random House Group Ltd Reg. No. 954009

The Random House Group Limited supports The Forest Stewardship
Council (FSC), the leading international forest certification organization.
All our titles that are printed on Greenpeace approved FSC certified
paper carry the FSC logo. Our paper procurement policy can be
found at www.rbooks.co.uk/environment

Typeset in 11/13½pt Giovanni Book by
Kestrel Data, Exeter, Devon.
Printed in the UK by
CPI Cox & Wyman, Reading, RG1 8EX.

2 4 6 8 10 9 7 5 3 1

For Barcelona

Acknowledgement

Laura Marney gratefully acknowledges the support of the Hawthornden International Writers' Retreat.

Chapter 1

What did I know about life? A wee heifer like me, a 22-year-old no-mates stay-at-home from the rump end of Cumbernauld? What did I even know about sex? Never mind drugs, or violence, or murder.

After I'd been there a few days I sent a postcard with views of the city: Gaudí chimneys, weird modern sculptures, the Olympic stadium. *Dear Lisa and Lauren*, it said, *Weather lovely. Recuperating nicely and working on tan. Had to buy new clothes (size twelve too big!). Enjoying sangria on La Rambla. Don't know if you'd like it here. The hot weather would be a nightmare for your athlete's foot and intimate itching – think of the thigh chafing! Nasty.* Hasta la vista, *Alison x x x*

And then I went back to flat-hunting.

I was a little anxious going into flats alone. For all I knew there could have been a psycho behind the door with a hessian sack and a packet of cable ties. The girl showing me this room was called Montse and looked about twenty-five. She was living there on her own with a baby. She spoke very little English but she was very accomplished at the word 'no'. No boyfriends, no smoking, no alcohol, no eating except in the kitchen, no staying out late, no TV after 8 p.m., it would wake the baby. This lecture was delivered in a whisper, the baby was sleeping.

It was a nice flat. The bedroom she offered was small but clean. Not luxurious but, unlike most of the other flats I'd seen, within my tight budget. It was clean. The fact that Montse didn't speak much English could be a plus point. I'd learn Spanish quicker, I'd have to. At least to begin with, conversation would be limited. Apart from no telly after 8 p.m. it would be the same as living with Mum.

The baby woke up and started wailing. Montse's face changed to a martyred expression. Did my arrival wake the baby? She came back into the room with the crying infant in her arms and repeated what she'd said, in case I didn't get it the first time: No boyfriends (boyfrens, she pronounced it), and then again in Spanish just to be sure: *hombres*, no.

The old me would just have taken the room. But the new slimline me knew there was more to Barcelona than this. With this figure, in this city, I was planning on having plenty of boyfrens.

'No thank you,' I told Montse, although I knew she didn't understand. 'If I'd wanted to live like a nun I'd have joined a convent.'

The next and final flat for the day was in Raval, a dodgy part of the city. I knew this because I was already staying there in a cheap hostel. Raval was the immigrant part of town: poor, dirty and run-down. Nearly everyone I saw there wore Arab or Asian dress. The narrow lanes were choked with garbage. Short-skirted high-heeled girls stood on corners. Shifty-looking men sat watching them from kitchen chairs on the pavement. There was nothing like this in Cumbernauld.

10

Despite the lax morals and hygiene of Raval, this next flat was the most expensive of all. I was hot and knackered and nearly didn't go, but it was on the way back to the hostel. If I did move in at least I wouldn't have far to lug my rucksack. And, as I navigated my way through the dog-shittered streets, I remembered that the Internet advert for this place had sounded the most promising. For a start it had none of the weird syntax I now realized was Spanish poorly translated into English, *'we look for ladies for to share apartament'* or *'to wash the clothes no is problem.'* This advert was obviously written by a native English speaker. *'Room to let for girl/guy, whatever. I'm single again so this is back to being the party apartment. Let the partying begin!'* It wasn't clear if the person placing the ad was a girl or a guy but it sounded fun. Even if I couldn't afford the room, maybe I'd get invited to the parties. It would be a way to meet people and make friends, another thing I was determined to do.

It was a door-entry system, upmarket for Raval. I pressed the buzzer for 4B and waited. Nobody answered. I checked the address and my watch, 1 p.m., right on time. I buzzed again, maybe he or she had been in the toilet. Still no answer. Perhaps they'd popped out for a minute. I waited ten minutes, leaning into the door to let people pass on the narrow pavement, and buzzed once more but nobody came.

They must have already let the room. Fair enough, but they should at least have the decency to tell me. What about the parties? They could still invite me. With the flat of my hand I pressed all the buzzers at once, pressing out an SOS dot dot dot dash dash dash dot dot dot.

Mayday.

It worked. At least three flats buzzed me in. Whether

4B was one of them I had no idea but I'd soon find out.

Inside the windowless stairwell I made for the light switch and pressed it but although I could hear the timer ticking, the light didn't come on. There was no lift in the building either, that was unusual. I'd have to walk up but it wasn't totally dark, I could see flights of stairs above me on the open staircase. I knew from my previous two days flat-hunting that there would be a light switch on every floor.

Halfway up the first flight my foot skidded on what I thought must be a banana skin or dog poo. Surely people didn't let their dogs shit *inside* the building? I looked down at my feet and it seemed I was standing in some kind of thick fluid which threatened to swamp my flip-flops. I curled my toes, lifted my foot and looked for somewhere dry to put it. There was nowhere, the next steps were covered in it too. I held on to the banister handrail as I made my way carefully up the stairs. It felt, through my thin rubber sole, like the liquid was viscous, like skidding on olive oil. I slipped and toppled forward, falling on to my hands and knees. For a moment the pain of absorbing the shock in my bones and the sting on my skin didn't let me think about anything else. But when it did, when the sensation faded, there was a worse one. Now I knew what was dripping from my forearms and shins. It was blood.

I scrambled to my feet and tried to clean it off in fast panicky swipes, as if I was trying to flick away a cockroach crawling on me: horrified to touch it but desperate to be rid of it. Then I noticed the boy.

He was lying at the bottom of the next flight of stairs. His head didn't make sense. It was at a weird angle, his ear touching his shoulder. I tilted my ear towards my shoulder to see if it was possible but it wouldn't reach. The blood was coming from the boy.

From this side he was handsome, with big brown surprised eyes and dark curly hair, but when I saw him straight on, the other side of his face looked as if someone had taken a sledgehammer to it. It was pulped mush, so battered it was difficult to make out his other eye. But it was there, almost buried in torn skin. Inside his crushed skull, his eye was intact.

It must have been shock, but at that moment the fact that he had two eyes was important to me. Like when a baby's born and its fingers and toes are counted by the midwife. He might only be a gruesome corpse but I felt better knowing he had the regulation quantity of eyes.

I didn't touch him, thank God. Later I'd be thankful for that. I heard a door opening on the floor above. I panicked, I turned and fled down the stairs, out of the building and on to the street. Straight into a crowd of Asian men.

They stared at me. I looked down. In the glaring sunlight they could see my arms and legs splattered in bright red blood. They were all talking, talking at me, asking questions, talking excitedly between themselves. I didn't understand. Their voices got louder as they crowded around me, shouting, demanding. They were angry. I looked back and saw my flip-flop shoeprints, bloody and incriminating, lead out of the building and straight to me.

13

Chapter 2

I wanted to run but the men were crowded round me, jabbering at me in Spanish and some other language, maybe Arabic. They towered over me, I couldn't see beyond them. Someone put a hand on my shoulder, a heavy hand, powerful enough to snap my skinny little body like a popadom. I felt warm breath on my neck. I don't know when I started screaming, maybe it was when I saw the boy, but I now realized I wasn't the only one screaming. Somewhere behind me there was another female voice shouting something in Spanish.

'¡*Dejala, cabrones!*' and then, 'Get away from her, you fucking assholes!'

An American voice.

A tall thin girl rushed at the man who had his hand on me and delivered a swift kick to his balls. He doubled over, going down with his hands between his legs. And then I was running down an alleyway with her. The girl sprinted easily in her rope wedge heels. Behind her I had an impression of thin bare shoulder blades flashing as she ran, long graceful legs covering the ground easily. My own short legs were no match; I couldn't keep up with her. Then she slowed, turned and smiled. She

14

extended her hand towards me. I didn't know who she was, I'd never seen her before in my life but she'd rescued me. She had appeared from nowhere, like some kind of angel of deliverance, and taken me out of that hellish place.

Gratefully I put my hand in hers. Her swift pace carried me through busy side streets full of rubbish stacks, men in doorways, parked motorbikes, dog shit, toddlers, old women, more rubbish. I held tight to her hand as we ran. After a few lung-busting minutes I felt like my heart was going to explode out of my chest. I pulled on the girl's hand like a brake. We stopped in a quiet lane. We leaned against old stone walls, our chests heaving. Through breathless gasps she asked me, 'Are you OK?'

I nodded.

'You sure? You're covered in blood.'

She rummaged in her bag and pulled out paper handkerchiefs and put them in my hand.

I nodded again. 'I'm fine, honestly.'

'What the hell happened back there?'

'I fell.'

'You fell?'

'On the stairs, they were slippy, I just slipped.'

I knew I probably wasn't making sense. She took the hankies out of my hand and began wiping the blood from my arms and legs.

'You have a cut under your knee and you've scratched both arms but it looks much worse than it is.'

'I just slipped, it's nothing,' I said.

'Jeez, you're quite a bleeder. We need to clean out those lacerations.'

'Are you a doctor?'

'Me? Are you kidding?' she laughed.

She didn't look like a doctor. She had shoulder-length blond hair, pale skin and a wide full-lipped mouth. She had American standard-issue straight white teeth and was thin everywhere except for her large shapely breasts. She wasn't exactly beautiful, her face was slightly too long, her mouth too big, but she looked healthy, abundantly healthy. An all-American girl. She looked like she could have been a cheerleader except that her super-sized breasts gave her an un-American stoop. She was slightly hunched, curled up, like a new leaf that hasn't fully opened yet.

'I thought those guys were trying to murder you.'

'No, I fell, that's all.'

'But you were screaming!'

'I just got a fright. They saw me and crowded round, I couldn't get away. I panicked, I'm really sorry.'

'Hey, don't be sorry. My bad, I'm the one that kicked the guy's balls.' She laughed.

I laughed too.

'Poor guy was probably trying to help you and I came along and smashed his nuts. He won't be having sex anytime soon.'

'He'll probably never have sex again. He'll be a eunuch,' I said.

'Yeah but he'll still have his tongue. He won't be completely useless.'

She laughed again. She seemed to like this kind of talk.

'Thanks very much for rescuing me.'

'*De nada*,' she said, waving her hand like she was swatting a fly. 'I only hope the poor guy isn't crippled for life. Listen, let's go to a bar and wash up, you don't want that getting infected.'

She took me into a dark underground bar. From outside it looked nothing, but inside it was like the headquarters of a comic-book villain. It was a huge cave, filled with noisy young people.

La Oveja Negra it said above the door. 'The Black Sheep,' she translated. 'The washroom's back here.'

The cuts on my arms and legs were minimal, scratches really, but I was worried. The dead boy's blood had mingled with mine. With my health record that was the last thing I needed. She filled the sink with hot water and poured in perfume from a bottle in her handbag. 'The alcohol will kill the bugs,' she told me.

'Lovely smell,' I said, wincing as she dabbed the solution on my arm.

'Yeah, it's Paris Hilton.'

I flinched. 'Doesn't that stuff cost a fortune?'

'Hell no,' she laughed, 'and it makes a pretty good antiseptic.'

She must be loaded.

'Come on,' she said once I'd got cleaned up, 'I could use a drink.'

She left me at the table while she went to the bar and ordered drinks in what sounded like fluent Spanish. She made out as if she didn't know that the boys at the pool table were staring at her, or if she did she didn't care. She brought back a tray with glasses of water, a jug of garnet-coloured sangria and a basket of popcorn.

'I'm sorry,' I said, 'I don't know your name.'

'Chloe,' she smiled, a big wide smile that took up most of her face. I was forced to admit that she was, in fact, lovely.

'Thanks, Chloe. I'm Alison.'

17

'Nice to meet you. You're English, right?'

'No, Scottish.'

She made a face. 'Sorry.'

'It's an easy mistake to make.'

'I'm American,' Chloe said. 'You guessed, huh? I've lived in about ten countries but I'm from California. My mom lives there, I guess it's home. Hollywood, Disneyland, all that shit. I'm sure you know what it's like. You've probably been there.'

I shook my head.

'Which part of Scotland are you from, Alison?'

'Cumbernauld. It's just a town, near Glasgow.'

Neither place seemed to register with her.

'It's quite near Edinburgh too.'

'Yeah, Edinboro.' She nodded. 'I haven't been to Scotland yet but it's on my list.'

'Well when you go, stick to Edinburgh and maybe the Highlands, they're the best bits. That's usually what Americans do.'

'OK. Thanks for the tip,' she laughed.

There was a silence. I drank most of my glass of water and didn't want any more.

'I suppose we both have time to see the world,' she said. 'We're about the same age, aren't we? How old are you?'

'Twenty-two. You?'

'Twenty-three,' she groaned.

Chloe was only a year older than me yet she'd lived in all those countries. She was taller, slimmer, with a better figure than me, if you liked that skinny big-breasted thing, which everyone did. She was amazing.

'How long are you gonna be in Barcelona?' she asked.

18

I shrugged. 'I'm not sure. I came to live here.'

'Good for you, Alison,' she said with a slow impressed smile. 'All right.' She poured us both large glasses of sangria. '*Enhorabuena*. Congratulations.'

It was probably raining in Cumbernauld right now. Lovely damp Scottish rain. If I was at home I'd be eating a crisps and fish-finger sandwich in front of *Richard & Judy*, shouting out the answers to *You Say We Pay*, pressing crumbs on to my fingers and licking them. I'd be looking out the rain-blurred window waiting for Mum to come back from the bakery and start making dinner. After seeing that poor bashed-head boy, after lying in his blood with him, Cumbernauld and rain and Mum was all I wanted.

Even before I got here I kind of knew something was going to happen. It was inevitable. My life had always been blighted, maybe it was always going to be. Might as well go home and accept it. Anyway, I was never going to find an affordable flat that didn't have a dead body draped on the stairwell. It wasn't fair. Lucky people, rich beautiful girls like Chloe who'd lived in ten countries, and had fabulous breasts, these things didn't happen to them. They didn't spend their lives dodging death.

'You?' I asked. 'How long are you here for?'

'Oh, you know, kinda the same, indefinitely.'

I lifted my glass. '*Enorbor . . .*'

'*Enhorabuena*,' she corrected me.

'Congratulations.'

We laughed and clinked glasses and took long swigs of sangria. Maybe in toasting her some of her good luck would rub off on me. The sangria tasted good, fruity and potent.

'Whoa!' I said, putting the glass down. 'That's strong. What's in it?'

'The usual stuff: red wine, fruit juice, but the real kicker's the gin. They use kick-ass gin here.'

'Right,' I nodded, smacking my lips and taking another slug. I wasn't supposed to drink at all for six months and after that only in moderation. Extreme moderation, Dr Collins had warned me, but the drink had already gone to my head.

The sangria relaxed me. Maybe I shouldn't rush home at the first hurdle, although Bashed-Head Boy was indisputably a pretty big hurdle. What if the murderer had seen me? Or if the police thought I killed him? There were plenty of witnesses who saw me covered in his blood. It wasn't fair. That boy was nothing to do with me. But I'd come to Barcelona to dwell, not to dwell on things. Dwelling on things wasn't healthy, I knew that better than anyone.

'My bad,' Chloe said, 'I totally misread the situation. But you know, guys come here all the time on bachelor weekends, the city's full of them. They get beered up and go wild. All I know is, I see a bunch of guys messing with a girl half their size and it makes me crazy. I thought you were Catalan.'

'Don't dwell on it, Chloe. It wasn't your bad, it was mine. The whole thing was my fault. I shouldn't have screamed like that. You thought I was what?'

'Catalan. You look like them, the same auburn hair. They dye theirs but yours looks real, is it?'

'Yes, but . . . that's why you rescued me? Because I have auburn hair?'

'No, I thought you were from around here! It's an easy mistake. Jeez.'

20

Chloe's shoulders hunched and she curled in on herself. I had offended her. Not knowing how to undo it, I sat with a stupid grin on my face.

'Right,' she laughed, 'I get it, you're joking. British sense of humour. I see a twinkle in your British green eyes.'

Relieved, I laughed too.

'You have great eyes,' she continued.

'Cheers.'

'Sorry, I didn't mean to embarrass you. You probably get that all the time.'

I nodded as if yes, I did get it all the time, but it wasn't true. Apart from old ladies on the bus telling me and then using it as an excuse to launch into how sick or lonely they were, I very rarely heard it. *'Oh, you've got lovely emerald eyes, hen, just like my Jack, God rest him. I miss him, so I do. But Jack's the lucky one, I wish God would take me.'*

'D'you speak Spanish or Catalan?'

There was that word again.

'Catalan?'

'The language of this region, Catalonia.'

'Eh, not yet, sorry.'

'Hell, Spanish is easy, you'll pick that up in a coupla weeks.'

'Really?'

'Sure.'

I wasn't.

'How long have you been here?' I asked her.

'Coupla months. You?'

'Coupla days. I arrived on Tuesday.'

'Where's your apartment?'

'Eh, I don't have one yet, I'm in a hostel in Raval just now.'

21

That was a thought. How could I go back to the hostel? I wouldn't be able to set foot in Raval ever again.

'Alison,' Chloe said, leaning forward across the table with her arms folded and a grin on her face, 'do you believe in karma?'

I nodded.

'Because maybe we were meant to meet today. Yeah, go ahead and smile, but it so happens we can help each other out.'

I didn't know I was smiling.

'You need somewhere to stay and I need someone to look after my apartment. For a few days. I'll be out of town three days, probably not more, but that should give you time to find your own place.'

I waited for her to continue but she'd stopped talking. I didn't say anything.

'Hey, no pressure. I totally understand if you don't want to.'

'Where is your apartment?'

'It's in Gòtic.'

'Is that near Raval?'

'No, I'm at the opposite end of Gòtic, going into Barceloneta, but it's a sweet little apartment, it's on the roof.'

'OK.'

'OK? You'll move in?'

'Yes please.'

'OK, excellent! Wanna come round now and check it out? I might have a Band-Aid for your arm.'

'OK.'

As we moved away from the table I staggered and narrowly missed stumbling into a boy carrying a tray of drinks. If Dr Collins could see me now.

'Whoa!' said Chloe. 'Sangria overload! We need to get you some coffee. Let's get out of here.'

I nodded carefully, not wanting my befuddlement to show. I didn't know if I could trust her. After what had happened, I didn't know if it was safe to trust anyone in Barcelona.

He was lying on me, his breath coming in loud gasps.

I was crying again.

'Shh,' he said, 'it's OK, pet. Don't worry, it'll be OK.'

He was too heavy, crushing my chest, I couldn't breathe. I tried to push him off, to wriggle out from under him but there was nowhere to go. If I moved he woke up and moaned, then I was too scared to move.

'Alison, don't tell your mum,' he said, as if that was the important thing, 'promise.'

Our faces so close together, I couldn't look at him. I knew he didn't want me to look at him. He started crying.

'I won't,' I said, 'I promise.'

Chapter 3

I let myself be led out of the dungeon bar into the sunlight. Chloe walked me briskly across La Rambla and into the maze of narrow streets of Barri Gòtic. This was a much nicer part of town.

At ground level the streets were corridors of bars, restaurants and shops. The shops sold mostly tourist stuff: fans, hats, rails of kiddies' flamenco dresses, Barcelona football strips, wee models of the cathedral, fridge-magnet dragons. Tourists clogged the confined space, taking photos. Bored shopkeepers hung about in doorways, keeping an eye on their kids playing in the street. Chloe drew my attention to a shop with a Day-Glo sign in English. 'Look!' she said laughing. *'Very cheap presents!'*

She caught me when I stumbled, my foot sliding out of my flip-flop on the cobbles. I managed to avoid knocking over the stacked cardboard boxes full of rotting vegetables and other folded cardboard boxes. Water occasionally dripped on our heads from washing strung on balconies above. At street level there was a potent smell of urine, but it was overlaid with the heavy chemical perfume of fresh laundry. We were at the bottom of a deep canyon. I had no idea where I was.

Chloe stopped outside an old building. She turned a key and we passed through a small wooden door within a much bigger wooden door.

'I'm sorry, the elevator isn't working. It hasn't worked since I got here.' Chloe smiled apologetically. 'We'll have to walk.'

She tried the light switch on the wall, popping it in and out three or four times.

'Shit, the light's bust too now. We'll have to feel our way upstairs,' she said in a thrilled voice. 'It's kinda spooky.'

I hung back.

'It's OK, it's only this one that's out. If you're nervous wait here and I'll get it on the next floor.'

She sprinted up to the next landing and turned the light on. I could now see all the stairs. There was nothing on them.

Chloe lived on the roof beyond the fifth floor. Five and a half flights of stairs. I was puffed out as she showed me in.

'Sit down and relax, get your breath back, I'll find the Band-Aid.'

It was a wee cottage plonked on top of a block of flats. A penthouse. It wasn't spacious; the kitchen and lounge areas combined were smaller than my bedroom in Cumbernauld. The walls were squinty, there were cracks in the plaster and bits had fallen off. The walls were painted with copies of famous paintings; I recognized one that I knew from a gallery in Glasgow. When I was nine I'd done a project on this painting when we'd gone there on a school trip.

As she rifled through drawers looking for the plasters I asked Chloe, 'Is that *Christ of St John of the Cross*?'

'Hey, you know Dalí, I'm impressed. I love his stuff.'

'Mmmm, yeah,' I said, nodding.

Some of the cracks and holes in the wall were incorporated into the artwork. There was one hole that had been filled with brightly coloured mosaic tiles and shaped like a dragon. I recognized that as the famous Gaudí lizard from Parc Güell, I remembered seeing it in my Barcelona guidebook.

'Gaudí,' I said simply.

I wasn't doing too badly. I knew more about art than I thought.

'Did you do this?' I asked. 'Are you an artist?'

I'd never met an artist before.

'Yeah, kinda, it's what I do.'

I didn't know much but I knew what I liked and I thought these were great.

'You're really talented.'

'Aw, stop,' she said, but I knew she was pleased.

'You've made the most of this place, it's brilliant.'

'Yeah, thanks. I totally fell in love with this apartment as soon as I saw it, even if it does have roaches.'

'Roaches?'

'Cockroaches, *cucarachas*.'

'How big are they?'

'Oh don't worry, just normal size. Don't you have cock-roaches in Scotland?'

'No, it's too cold, I think. Is this your own place?' I asked, wanting to change the subject from cock-roaches.

'No. I was gonna buy it but there was a problem with the real-estate survey. The building has subsidence, but most of Barri Gòtic has, it's real old. The Aged P wouldn't release the funds.'

'The Aged Pea?'

'The Aged Parent. My dad. He's such an asshole, he just doesn't get it that I love this place *because* it's cracked, it has character. I only have a short rental lease but I'm never gonna leave this apartment.'

'Quite right,' I agreed, 'it's lovely.'

She had found the Elastoplast now.

'Come over here and I'll put these on you.'

She indicated that I should sit on the couch. She knelt on the floor and dressed my cuts. I'd been out all day running around in the heat, I was dirty and smelly but she was determined to put plasters on both my arms and legs.

'So, you're going away for a few days,' I said, 'where are you off to?'

She pushed her breath through closed lips. 'I have to go to Berlin.'

'That sounds great.'

'No, I have to go see the Aged P. I have to spend the Fourth of July holiday with him. It's a duty call.' She pronounced it 'dootie'.

'If I don't check in with him he stops my allowance. He likes to keep me on a tight leash. Fucking pervert.'

Alarm must have registered on my face because then she said, 'No, I don't mean like that. I mean he's a control freak. I'm twenty-three for Chrissake. I inherited my grandfather's estate when I was twenty-one but my dad told the court it wouldn't be good for my health. So now, thanks to Aged P, I'm dirt poor. I mean, hello? Like, being a multimillionaire is *bad* for your health?'

'Are you mega-rich then, like Paris Hilton?'

28

'Paris Hilton doesn't have to live on a lame allowance like a little kid, it's embarrassing.'

'That must be tough.'

As soon as it was out I realized she might think I was taking the piss, but I hadn't meant it that way.

'Yup,' she said cheerfully, 'I suppose there are worse things.'

She finished putting the Elastoplasts on and eased my leg down to the floor. She had a very gentle touch.

'There you go, all done.'

'Thanks very much, Chloe.'

I sat back in the huge couch piled with luxurious throws. There was an enormous plasma TV and on the shelf beneath, a digital frame flashing up different photos every few seconds. All the photos were of the same person. At first I thought I recognized her, a film star I couldn't quite bring to mind, but I was mistaken. They were simply high-quality photographs of a very beautiful woman. These weren't snaps from the family album, they'd been taken by a professional photographer in a proper studio. In every shot the woman was alone. She was stunning: long blond hair, pale blue eyes, full lips, perfectly proportioned cheekbones, nose and chin. Some of the shots were slightly soft focus but even in the close-ups she had not a line or wrinkle or sag, and she was pretty old, she must have been over forty at least.

'Is this your mum, Chloe?'

'Yup, that's my mom.'

She sounded proud.

'You look like her. She's beautiful.'

'Yeah, well, she gets her looks from me, but thanks, I'll be sure and pass her the compliment,' she said, getting up from her knees. 'You look like you could use some coffee.'

Chloe gathered the bits of backing paper from the plasters off the floor and went back to the kitchen. She immediately returned and flicked a switch that began a low hum.

'Thank God for air con, huh?' she smiled.

The air was suddenly noticeably fresher.

'Help yourself,' she said, 'check the place out.'

Compared to the other flats I'd seen in Barcelona, this place was fabulous. The bedroom had a huge bed, king-size or even larger. It was the biggest room in the flat and the most untidy. There were three empty glasses on the bedside table and the easy chair was buried under a pile of clothes, but it was a great room. There was what looked like an antique wooden bedroom suite with a massive carved mirror. On the unmade bed lay a small back-pack with its contents spilling out: pants, a bra and two crumpled tops. Beside that, an airline ticket. I could hear Chloe banging about in the kitchen so I risked a quick peek and saw that the ticket was made out to Miss Chloe Taylor. It was for Berlin. First class. One way.

Chapter 4

My inspection of the flat only took a few minutes but I was already looking forward to moving in here, even if it was only for three days.

'Take a look at the terrace,' Chloe called from the kitchen. 'I'll bring the coffee out there.'

The terrace was three times the size of the flat. Sliding glass patio doors led out to the roof from the living room. There was a massive chimney with four chimney pots that rose up out of the terrace, about eight feet tall. I had no idea chimneys were that big, I'd never stood next to one before. There weren't any roof terraces in Cumbernauld. All the Cumbernauld roofs had steep gradients to let the rain drip off the mossy tiles. But the most impressive thing about being up here, apart from making me feel like Mary Poppins, was how quiet it was. There was no more than a background buzz from the noisy street five flights below. From up here it was all neat squared-off terraces. Beyond the pleasantly hazy green patches of roof gardens, there was a thin bright blue line on the horizon. A stripe of Mediterranean. It was close enough to smell, a nice change from the rank street odours.

Along one side of the terrace Chloe had rigged up

some kind of shade with white sheets pegged across two washing lines, making a ceiling and three walls. Inside the makeshift tent there was a low table and another pile of large silky cushions. I poked my head inside but was quickly driven out again by the strong musky smell. It smelled like something nasty had crawled in there and died.

Chloe brought out the coffee on a tray.

'Ah, so you've found my Bedouin yurt,' she said.

'Yeah,' I said, 'it's brilliant.'

'If you liked my dragon you're gonna love this.'

Chloe led me round the other side of the chimney to a pile of stuff: a pair of ladders, dust sheets, bags of plaster, cement, a basin, a toolbag and a bundle of ceramic tiles.

She bent down and fanned out the tiles like cards in a pack.

'Check out these colours!' she said, as excited as a kid.

The tiles were iridescent blues and greens and yellows.

'Oh, they're absolutely gorgeous!'

'You like 'em?'

'I love them!' I squealed.

'I'm gonna do *una chimenea.*'

'Cool. What's that then?'

'A chimney. This one. I'm going to have my own Gaudí chimney up here.'

The chimney was square and boring, nothing like the ones in the guidebook, which contained pages and pages of colourful mosaic-tiled Gaudí chimneys. I knew nothing about Gaudí except that he had designed a fancy cathedral that, a hundred years later, was still nowhere near finished, oh, and that he was a maniac for mosaic. And chimneys. There were lots of Gaudí's crooked chimneys on the posh buildings around Barcelona, buckled mosaic things shaped like ice-cream cones or turrets on a fairy-tale castle. I couldn't see how this ordinary straightforward chimney was going to look like one of those, but I didn't say so.

'That's a great idea.'

'It's not the right shape, obviously, yet. It'll be based on one of the Pedrera *chimeneas* but different. Mine's gonna be unique.'

Chloe took out a metal hammer from the toolbag and balanced a green tile on two bricks. With a decisive tap the tile fell into sharp-edged pieces.

'Now you try,' she said, handing me the hammer and a shimmering blue tile.

I lifted the hammer and started to bring it down but I couldn't follow through.

'It's too beautiful, I . . .'

'Go ahead, it's fun.'

I brought the hammer down hard. Pieces of tile flew out and ricocheted across the terrace.

'Wow! You're meaner than you look! Fun, isn't it?'

'Yes,' I smiled.

'And when the work gets too hot I cool off in my nice new rooftop pool,' Chloe boasted.

'You have a pool on the roof?'

'Who doesn't? It's right over there, right behind the yurt. I got it yesterday in Corte Ingles.'

She led me behind the tent and showed me a large plastic kiddies' paddling pool, filled to the brim with water. The inside of the pool was a pale blue colour which made it look really cool and inviting.

I laughed. 'Another great idea.'

'Oh yeah, I'm full of 'em.'

Chloe seemed pleased that I liked her little joke.

She lifted the coffee tray and we went back to the yurt. The hot dirty smell was still as strong, but Chloe didn't mention it. To avoid gagging I had to mouth-breathe. In the tent Chloe turned around slowly, all the while looking down at her feet. She seemed nervous of lowering herself on to a cushion while holding the hot coffee. Trying to help, I reached to take the tray, but she continued to turn.

'Where is she?' she said. 'Juegita, Juegita, where are you, darling?'

Before she'd finished speaking a sweet-faced little dog had emerged from a sleeping bag bundled at the back of the tent. The dog approached and flopped down beside Chloe. It was a lovely little thing, a mongrel with delicate intelligent features. Underneath, along the length of her chest and belly, she had two rows of large droopy teats. Juegita lifted her head to be stroked but her body lay splayed out uncomfortably on the rows of breast.

Chloe put the tray on the table. 'Poor Gita, your titties are too hot,' she said, caressing the dog's head and breasts. 'What a rack, huh?' she joked.

'Massive mammaries, poor dog,' I said.

Chloe laughed and opened out the sleeping bag.

'Ta da!'

This at last explained the smell. Inside the bag there were eight tiny squeaking puppies.

'And every one of 'em female.'

'Oh, they're so cute!' I blurted.

All of them were, like their mother, chocolate brown with white patches. They were chubby little girls with huge eyes, big heads, short legs and round little tummies. At first glance they all looked the same but after a few moments I could see each one's distinguishing marks:

34

white socks on their legs, or patches on their heads or backs. I couldn't decide which one was the cutest and I'd stopped noticing the smell. When they walked, or waddled, they lurched to the side like drunks. They were great fun to watch, climbing over each other, pulling each other's tails. They fought for access to their mother, who sat patiently while they tugged at her swollen breasts.

'You guys should leave Mommy alone,' Chloe gently chided them, 'give her a break.'

While we watched the pups Chloe told me the story of how she came to have so many dogs. Juegita, meaning 'little toy', had apparently been abandoned. Chloe had found her on the beach looking sad and bedraggled and brought her back to her flat. She hadn't realized at the time that Juegita was pregnant.

'I thought she needed to lose a few pounds. What a doofus! She gave birth two nights ago, in the middle of the night. I was supposed to be vacationing this week in Vietnam with my dad and my boyfriend but I couldn't leave her.'

'You gave up a holiday in Vietnam?'

'Yeah, Dad was pissed about that. He'd already bought the tickets.'

'D'you make a habit of rescue missions?'

Chloe laughed. 'I'm starting to.'

First impressions are lasting ones, so they say. What with the horrible hostel I was staying at and the grotty flats I'd viewed, not to mention the murdered boy with his head stoved in, I'd had a rough few days. Chloe, with her overflowing kindness to waifs and strays, and her shining beauty, seemed to me like an angel.

'These are nice,' I said, pointing to neat rows of identical pot plants.

'Maria,' she said offhandedly, 'it's going to be a bumper crop.'

'Maria?'

'Marijuana,' she said with a strong Spanish accent. It took me a moment to realize what she was talking about. She was growing hash in her home, lots and lots of it, there were ten or more big leafy plants.

'This is the highest terrace around here so I have privacy, but the police helicopters sometimes buzz the neighbourhood. They don't care, everybody does it.'

'Everybody does it?' I asked, 'everybody grows marijuana?' Anxious to use the Spanish pronunciation, I pronounced it mareehwhana.

'Pretty much.'

'Cool.'

We giggled.

'Man, I love Barcelona,' said Chloe.

Once all the pups had taken a turn feeding from poor exhausted Juegita, I helped Chloe put them back in their little bed in the yurt. Just as we popped the last one in, Chloe's phone rang. When she saw who the call was from she rolled her eyes.

'Yeah, I picked up the ticket, Dad, I told you already.'

It wasn't so much what she said but the way she said it: bored, impatient, barely tolerating him.

'Duh, same terminal it always comes in.'

Rather than eavesdrop, I lifted the coffee tray to take the cups back to the kitchen. I could make myself useful and wash up; I'd linger there until she'd finished her call. As I started to move out of my cross-legged sitting position Chloe held out her hand, a signal: halt. She held my eye forcefully. With the tray in my hands, I froze. She raised her voice. 'I told you, Daddy, the puppies stay with me.'

It felt like she was shouting at me. I smiled but she wouldn't release me and there on the floor, halfway between sitting and standing, back aching and legs quivering, in a weird yoga position, I was forced to squat.

'Of course I've made fucking arrangements!'

Chloe barely allowed a reply and then crowed triumphantly, 'Yeah, well, you're so wrong, Dad, as usual. My friend Alison is going to feed Juegita.'

She nodded to me for confirmation. Without hesitation I nodded back.

'I am not! She's right here.'

Chloe suddenly thrust her phone at me, but as my hands were full with the tray I couldn't take it from her. She held it to my ear.

'Alison?'

Considering the venomous way she had spoken to him, I was surprised by the friendliness of Chloe's dad's tone. He had a nice voice, grown-up and laid-back American.

'Yes?'

'Chloe says you've offered to feed the little dogs?'

Chloe was still holding my eye with an unblinking stare.

'Eh, yes, that's right.'

'Thank you so much, Alison.' He sounded surprised. 'That's very kind of you. Chloe's not always quite so organized. That's an interesting accent, where are you from?'

'Thank you. I'm from—'

Chloe pulled the phone away from me and put it back to her own ear.

'Satisfied?'

37

I stood up and took the cups into the kitchen. I was rinsing them under the tap when Chloe came in.

'Juegita isn't the problem,' she explained.

She didn't seem angry any more. I was relieved.

'So long as I leave her enough food and water she can take care of herself and the pups. She's still feeding them so they pretty much get everything they need from her. I can't tell him that someone has to be here to water the maria. In this heat the plants need watering at least once a day. If I left them three days I'd come back to a bunch of dried-up stalks.'

Chloe was leaving me in charge of her flat, her dogs and her drugs. *Dear Lisa and Lauren, Staying at my American-heiress friend Chloe's penthouse in the fashionable Barri Gòtic area of the city.*

'OK,' I said.

'You sure? You don't mind staying a coupla days?'

'No problem.'

'You can't smoke the maria though, you know that, don't you? It won't flower for weeks yet.'

'I know.'

I didn't.

'But you get first toke of the first joint. Deal?'

'Deal.'

'And we'll get so stoned!'

Sangria laced with kick-ass gin might have been a bit much for my delicate recovering liver, but Dr Collins hadn't said anything about smoking dope, moderately or otherwise.

Juegita staggered in from the terrace, her multiple nipples scraping the ground. She made a beeline for me and began nuzzling me like an old friend.

'She loves you!'

Just playing with gorgeous puppies, watering the hash plants, chilling out and enjoying the sunshine and the rooftop view. Is it drizzling again in Cumbernauld? The dampness gets to you after a while, doesn't it?

Chloe rummaged in the kitchen drawer and tossed me a set of keys.

'You're happy with this, looking after the farm? I'll be gone three days max.'

'Sure, if you think you can trust me,' I said.

She was so open-hearted, leaving her home and her pets in the hands of someone she'd only just met.

'Sure I trust you. If you trust me,' she said with a wink.

Chapter 5

Having friends had not been something I'd excelled at so far. I blamed my family. If it wasn't for their over-protectiveness I would've had the normal healthy relationships I was supposed to have. Instead of which I'd hung around with my mum and my brothers. Or, not so much hung around *with*, just hung around and watched while they got on with their normal healthy relationships.

Their relationship with me was not so normal: Charlie babied me, Joe and Jim resentfully gave in to me and Mum quietly ignored me. It had been like that since Dad died. But of course it was Dad who started all the unhealthy-relationship stuff. I blamed him, even if he was dead. Especially as he was dead.

By meeting Chloe I'd increased my circle of friends by 100 per cent. Alone in this big city it felt good to have a pal. The last time I'd had friends was at college.

Cumbernauld College didn't offer me much of a challenge academically. Within the first month I'd read the course books cover to cover and started wading my way through the library stock. I only went to classes so I'd qualify for the study grant, and they were boring.

The most interesting thing about college was the social life. For the first time since primary school I was socially sought after and quickly acquired two friends. Both were marginally less fat than me.

The first, Lisa, a girl in my economics class, was obviously in the market for a best friend. Those who had arrived at college knowing no one had circled each other warily, checking for signs of best-friend material or at least compatibility. I didn't. Too shy to actively participate, I let them circle. Unfortunately for her, Lisa didn't shop around sufficiently, panicked, and settled too quickly on me. We had a lot in common: we were the same age, on the same course and on the same high-carb low-veg diet. We were similarly unattractive but while I was fully aware of my lack of allure, Lisa was blissfully ignorant. She drew attention to herself with a high-pitched laugh and a nervous habit of touching her chin when she spoke as though she was afraid that, with the movement of her jaw, her chin might drop off.

Another chubby girl in our class, Lauren, had loftier ambitions, at least to begin with. She wanted in with the Beautiful People. After she had fumbled a few overtures, keeping seats, sandwich bribes at lunch, overeager giggling at weak jokes, the Beautiful People rejected her and quickly froze her out. Adrift and friendless, by the end of the second week Lauren had attached herself to Lisa and me.

Lauren was almost as fat as me but she had beautiful thick black hair, and ownership of such glossy tresses made her eligible for an attitude. This amounted to her widening her eyes, tilting her head and prefacing everything she said with 'I'm sorry, but' even when it was uncontroversial and no apology was required. For instance she'd say, 'I'm sorry, but *X Factor* was the best programme on telly. And I mean ever.' Or, 'I'm sorry, but I use hot oil on my hair. I *only* use hot oil.' Her delivery was challenging; she was anything but sorry.

It was my own fault. Courted by Lisa, unused to this kind of attention, or any attention, I overplayed my hand and made the extravagant gesture of inviting Lauren into my gang. For a brief three-week period I was queen bee, both of them jockeying to become my best friend. At the time I thought my mistake had been to hesitate too long in choosing one over the other, but with hindsight I realized that it would've happened anyway.

Lisa began to talk about us all getting a flat together. Lauren was the keenest, phoning the agents, arranging viewings. Once, between classes, I was in the ladies' toilets and Lisa and Lauren came in. I was already in the cubicle and they didn't know I was there. I overheard them talking. I could have announced my presence but I was interested to know what went on between my new best mates when I wasn't around.

'I'm sorry, but it's a brilliant flat,' said Lauren, 'but how are we going to afford it?'

'We can afford it,' said Lisa.

'And more to the point,' continued Lauren, 'what the hell are we going to tell the Hump?'

They both giggled.

'It's not the Hump, you idiot, it's the Hulk,' sniggered Lisa. 'We'll tell her it's to do with fire regulations, that only two people can live there and she can't come.'

The Hulk.

I was only marginally fatter than those two great fucking fatties.

Holding the moral high ground, I bowed out gracefully.

I told them I'd thought about it and preferred to stay at home with my mum and my brothers. Lisa and Lauren never bothered to disguise their relief. They gushed and showered me with invitations to their new flat that I never took up. A new order was established. It was OK. I was glad I'd overheard them. It was more comfortable returning to the hanger-on zone than being centre stage on a wobbly throne. At least I still had lunch with them.

That was the important thing, to be seen to be part of a group. Hanging around the edges of their bestfriendship was a humiliating reminder of my lower status, but it was better than being a friendless freak. By the time we got to third year, Lisa and Lauren could barely conceal their embarrassment at being seen with me. We were all relieved when graduation came. Of course they made effusive promises to stay in touch.

When I suddenly became gorgeously thin the first thing I did was join Friends Reunited. I posted photos of me in tight jeans and a gypsy top, and mailed them to every name I recognized. I was disappointed that Lisa and Lauren weren't registered, but I looked on the bright side. Perhaps they were still lard-arsed losers and were too ashamed to join. Friends Reunited did hold one surprise.

Sarah Anderson, the mousiest girl in my primary school class, was now a seasoned world traveller. She casually listed Morocco, Western Samoa and Vladivostok as places she had worked teaching English. She even boasted that she didn't have any proper teaching qualifications. All she had was a degree, and not even an English one. Hers was an even more Mickey Mouse degree than mine: media studies.

'It's just an accident of birth that I'm an expert in

English, the language that is, luckily for me, the world's most important business language,' said her profile. 'It's such a great gift and I love passing it on with my teaching.'

I'd been blessed with the gift of English too, and more abundantly than her, I seemed to remember. I was the best reader in the class, way ahead of Sarah Anderson; she was in the remedial group. I could use my gift and teach English abroad.

Perhaps Western Samoa was taking things a bit far. What I needed was somewhere they didn't speak English – the poor unfortunates – but near enough that I could come home if it didn't work out. Sarah had been generous enough to attach links to English-language schools and agencies all over the world.

Within two days I had received notice of my interview with a business school in Barcelona. Booking a flight took about twenty minutes. It was that simple. Rather than have another pointless argument with them all I copied an email to Charlie, Jim, Joe and Mum. Mum was downstairs watching *Coronation Street*, but she'd read it later.

I was on the point of booking a hostel when Charlie, my oldest brother, phoned.

'Good stuff,' he conceded graciously, 'Barcelona's a brilliant place.'

He went on to explain, in his long-winded way, that provided I promised to look after my health, he'd resign himself to my going. I was then treated to Charlie's glory days backpacking through Europe. Anyone would think Spain and France were on some dark and as yet undiscovered continent the way he went on. My other brothers, Joe and Jim, had also been to Europe. Even my nan, who was seventy-three and had a colostomy bag, had been to Spain.

'I wonder if Ewan's still in Barcelona,' Charlie mused. 'Last I heard he was running a hostel out there. You could look him up. I used to hang about with him at school, Ewan Moffat, d'you remember him?'

'Eh, not really.'

'Well, I suppose you were only wee at the time.'

'But Charlie, how spooky is that? I'm looking at hostels right now.'

'Spooky,' he agreed. 'Anyway, I can't remember the name of the place. I think it was something to do with music. Is there one called Music Hostel, or Hostel de Music, something like that?'

I quickly scanned the web page.

'No, but I'm only seeing the ones that have websites. Wait, there's one here called Blues Hostel, is that it?'

'Could be.'

'Here's another one, Jazz Hostel.'

'Jazz Hostel! That's it. We called it Jizz Hostel because Gary and this wee Irish burd . . .' said Charlie, tailing off. 'Eh, no, sorry, inappropriate. Jazz Hostel, that's the one.'

'It's cheap, fourteen euros a night, that's the cheapest I've seen.'

'Aye well, Ewan might give you a discount if you mention my name. If he's still there.'

'When did you last speak to him?'

'Eh, three, four years? He's never come back to Cumbernauld, I would have seen him. Maybe he's still in Barcelona.'

I booked for three nights. Charlie seemed relieved. He didn't say so but I knew he was worried that I wasn't recovered enough yet, that I might have a relapse. At least this way he'd have his old friend Ewan keeping an eye on me. Without Charlie's dubious recommendation I'd probably have booked Jazz Hostel anyway, it was the cheapest, but maybe it was a good omen.

When the taxi pulled up outside the hostel I saw why it was only 14 euros a night. And when I lugged my rucksack inside there were more disappointments to come.

'You're booked for three nights, aye?' asked the receptionist from inside his reception box.

He was Scottish, but there was no way this guy was Ewan. This guy looked at least five years older than my big brother Charlie. He was older, but he wasn't bad-looking. The bare bulb in his wee booth shone down on his long red dreadlocked hair. He had a good bone structure, his cheeks tapering nicely to his jaw. When I came in he was looking down, consulting the register. I put on the new smile I'd been practising and waited for him to look up.

He wasn't quite so attractive when he did so. His face was pink, his bright eyes suspicious and his mouth was as tight as a cat's arse.

'Fifty-six euros,' he said, 'three nights' accommodation and one night's deposit returnable on day of check-out. And I'll need your passport.'

He spoke with a pronounced West of Scotland accent, for instance saying 'out' as 'oot', as if he was trying to emphasize his Scottishness. He must have recognized my Scottish accent but he didn't mention it. He probably had Scots coming through here all the time.

'There you are,' I said, handing over the money, 'thanks very much.'

I turned towards the dormitory, but it was too much of a coincidence that this guy was Scottish.

'Excuse me,' I asked, 'what's your name?'

'The name's Ewan.'

'I know someone who knows you.'

'Really,' he said flatly, looking down again at his register. 'A lot of people know me. They *think* they know me. Check out on day of departure before ten a.m. or you lose your deposit, OK?'

'OK.'

Since that rather sour introduction I'd spent two nights in his sweaty low-rent hostel. Now as I got out of another taxi, this time to move into Chloe's luxury penthouse, I couldn't wait to tell Ewan exactly where he could stick his manky hostel.

Chapter 6

Charlie had been baffled.

'Well if it *is* him, he's a changed man,' he said sadly.

'It's him.'

I'd seen his full name on the registration sheet when I picked up my passport the next morning. Ewan Moffat, it was him all right. Ewan Moffat had been working here for all these years. It had made him a bitter man, and no wonder.

The first night I arrived at the hostel I had been unprepared for the squalor. Once I'd got my head round the cramped conditions of the dorm, I lay down carefully on the bunk I'd been allocated. There was nothing I could do about it; I'd paid upfront. I kept my clothes on. Since there seemed to be no private space I wasn't about to change into my nightie in front of a lot of strangers, boys as well as girls.

My room-mates had no such anxieties. People were whipping their kit off right and left. An inhibition-free zone. Naked and nearly naked bodies of both sexes were strewn around like the aftermath of a particularly exhausting porn movie. And the smell.

Before my nostrils became thankfully immune to the

rank stench I could make out urine, garlic breath and smoke-singed clothes, but these were way outranked by the whiff from unwashed body parts: pits, groins, and worst of all, cheesy feet.

It was an orgy of exhibitionism. Hot as it was in the overstuffed, low-ceilinged, bunk-crammed dorm, I wouldn't be getting naked.

An argument was taking place in two languages. A girl speaking what sounded like some kind of Eastern European was going at it with a Frenchwoman. The dispute was over whether the window should be open or closed. It wasn't until they began to tussle, the Balkan girl opening the window and pulling the Frenchwoman's pigtails and the Frenchwoman closing it and smacking the Balkan's face, that it became clear who wanted what. It escalated to the point where the Frenchwoman poked the other girl's eye. Nobody intervened. After that, the window stayed closed.

Half asleep and barely conscious, instinct took over. I had to cool down. I peeled my damp dress off my clammy skin and over my sweat-soaked head. The relief was instantaneous. I wafted the dress above me a few times before laying it lightly on my body and going to sleep.

The next morning I awoke to find my dress on the floor, my limbs spread north, south, east and west. My mouth was dry and wide from snoring, my top lip stuck to my teeth. One breast had spilled out of my bra. Luckily there was no one there to see it. Apart from a few still sleeping at the other end of the dorm, everyone had gone.

'Right,' said Ewan, bounding into the room, 'it's five to ten. Check out in five minutes or you lose your deposits.'

By the time he'd made it along to my row of bunks I'd managed to pop the rogue breast back in my bra and was working my mouth trying to regain the use of my top lip.

'Check out in five minutes,' he repeated.

'Ewan,' I said, pulling my dress in front of me, pinning it under my arms to hold it in place, 'I'm booked in for three nights.' Panic had crept into my voice. 'I've another two nights to go, I've already paid.'

'Aye, *calmate*, calm down, I'm not talking to you.'

He was a charmer all right. It was hard to believe that only two days ago I'd been so scared of him. Now that I was preparing to leave the hostel Ewan could no longer wield such power over me.

As I entered the hostel he was enclosed in his little reception box as usual, arguing with someone.

'Haw you!' he bawled at the bemused hosteller who was attempting to bring a bike into the building. 'You cannae bring that in here!'

'But only to bring ze bicycle here?' suggested the guy, indicating the lobby area.

The hosteller/cyclist was wearing only a few key garments: army shorts with grease-bordered pockets, dust-coated open-toed sandals, thick socks and a long straggling Taliban beard.

'Ze bicycle vill be stole if it stay outside.'

He was a perfect example of the unwashed types who stayed here.

'Not my problem pal, get it out!' shouted Ewan, pointing to the door with his pen.

There was an embarrassing kerfuffle as the cyclist awkwardly heaved himself, his huge rucksack, his bike and his beard through the narrow doorway. As he exited he shouted something foreign and, by its tone, offensive.

'And you!' retorted Ewan cheerfully.

I would have slunk upstairs and picked up my stuff but as I passed his booth Ewan cried, 'Alison, it's wee Alison Donaldson!'

Charlie. He must have emailed Jazz Hostel.

'How are you doing, Alison, have you had a nice day?'

'Splendid, thank you,' I said without a smile.

When I came back down a few minutes later with my rucksack ready to do battle with the front door, he seemed alarmed.

'Hey, where are you going?'

'I'm checking out.'

'No, but Alison, you're booked in for another night, plus deposit.'

'Goodbye,' I said as I strode past.

The impact of this parting shot was lessened by me having to stop at the door. A large group of students was now blocking the exit as they came in. A cloud of communal body odour engulfed me as they passed. They would have been my room-mates tonight, my scratching, snoring, farting *compañeros*.

'Ho!' Ewan bawled, and then emerged from the reception box and followed me to the door. 'Where are you going?'

'None of your business.'

'D'you not remember me? I'm Charlie's pal, I used to give you money for a cone when the ice-cream van came round, d'you not remember?'

'Nope.'

I kept my back to him and he tried to sneak around me.

'Aye you do. Me and Charlie, up in the room playing music.'

I shook my head.

I did remember, I remembered all too well Charlie's porno mags and his ruses to get rid of his kid sister, but I was anxious to get out of Raval before anyone recognized me and connected me with the Bashed-Head Boy murder. The taxi was waiting.

'Well I remember you, course I do. How could I forget those beautiful green eyes?'

My beautiful green eyes flicked him a dirty look.

'You can't go, I told Charlie I'd look out for you, show you round town and that. Anyway, what's the rush? You've still got two nights to go, and you can stay an extra four nights, no charge. I'm doing a buy-one-get-one-free, just for you. Fancy it?'

'Sorry, Ewan, I've sorted out something else.'

'Where? You'll not get a cheaper deal than that.'

'An apartment,' I said vaguely. I didn't want anyone in Raval to know where I was going.

'Well, OK.' He sounded crushed. 'But I'll need a forwarding address before you leave, or at least a contact number. Sorry, Alison, it's the law.'

I thought about this while the straps of my rucksack bit into my shoulder and the taxi waited outside. A taxi idling so long was conspicuous and the meter was still running.

'D'you promise you won't give it to anyone else?'

I was cold. He lay between my legs. The bits of me that he wasn't lying on, my face, my left arm and foot, were cold. The other bits were numb.

Stuff was on my face. I tried to reach up with my free hand to wipe it away but he was too big, too wide, I couldn't get round him. It dripped on my face. First it was warm, then cold, then it dried hard. Like the cucumber face mask Mum used on a Friday when I was wee. Not every Friday, just special Fridays when we prepared a special dinner and waited for the Aberdeen bus to get in. After she'd smeared it on herself, her face a stern and ghostly pale green, Mum put what was left on me.

'Don't laugh, and don't dare cry or your face'll crack,' she told me. 'I won't,' I said, my face set like rigor mortis, 'I promise.'

Chapter 7

Bad dreams, too much excitement, but as I woke up I remembered I was now in Barcelona. The light was different here, the sunshine bright and cheerful. I lay enjoying my privacy and celebrated my solitude with a long plangent fart. I could see myself reflected in the big carved mirror.

I saw a girl, a Euro traveller. A girl who'd grow dope and lived in Barri Gòtic; who'd have American girlfriends and Spanish boyfriends. A girl with green eyes and a great figure.

I hooked my toe round the sheet and stretched, pulling it down, slowly, teasingly revealing the slim body that was attached to my head.

I was still getting used to the slender arms and legs that had emerged from the sausage casing they'd been trapped in for so long. I couldn't take my eyes off them. I turned sideways to give the mirror an appreciation of my peachy bum. Glandular fever had been the best thing that ever happened to me.

Juegita was on at me as soon as I got out of bed, so I filled her bowl with the dried cereal Chloe had shown me and topped up her water. The pups were still sleepy and lay curled in comical upside-down positions in the sleeping bag. When they woke they clambered over each other, tiny paws on tiny necks, tummies and ears. They squeaked in the high-pitched tone of soft toys. While Juegita suckled them, one of the pups was too sleepy to open her eyes. Instead of her mother's nipple, she sucked happily on one of her sisters' tails.

The earth in the marijuana pots slowly became an inky black as I watered them. I pulled out weeds as I went. It was pleasant work, before I'd even finished I was looking forward to the next watering. The next job wasn't so pleasant. I swept up the cockroach bodies from outside the front door and shook out more bug powder the way Chloe had shown me. I was careful not to drop any inside the flat. It could poison the puppies, she'd warned.

The chores done, I began sorting my own stuff. In my hastily packed rucksack my dirty clothes had got mixed up with my clean ones. I started to sift through them but then gave up and slung everything in the washing machine. I didn't know when I'd have access to such good facilities again.

She probably wouldn't mind if I borrowed something of hers, just until my own stuff was dry. I looked through the cupboards and drawers. I didn't really have to look in the cupboards; there were plenty of Chloe's clothes on the chair and on the floor, but I wanted to find out about her. All her clothes were gorgeous. Even those with names I didn't recognize on their labels looked like they were designer. I tried her perfumes and found a make-up bag full of expensive products. A bottle of foundation had burst in the bag. Everything was stuck together and a grey-green fungus was growing in the gunge.

It was easy to tell which clothes Chloe had worn and which were clean. The dirty ones smelled like the inside of the yurt: a powerful doggy stink. Most of her clothes needed washing. I considered putting a load of hers in the machine when mine came out, but I didn't want her to think I'd been snooping.

Some skirts were a bit long on me but otherwise everything fitted. Chloe was at least six inches taller than me but we were the same size everywhere else, even shoes. I tried tops and skirts and trousers in different combinations. If they looked this good on me, how amazing did they look on her? In the bottom drawer there was a gorgeous white lace bra and pants set wrapped in tissue inside a Victoria's Secret box.

My phone rang.

I panicked.

I had to get out of the bra and pants. If I answered the phone in them I might give myself away. I whipped the pants off and threw them across the room, distancing myself from the evidence. They landed somewhere at the back of the shoe cupboard. The bra was too tight to come off easily. My fingers fiddled behind me but I couldn't unfasten it. I pulled the straps, yanking my arms free and forcing the delicate material down. The elasticated part was dragging and becoming embedded in my belly flesh. I tugged at it again and heard the expensive white lace rip.

'Hello?'

'Hey! How's my darlin' girl?' said Chloe.

'Eh, fine, I just woke up,' I said, trying to disguise my fright as sleepiness.

'Actually I meant Juegita,' Chloe laughed, 'but OK, Alison, you're my darlin' too.'

She laughed again and I felt an unpleasant flush across my naked skin.

'Juegita's fine,' I said, all bumbling, 'I've filled her bowl and given her fresh water. And the pups. They're fine too. Everything's fine.'

At the mention of her name Juegita toddled into the bedroom and looked me over, her expression hovering between confusion and envy. She must have longed for some multicupped dog bra to support her long pendulous breasts.

'Great,' said Chloe, sounding relieved, 'and the other matter?'

Dizzy with confusion, I had no idea what she meant. The lacy bra cups drooped like empty holsters from my hips.

'The other matter?' I repeated.

'The *vegetable* matter.'

Finally I hauled myself clear of the torn bra, the elastic snapping painfully against my skin. I lifted it at arm's length and moved to the shoe cupboard to recover the pants. Chloe was still talking.

'You know, the vegetables I'm growing,' she said, putting extra emphasis on the word 'vegetables'.

I rummaged in the back of the cupboard, pulling a tin box aside to get at the pants.

'The vegetables in the pots on the terrace. The ones I asked you to water?'

'Oh!' I said, 'that vegetable matter! Yes, yes, I've watered the mareehwhana, it's fine too. Sorry, I was thinking of another matter entirely.'

Chloe laughed again.

'British humour, I love it!'

I pulled out the tin to get at the pants. It was an

old-fashioned biscuit tin with a picture of a flamenco dancer on the lid. The dancer's dress was vivid red and yellow.

'So, do you have plans today?' asked Chloe.

'Yes, I've got an interview with the Valero Business English Centre.'

'Good luck with that.'

'Cheers.'

As I reached in behind it the tin fell off the cupboard shelf and on to the floor.

'I'm so jealous. I'm stuck with old Aged P and he is just *soo* depressing. I swear to God, he's actually wearing golf slacks. Golf slacks in Berlin, what a moron.'

The tin had emptied at my feet. As we chatted I bent to pick up and replace the contents.

'Thanks for looking after everything, Alison, I really appreciate it.'

Amongst other stuff there was a small plastic bag with maybe eight or ten bright pink pills. I didn't know for sure what these were but I had a pretty good idea. I knew immediately what the other stuff was. Money. The box was full of it, large solid bricks of cash, all in crisp clean hundred-euro notes. Juegita waddled across and sniffed at it.

'Are you comfortable in the apartment?' asked Chloe. 'You got everything you need?'

There must be thousands of euros here. I pushed the dog away and began to gather the bundles of cash.

'Alison?'

'Eh?'

'Is everything OK?'

'Oh yeah,' I reassured her.

I didn't know Chloe at all. I didn't know how she might

react to her stash being uncovered and her underwear being defiled.

'Yes, everything's fine, absolutely fine.'

'Well, just make yourself at home. You want anything, Alison, just help yourself.'

'Cheers, Chloe,' I said, feeling the weight of the cash bundles in my hand, 'I'll do that.'

Chapter 8

The only person in the Valero Business English Centre was the man himself, Señor Jorge Valero. He welcomed me warmly. It was a relief to find he knew who I was and why I was here.

'Ah, Señorita Donaldson, so nice to meet you,' he said.

The first thing he did was pour me a coffee and insist I try a piece of *turrón*, a soft nutty sweet. He watched my face closely while I nibbled at it. It was OK, if a bit over-sweet, but I nodded and made appreciative noises.

With the niceties taken care of, Señor Valero got down to business. He didn't seem too bothered that I didn't yet speak Spanish. He said that this was sometimes advantageous, forcing the students to find ways to make themselves understood in English. Señor Valero complimented me on my charming Scottish accent but admitted having a little trouble with it. This alarmed me.

Since arriving in Spain I had been forced to abandon my broad west coast brogue. Nobody understood me. In the last few days I had begun to speak slowly and carefully, softening my vowels and rounding out my consonants. Now I sounded more like a posh BBC newsreader. But,

Señor Valero reassured me, it was good for students to be exposed to all kinds of regional English accents.

'Scotland is same as England, yes?'

'Well, not exactly, Señor Valero.'

I explained that Scotland was a separate country with our own Scottish parliament and judiciary.

'It's quite a different culture,' I told him in my new cut-glass Home Counties English accent, 'we're very proud of our Scottish national identity.'

'*Bueno*,' said Señor Valero, looking bemused.

To change the subject I handed over a copy of my CV. I'd spent ages padding it out and paid a fortune for the folder. I hoped this would distract him from the absence of any teaching qualifications and experience. It seemed to do the trick. Except for a nod to the obvious quality of the expensive folder, he barely glanced inside. It was exactly as Sarah Anderson had said: all you needed to teach English was to be a native English speaker.

Señor Valero appeared to be satisfied and went on to discuss terms and conditions.

'Your NIE number?' he asked, having progressed to filling in a form.

'Sorry?'

'NIE Employment number.'

'Oh right, my National Insurance number? It's on my CV.' I opened up the folder and pointed.

Señor Valero put down his pen.

'Is your English number, no?'

Not wanting to quibble, I simply nodded.

'You have Spanish number, from Spanish government? You no have NIE?'

'Well, not at the minute,' I blustered, 'I wasn't aware . . .'

Señor Valero smiled.

'Is no problem. Scotland is same as England. Is in European onion, yes?'

'Yes,' I nodded enthusiastically.

Never before had I felt so grateful to be a member of the European onion.

'*Bueno*, no problem,' he said with a careless wave. 'There is time; I give you letter and you get NIE for September, yes?'

'Yes,' I said, letting out a long-held breath.

'Your address please?'

I gave him Chloe's. I'd amend the details when I found my own place.

'OK, you sign here.'

At this stage, the form was only partially filled in. As it was written entirely in Spanish it didn't make much difference anyway. I could have been signing permission for open-heart surgery without anaesthetic for all I knew, but I signed.

'*Bueno*,' he said, placing the form with my CV. 'Good.'

Señor Valero saw the look of expectation on my face and was quick to react.

'Sorry. You have questions?'

I smiled as I said it, the old job-interview cliché: 'When do I start?'

'*Sí*,' said Señor Valero, 'classes begin in September.'

'September?'

I'd wondered earlier why he'd mentioned September. It was now only early July, two months until the beginning of September.

'But I'm available to start now. I'd hoped I could start immediately, or at least soon.'

Señor Valero laughed. 'No classes in summer, is impossible,' he chortled. 'All is on vacation, at the beach. You want to teach English at the beach? In the sea? With the swim clothes on?'

I laughed too. How silly of me.

Señor Valero showed me out of the office, still chuckling at his little joke.

'You call in September, when you have NIE. We fix classes.'

As I walked back to Chloe's apartment I calculated how much money I had and how long I could make it last. Not till September. Even if I found a cheap place and I lived very carefully it probably couldn't be done.

I dug out my phonecard and phoned home. After a few minutes' small talk I asked Mum.

'It would only be a loan; I'll pay you back as soon as I get paid.'

'What did I tell you? I told you you didn't have enough money, didn't I? I bloody told you.'

'I'll send it in September.'

'Alison, you're not fit for this. Are you forgetting that a couple of weeks ago you nearly died of glandular fever? You have my heart roasted so you do.'

'It's only a few hundred.'

'A few hundred! D'you think I'm made of money? This is a piece of nonsense. You get yourself on a plane home right away, young lady.'

'I've told you, Mum, I'm not coming home.'

'Look, come home and get yourself up to that hospital for your check-ups. If Dr Collins gives you a clean bill of health and you're still hell-bent on it then you can always go back in September.'

'Please, Mum, I wouldn't ask but—'

'Then don't. Don't do this to me. You can't be gallivanting about Spain, not with your liver, and I can't be encouraging you. You know I'd do anything for you, Alison, but this isn't good for your health. It's not good for mine either, I'm worried sick, you've got my heart roasted.'

She was about to start crying again about how she missed me, how the house was empty without me, I could hear it in her voice.

When I first saw the money I put it all back in the tin the way I'd found it: fat bundles of notes held together with elastic bands just chucked in higgledy-piggledy. Now when I looked at it again and began to count it I realized that what had looked like solid blocks of same-denomination notes was a mixture of fives, tens, twenties and even the occasional fifty or a hundred. There was no order to it. Chloe probably had no idea how much was there.

She'd get it back, I wasn't a thief. In September I'd find a way of getting it back to her. She'd have to visit her dad again sometime. Wasn't Thanksgiving around that time? I'd offer to look after her plants again. I could put the money back then.

Dear Lisa and Lauren, Gallivanting around Spain with my liver. Essential kit, I wouldn't be without it. Had to decide whether to become a pavement vagrant or a high-society thief. Guess which one I picked? Life here is filled with exciting challenges. Only yesterday I saw a murdered boy with his head stoved in. Brains looked like raspberry jam. You couldn't make it up. Are you still so into sudoku?

I'd already binned the Victoria's Secret underwear and box. The bra was beyond repair, the pants slightly soiled. There was no way I could put them back in the drawer. Chloe had so many clothes and posh underwear sets I'd have to hope she wouldn't miss it.

My heart was racing. I took four fifty-euro notes, each from a different bundle. Two hundred euros wasn't a huge amount, and nothing compared to what was in the tin. I'd still have to live carefully, but at least this way I might not starve.

Chapter 9

I remembered the first time I found out the truth about
sex. I would have been about nine or ten at the time.
My brothers had rented a DVD and were watching it in
Isabelle's house. Isabelle was our next-door neighbour
and Mum's best friend. She didn't have any kids of her
own. Dad was away on the rigs, Mum worked full-time at
the bakery and Isabelle childminded us after school until
Mum came home.

Me and my brothers and Isabelle would watch *The
Simpsons* every day. The boys only ever wanted to watch
TV but Isabelle and I did loads of things together. We
talked about everything: school, my teacher, class
projects, Mum and Dad, her husband Graham, visits to
my nan. Every day she brushed my hair, one hundred
strokes to bring out the shine. Sometimes we went out
to the shops or the spiritualist church. Occasionally
Isabelle let me bake cakes so long as we ate them up
before Mum got home. If Mum brought cakes home that
night from the bakery Isabelle told us we weren't to say
anything. She didn't want Mum's feelings hurt. Isabelle
was considerate, a warm loving person in my life. She
was a wee fat woman, always tickling me and hugging

me tight, and she was always honest and open. I could ask her anything.

'Go on,' she'd say, 'ask me anything.'

One day I asked her about sex. My brothers were watching a DVD and laughing.

'Isabelle,' I said, 'why are the boys laughing at that film?'

I already knew why they were laughing, it was because I'd said that the man in the film was doing press-ups on top of the lady, but I couldn't understand what was so funny about that.

Isabelle made the boys turn it off and whisked me into the kitchen and gave me a Caramel Log.

'He isn't doing press-ups, Ally love, the lady and the man are having sex.'

Isabelle assured me that this was nothing to worry about.

'Sex is when a man and a lady who love each other very much have a special cuddle,' she said.

I thought about this while I scraped the coconut off my Caramel Log with my teeth.

'Did you have a special cuddle with Graham?'

'Oooh! Many's a time and often,' Isabelle said laughing.

Isabelle's husband Graham was dead, but we often discussed him. She loved to talk about how Graham died. I knew the story well but I always enjoyed it. A lady was crossing the road and she had a wee baby in a pram and the bus driver lost control of the bus and drove straight at the lady and the baby, but Graham ran on to the road and pushed the lady and the baby away and the bus ran over him and he passed.

'He died a hero, you can't ask any more of a man than that,' Isabelle would say.

During the school holidays, if there was a visiting medium, we sometimes went to the spiritualist church for the afternoon sessions. Isabelle often got messages from Graham, usually telling her he was well and not to worry, but one day he sent a message for me.

The medium was a small beak-nosed lady. Her method was to move around the hall trying to pick up messages as though she was trying to pick up a radio signal.

'I have a message for someone in this row, someone in green, no, that's it, green eyes. The little girl on the end there. I have a message from, I think it's Gordon, or is it Graham? Yes, Graham. Graham sees an illustrious future for this child; she will travel far and know riches beyond her wildest dreams.'

Delighted, Isabelle dug me in the ribs.

'What's that, Graham?' said the medium. 'Yes, thank you. Graham sends a warning: but first she will be deceived, she must face many trials and betrayals but she will triumph! She shall be entered into glorious halls and receive bounteous riches!'

I wanted more but the medium collapsed and had to be brought a glass of water. Isabelle said we should go.

'I think we'll give the spiritualist church a miss for a wee while, eh, Ally?' she said as we walked home. 'Some of those mediums talk a lot of nonsense. Don't say anything to your mum, eh, pet?'

Isabelle never again took me with her to the spiritualist church but she continued to go alone in the evenings, and she always told me whenever she got a message from the other side.

That day after she had explained what the man and

lady in the DVD were doing and she was brushing my hair, I asked Isabelle another question.

'Isabelle, when you pass to the other side?'

'Yes?'

'Will you be able to have special cuddles with Graham on the other side?'

'I certainly hope so,' said Isabelle and then seemed a bit uncomfortable, 'if Graham still wants to. Now come on, finish your biscuit. *The Simpsons* will be on in a minute.'

Chapter 10

Ewan took me to a noisy café.

'This OK here?' he asked.

'Yeah, sure.'

The place was busy but it was nothing to look at. The tables and chairs were old dark wood and the only planned decor seemed to be the ornate blue and yellow ceramic floor tiles. Along one wall were stacked dark wooden wine casks with silver taps and names and prices chalked on them. Wine dripped from the taps and a dark reddish-brown stain built up on the floor. I couldn't look at it and had to turn away.

I'd have gone crazy if I'd had to stay alone in the flat. Mum ranting down the phone at me about check-ups and Dr Collins hadn't helped, she was going on as if I was about to drop down dead. With Chloe away Ewan was the only person I knew in Barcelona. He was also the only man, so far, ever to have asked me out.

No doubt this would turn out to be, like my relationship with Lisa and Lauren, a friendship of convenience, but I wasn't in a position to be fussy. Ewan was from home, if we ran out of things to say we could talk about Cumbernauld.

Ewan ordered two glasses of wine from the most expensive cask.

'Thank you. Mmm, lovely wine,' I nodded.

Ewan nodded back. He smiled at me and I smiled back. We both spent a few minutes nervously looking at everything all around the bar, then we smiled at each other again.

'How are things in Raval?' I shouted into his ear.

'Smelly backpackers coming and going.' He shrugged. 'It never changes.'

'Yeah, but in Raval, anything interesting happened lately?'

'Not as far as I know. Are you OK, Alison?'

'I'm fine.'

We looked around the bar again.

'We could reminisce about the Nauld,' I said.

Ewan looked confused.

'The Nauld, you know, the old country, Cumbernauld.'

'Cumbernauld!'

Ewan laughed. He laughed hard and for ages which relaxed me. Somebody in Barcelona got my jokes.

'I haven't heard that for years. The Nauld.' He shook his head appreciatively. 'What would I know about the Nauld? I haven't been back for years. You know more than me, you tell me.'

So I did. I told him about the sad gits he remembered from school. They were all still living in council flats, still working in the same shops and call centres. They were still meeting the same grey faces every weekend in the local pubs, breeding a new generation of sad-git grey-faced Naulders. Ewan laughed his head off.

The wine had gone straight to my legs. I wanted a seat

but the place was packed, three or four deep at the bar. All the tables were taken. At each small table people were huddled together over shared dishes, stabbing at communal plates with toothpicks. Even on the bar, space was mostly taken up with food which was displayed in a long glass case.

The air was clammy with fried fish and cigarette smoke. Plates clattered, Spanish was called from table to bar to kitchen and back again.

'This shouting-the-orders-in system they've got,' I said, 'it's very atmospheric.'

'That gets on my tits,' said Ewan. 'It's noisy enough in here with everything else that's going on. But that bawling for the food makes you feel like you're in court when the judge is calling the witnesses.'

I laughed.

'Call Patatas Bravas!' he shouted above the other noise.

People around us stared but Ewan didn't give a toss.

He was right, there was a lot happening in the crowded bar. Not everyone standing around was waiting to be served. Some were waiters, moving amongst the tables, stopping to chat and joke, aware of waiting customers but apparently immune to pressure.

Some were strolling musicians, three of them with guitars and accordions servicing the tables, playing old international hits that everyone could join in. While one table sang, *quizás, quizás, quizás*, the next sang, 'perhaps, perhaps, perhaps'.

Some were beggars, gypsy women in long skirts and trainers, always with a baby on their hip. The women made hungry gestures: thumb and fingers pushed towards mouth. Some tourists mistook this as a plea for food, offering a share of their meal, but it was money the women wanted. Waiters were quick to eject them.

Some were vendors, Asian boys, selling flowers: formally wrapped individual red roses or haphazard bunches. The boys spoke in wheedling voices, appealing to men to buy a rose for their lady friend and making disappointed disapproving faces when the men refused. One of them approached us.

'Buy a flower for the lady?' said the guy, grinning at Ewan.

'Sanj!' said Ewan. '*Hola chaval.*'

'*Hola* Juan,' said the flower seller. '*¿Qué tal?*'

They made a show of their friendship with a long elaborate boys-in-the-hood-type handshake. They spoke in Spanish while I stood with a formal grin on my face. It was Sanj who spotted my isolation and switched to limited English.

'Please with meet you,' he said, smiling.

He was a good-looking lad, about my age, maybe younger, with shiny black hair falling over dark eyes. He had really long lashes and a big innocent smile, like a bhangra dancer in a Bollywood movie. He was small, only slightly taller than me, and thin, a featherweight. Being a flower seller suited him. He wasn't begging. I'd watched him move around the tables calmly, a chilled-out hippy.

'Pleased to meet you,' I said.

'Sanj, this is my friend Alison,' said Ewan, enunciating slowly and carefully, 'she is from Scotland. Like me.'

With the introductions over Ewan returned to speaking Spanish. Rather than stand there smiling, I took the opportunity to go to the toilet. When I came back Sanj had moved off to work the rest of the tables and Ewan handed me a fresh glass of wine and a bunch of flowers.

'Thought these might straighten your face,' he said gruffly.

No one had ever bought me flowers before. No, that wasn't true. My brothers had brought armloads when I was dying in hospital, but that was different. When I was dying in hospital I couldn't understand how these beautiful dead things, cut off in their prime, were supposed to make me feel better. Death was ugly and frightening, I'd come to Barcelona to get away from it. But perhaps Ewan had only bought them to help out his friend. I'd watched the previous vendors work hard to sell even a one-euro rose. I couldn't see how there was any money in it. But even so, I was grateful to Ewan for the gesture.

'Cheers,' I mumbled.

'Have you eaten?' asked Ewan.

'Not yet.'

'Well we can't let you go hungry. Your big brother would kill me.'

Dear Lisa and Lauren, Having dinner in a café with my date. He has just bought me flowers. On my second glass of wine. Mum and Dr Collins can go fuck themselves. Wine here is poured from the casks, nice and fresh. Are you still buying boxes of Morrison's own brand?

While Ewan organized us a table he asked me to choose something from the food piled in the glass case on the bar. This system was different from the Spanish restaurant I'd been to in Cumbernauld. In Cumbernauld minuscule portions of sausage or prawns, bobbing in pools of green oil, were ordered from a menu.

Apart from sardines, which I didn't like anyway, I didn't recognize anything. Ewan pointed towards something he called *chipirones* and I nodded, only because the batter it

74

was coated in was familiar-looking. When it came it had eyeballs, two of them I was careful to note. And tentacles, loads of them. It was whole baby squid, Ewan explained. I hadn't eaten since yesterday afternoon, I couldn't face food but I knew I should soak up the alcohol. Suddenly my mouth flooded with saliva.

'Wolf in,' said Ewan.

I closed my eyes and crammed a baby squid into my mouth.

'How is it?'

'Mmm, crispy on the outside, chewy on the inside. Reassuringly greasy and salty. Like my mum's cooking but absolutely nothing like it at all.'

Something else arrived at the table: small fried and salted green peppers.

'*Pimientos de Padrón*,' said Ewan.

An amused smile played around his lips as he watched me eat, closing my eyes to scoff the *chipirones* and tearing out the pepper stalks with my fingers and teeth.

'*Pimientos de Padrón, algunos picantes, otros no*,' he said as though reciting a nursery rhyme.

By my expression he could see that I didn't get it.

'Some are hot, some not,' he explained, 'just be careful, you'll know all about it if you get a hot one.'

It wasn't until my tongue exploded in a firestorm that I got it. The heat in my mouth became apparent on my face. Ewan found this hilarious. He'd obviously been waiting for this, playing Russian roulette at my expense, watching to see which innocent-looking pepper would turn out to be edible dynamite.

My face was purple with embarrassment and smothered coughing, but I didn't want to give him the satisfaction of seeing me choke. I pulled my stomach muscles tight and swallowed the fiery pepper. I reached for my wine-glass, drained it and walked out. Outside in the street, out of sight and earshot of Ewan, with my eyes and nose streaming, I allowed myself a good cough. This was a sustained and productive cough, so productive I nearly vomited, but instead of clearing my lungs, my windpipe became narrower and I found it increasingly difficult to breathe.

I wasn't surprised by this fit, it had happened before. It had begun after I got out of hospital, some kind of stress reaction. I'd managed to hide it from Mum and the boys, but I'd noticed the coughing fits were becoming more frequent and more intense. There was no doubt that this one had been induced by the Bashed-Head Boy incident but there had been loads of other times when it had come on for no apparent reason. One of these days my throat would close completely and that would be the end of me. Death would finally get me: I'd wilt and die like a cut flower.

Ewan came out after me with a glass of water. He wasn't laughing now.

'You OK? Here, drink this.'

I had my back to him. I leaned into the wall, resting my head on my forearm, coughing hard. He held out the water but I shook my head, my only means of communicating. I leaned forward, resting my hands on my thighs, blocking him out of my line of sight. He kept his distance and I was grateful.

Sanj came out and was surprised to find us there. Ewan grabbed him, whispering instructions. Sanj went back into the café and came out with half a baguette. As he approached he was already burrowing into the bread with his bare hands. He scooped out a lump of dough and kneaded it before passing it to Ewan. Ewan approached me and put a hand on my back.

'Here, chew this and swallow it slowly,' he said gently.

I shook my head. There was no way I was going to swallow a lump of dough that had been mangled in the hands of these two. And besides, I'd tried bread before, and water, neither of them worked, nothing worked. I just had to hack my guts up until the fit passed. I just had to hope that this wouldn't be the time I'd keel over and die.

When it became clear that they could do nothing for me, Ewan quietly dismissed Sanj. Ewan continued to stand guard at a discreet distance but it was ten minutes of gagging, heaving and choking before I could afford to take even shallow breaths. I knew I was over the worst when the tears started. Ewan passed me a napkin. I kept my back to him and tried to disguise my fear, relief and mortal embarrassment by blowing my nose and wiping my face.

'C'mon back inside,' he said softly, putting his arm around my shoulder. He ordered me a large brandy.

'Drink it slow, it'll relax you,' he said.

He was right. It did relax me. I laughed.

'What's funny?' said Ewan, with an unsure smile.

It wasn't funny, it was tragic. My first ever date and I'd made a huge fool of myself. It was so tragic there was nothing else to do but laugh.

'Your friend Sanj called you Juan.'

'Aye,' he sighed, 'people here can't say Ewan. It's hard for them to pronounce. No matter how many times I tell them they always end up calling me Juan.'

To Ewan's surprise and mine, I snaked my arms around him. It could have been the brandy that made me do it, on top of the wine. Or maybe it was the flowers he bought me or worrying about the lack of stair lighting in Chloe's building, but it was none of these things.

It was death; death made me do it.

In hospital, when I was close to being measured for a shroud, I was scared. Scared and horny. That was probably why my recovery was so rapid. Dr Collins told my family I had a good attitude, a strong life force. But I just wanted sex. I spent every waking hour in my narrow hospital bed fantasizing about what the buck-toothed hospital orderly Frank would do to me. I could have picked any one of the handsome young doctors, including Dr Collins, but it was always dirtier to dream of Frank. I was terrified of death but I was even more scared to die a virgin.

On the staircase with the dead boy I'd felt fear, but also lust. Not for him, I had pity for him, and a kind of fellow feeling. He was the corpse I should have been, on more than one occasion. I might fancy ugly guys but I didn't fancy dead ones. I wasn't a complete pervert. Seeing the dead boy had reawakened what I'd wanted when I was in hospital: a warm breathing body next to mine.

I could feel Ewan's hesitation, I was Charlie's wee sister after all, but I also felt the warmth of his skin and the tensile strength under it.

'So,' he said with a nervous laugh, 'what d'you want to do now?'

I smiled and pressed my stomach and my breasts against him and my face close to his.

'Want me to show you some puppies?'

Chapter 11

It was a hot night as Ewan and I walked from Barceloneta
to Barri Gòtic. The main streets with the bars on them
were busy, swarming with people smoking and laughing,
but some of the smaller streets we passed through were
dark and deserted. I was glad I wasn't walking here alone.
I kept to the pavement to avoid being hit by the mopeds
that occasionally roared past, but Ewan strode up the
middle of the street.

'Where is it you're staying?' he asked me, again.

'You asked me that a minute ago,' I giggled.

'Sorry, so I did. Come here, you, to me,' he said softly,
seductively, opening his arms.

Ewan was at least as drunk as me. Another bike came
down the street, the girl riding it ringing her bell as a
warning.

'Ewan, be careful you don't get run over,' I said.

'I'll walk where I like. Don't you stand under there,' he
moaned, 'you'll get soaked.'

It was true, as I walked beneath the balconies of the
flats above, water was dripping on my head and down
my neck.

'Where is it coming from?' I asked him.

'Well, if you're lucky it's the run-off from somebody doing their washing or watering their plants.'

'And if I'm not?'

'Then it's their condensed sweat. See those wee boxes up there? They're gathering up people's sweat and spilling it on to your head.'

'Eeuch!' I squawked, moving off the pavement.

'Come here, you, to me, you lovely wee thing.'

This time I came to him. We walked down the middle of the road with our arms entwined.

'Aye, your big brother Charlie's doing all right then, eh? Electrical engineer? He was telling me he's got his own business. Must be making good money. Good on the boy, I always knew he'd do well.'

'You sound like you miss Scotland.'

'*Claro*. Of course I do. It's my homeland, I'll always feel that way about it.'

'Would you ever go back?'

'And do what? Work in a hostel? There aren't any in Cumbernauld. And there's no call for fluent Catalan speakers either. I'm not trained for anything else. I couldn't go back to living in a council flat and signing on. I've stayed away too long. I can't go back to Scotland, but that doesn't mean I don't miss it.'

Ewan looked as though he might start crying, but I was wrong.

'*Oh flower of Scotland!*' he sang,
'*When will we see,*
your likes again?
That fought and died for,
your wee bit hill and glen,
and stood against him.'

Ewan aggressively interrogated himself.

'Against who?'
And then vigorously replied, '*Proud Edward's army,
and sent him homeward,
to think again.*'
Having sex with Ewan tonight might not be a good idea after all. Maybe I should wait until I got to know him a bit better. So far he was grumpy when he was sober and maudlin when he was drunk. I was mulling this over when a river of dark blood came rushing down the hill towards us.

I couldn't believe this was happening; it was like something out of a horror movie. I screamed and dug my nails into Ewan's arm.

'Calm down!' he said sharply. 'It's only the binmen. They're cleaning the street, they do it every night.'

And then I saw that it was indeed the binmen. They were washing the ground, aiming a fat hose into dark corners, flushing the muck out along the street and down into the drains. Even though rationally I knew this, I was still terrified of the black water touching me. I tried to run in the opposite direction but Ewan held tight to my arm.

'Here, get on.'

He bent his knees and invited me to jump on his back.

As I leapt on him the filthy water flowed over the soles of his flip-flops and between his toes. I held tight, my arms and legs clamped around him, my face against his.

'Jesus,' he complained, 'will you stop that bloody squealing? It's right in my ear!'

'Wow, nice place,' Ewan said after we'd walked up the five flights. 'This must be costing a packet.'

'Indeed,' I replied enigmatically.

I showed him into the living room.

'No, but really, how much is this place costing you?'

'Nothing, it's free.'

'How d'you mean?'

'I mean, it's free. I'm looking after it for a friend who's gone to Berlin for a few days.'

Ewan looked confused.

'Charlie said you didn't know anybody in Barcelona.'

'Well, it goes to show that Charlie doesn't know everything.'

'And this "friend" just left you their flat, just like that? Just went to Berlin and left you the keys to a penthouse apartment, for nothing?'

'Ah well, it's not entirely for nothing. I have to earn my keep.'

'Oh aye?'

'A bit of gardening. Crop management and animal husbandry,' I said. 'Come and I'll show you.'

I took him out to the terrace and showed him the marijuana plants.

'Ah,' he nodded.

We sat on the plastic chairs and looked out over the terrace towards the sea.

'Sea view,' I indicated, but it was too dark to see anything. 'If you concentrate you can feel the wind off the sea.'

We closed our eyes on the stiflingly hot night and concentrated on the breeze.

'The maria's not ready yet,' I said with a backwards glance at the plants, 'it'll be a few weeks before the buds are out.'

'Just as well I brought my own then.'

Ewan reached into his trouser pocket and pulled out a lump of hash.

'Not as good as home-grown, but you have to take what you can get when you buy it in a café.'

'You bought that in the café tonight?'

'Those boys don't just sell flowers, you know.'

'Really?'

'Whatever you want, if you know the right people: coke, eckies, grass, anything.'

'Cool. Is your friend Sanj the right people?'

'Could be. He's certainly well connected. Sanj's uncle Mahmood runs the street vendors.'

'Sounds dodgy.'

'Och, it's not like that. Mahmood keeps everybody in a job; he takes care of his community.'

'Like the Godfather?'

'Kind of like the Godfather, only Asian. Mahmood's more of a businessman than a gangster. And a successful one, he owns half the property in Raval. But it's true, he's shady. You hear rumours. I wouldn't like to cross him. Nobody messes with Mahmood.'

Ewan produced a tin containing tobacco and cigarette papers and began rolling a joint. He licked the paper and twisted the joint closed before handing it to me to light.

Weeks ago, resisting the temptation to invite the buck-toothed Frank into my hospital bed, I'd decided that the first man I slept with would be gorgeous and sexy. Was Ewan a worthy recipient of my favours? The criterion, like my gloriously intact hymen, was tight. Since we'd been chatting I'd watched Ewan's mouth closely, imagining kissing it. It was a small mouth, one that I'd previously compared to a cat's arse, but I'd been unfair. His lips were full, pouty even, especially when he smiled. He smiled slowly, the left side of his lips curling slightly before the right, giving him a crooked, mischievous expression. That was sexy, so was his gold hair and firm body.

But good looks weren't enough. The man who deflowered me would have to be a kind, considerate lover. I'd read enough in magazines to know what that meant. Ewan had shown kindness and consideration when I'd had my coughing fit. And he'd gallantly carried me across the dirty water in the street.

Most important of all, my first lover would have to be discreet. Ewan scored highly here too. I doubted he would tell anyone, not Charlie anyway, who would probably kill him for breaching the sanctity of his wee sister.

As I puffed on the joint I weighed it up. Perhaps before the night was out Ewan and I would be doing the mattress mambo.

'No! Suck, don't blow! That's a waste of good dope,' he said.

'Sorry.'

On the negative side, he was a grumpy git. I took another draw and the smoke slid into my lungs quite pleasantly. I passed the joint back, pulling a face I'd seen professional hash-heads make.

'Sorry, I was worried I'd start coughing again.'

'Jesus. Sorry, Alison. I'd forgotten about that. Yeah, you're right, you should take it easy. We don't want that to happen again. I thought you were going to have a heart attack.'

'It was only a cough. It wasn't that bad.'

'Still and all, maybe you should take it easy tonight until your lungs clear out.'

'Oh, you think so?' I said taking the joint from between his fingers.

'Look, if you're going to smoke, put it between your lips, but keep them open at the sides, like this.'

Ewan demonstrated. He moved close to me and gently held the joint to my lips while I inhaled. He was now studying my lips the way I'd studied his.

'That'll cool the smoke down.'

It did. I took a deeper draw than the last.

'Easy, don't take too much.'

'I'm starving,' I said suddenly. 'I'm going to see what's in the fridge.'

Ewan smiled benignly. I left him facing into the sea breeze with his eyes closed.

In the fridge I found a bag of cherries, black cherries, engorged and ripe, the most delicious I'd ever tasted. I had eaten more than half of them before I remembered Ewan.

'Ewan, you have got to try these. These are the best cherries in the world.'

Ewan still had his eyes closed. He was still smiling.

'The wind's got up, can you feel it?' he slurred. 'It feels good.'

I stood still and felt a faint stirring of wind across my face. It occurred to me how wonderful it would be to feel it across my belly and before I knew it I'd pulled my top over my head. Ewan's eyes were still closed.

'Oh, I can feel it, it's fantastic!' I gasped.

I was wearing a magenta-pink bra of Chloe's that I'd found in her drawer. Like the other one, this bra was a bit tight, but it pushed my tits up to just under my chin. The breeze tickled and played across my skin.

Until the glandular fever my torso had been a sweeping panorama of featureless flesh. Now there were distinct regions: the mountainous peaks of my breasts, the flat plain of my stomach, the twin promontories of my arse cheeks. I was shaking from my shoulders to my finger-tips. I had never stripped in front of a boy before. I wasn't comfortable, it wasn't me. I reached to pull my top back on and Ewan opened his eyes.

'I like you better like this,' he said quietly.

I hunched and put my arms across my chest, but Ewan gently opened them. 'Look at the shadow you're cast-ing.'

I turned and saw my silhouette on the wall.

'See? You're like a Bond girl.'

I stared at it and laughed. The shadow had a slender graceful figure.

'Did you have a nice night out?'

'Yes I did, thank you, Ewan.'

'You know, I feel a bit bad. When you gave me your number: it's not a legal requirement to take a contact number. I wanted to see you again, I hope you don't mind.'

'No, I don't mind.'

Ewan saw the Elastoplast on my arm. 'What happened to you?'

'It's nothing,' I mumbled. 'I tripped.'

'Come here, you, to me, I'll kiss it better.'

Suddenly I was aware of a snuffling at my feet. The smell of the hash must have woken Juegita. She and all her puppies were standing looking up at us expectantly. Ewan laughed.

'Puppies!'

He lifted one of the pups and held her to his face, kiss-ing and hugging her.

'You really do have puppies!' he said. 'I thought that

was only a ruse to get me here. I thought you wanted to take advantage of me.'

I leaned over and kissed him, open-mouthed.

'I do,' I said.

Then I kissed him again.

Something was sticking out of his eye, a twig, from a branch. He was blinking and blinking, but his eye wouldn't close properly, his eyelids meeting around the twig like lips kissing, making a puckering, kissing noise.

He was crying and groaning. Stuff was coming out of his eye, slower and thicker than tears.

When I was small and I cried she used to sing a song to cheer me up. She put her finger in her mouth, sliding it across the inside of her cheek and out through her lips. It made such a funny noise that I'd laugh and forget to cry. Pop goes the weasel.

He found the twig. He touched it and screamed, his hand flailing about in front of his face. And then his hand moved to explore it again.

Chapter 12

The next morning I woke up on the couch. I groaned when I realized I had that stupid song 'Pop Goes the Weasel' running round in my head again.

Every time I tried to lift my head two things happened: an invisible mallet fell on my skull and an invisible horse blanket of shame was thrown, heavy and suffocating, over me.

Stupidly I continued to try.

Not only was it incredibly painful but it didn't even have the benefit that hangovers were supposed to have: I could remember everything.

Last night, after a snuffle and a hug, the dogs had gone back to sleep. Ewan and I had advanced from sitting in the plastic chairs to lying on the terrace floor looking at the stars. We had kissed some more. At some point my jeans had been removed and Ewan had taken his shirt off. It was still very hesitant. But we had all night, we weren't going anywhere, and I was loving the sensation of being stoned.

I asked Ewan to roll another joint.

'Eh, excuse me,' Ewan said pointedly, 'I think you've had enough.'

'Eh, excuse me,' I retorted, 'I don't think so.'

'Easy, you're already monged.'

'I'm not monged! Whatever monged is, I'm not it.'

Ewan laughed.

'Of course you are. Your green eyes have turned a lovely shade of pink.'

I giggled. 'Which one?'

Ewan sniggered. 'What d'you mean which one? Both your eyes are pink.'

I hooted with laughter and slapped the ground. 'No, not which eye, you idiot, I meant which shade of pink?'

'Magenta. You idiot,' he replied, sourly.

'The same shade as my bra!'

I started to pull myself up, curious to find a mirror and see what my eyes looked like.

'Hey,' said Ewan pulling me back down, 'don't worry, they're still gorgeous.'

He leaned forward to kiss me. At that moment this struck me as a preposterous thing for him to do. I pushed him away and giggled.

'You're off your face, girl.'

He lay back and didn't try to kiss me any more.

'Ewan, don't get all serious.'

I leaned over and slid my fingertips across his chest.

'It's OK, I'm not monged, I feel nice,' I whispered, but even as I whispered, I felt the impulse to laugh. Everything I said sounded ridiculous.

Ewan looked me in the eye. He lifted his bum off the ground and pulled down his jeans. As he tugged his jeans past his crotch his penis sprang out and bounced a few times against his belly. I bit into my cheeks and managed to resist laughing, but I shouldn't have looked down. There, fully erect and weirdly asymmetrical, was his hilariously misshapen penis.

How could I not laugh?

I must have been monged after all, how else could I explain the irrepressible waves of mirth that washed over me at the absurdity of a penis? That and first-night nerves.

It had been no stifled titter. It had been a pretty intense attack of the giggles: shoulders heaving, slapping the ground, pointing. I groaned again at the mental replay: *pointing*.

I'd seen a naked penis before. In magazines admittedly, but nevertheless, I knew what they looked like. *Cosmo* had run a feature celebrating the fact that no two were the same. They had photographs of long ones, thin ones, long thin ones, pointed ones, tulip-shaped ones, bent ones, short stubby ones that resembled doorknobs, ones that veered to the left or right or curled back or forward, tiny ones difficult to detect with the naked eye, huge ones like Hoover attachments.

As I lay groaning on the couch I racked my brains to think which category Ewan's fitted. On reflection it seemed like it was of a reasonable length, a bit bell-ended and definitely curly. It was the curliness that had started me off laughing, the way it curved outwards and sideways, like a friendly puppet that lived in Ewan's pants. Apart from the curliness, it wasn't that bad. It was certainly no reason to ridicule the poor guy.

It was first-night nerves, I told myself, simple first-night nerves, but Ewan wouldn't have known that.

He'd stormed off to the bedroom last night, perhaps thinking that, despite my hysteria, I'd follow him. I would've if I'd not felt so ashamed; if I'd not been so nervous about actually doing The Deed.

As my hangover began to lift I thought of ways to get back on track with him. I'd bring him a cuppa. The only tea I could find was some foul-smelling herbal stuff. That would have to do. There was no milk, I hoped he could take it black.

'I've brought you a cuppa,' I said as chirpily as I could.

Ewan grunted. He opened his eyes and sat up.

'Cheers,' he said.

There was no rancour in his voice. Perhaps he'd been as stoned as I was; perhaps he'd no memory of last night. More likely he was as embarrassed as I was and preferred to forget it.

'Jesus Christ!' yelled Ewan. 'What the hell is that? It tastes like rat poison.'

Not being able to understand Spanish, I hadn't stopped to read the label. I'd assumed it was tea; perhaps it *was* rat poison.

'Sorry,' I said meekly. 'Don't drink it if you don't like it.'

We fell quiet. This was embarrassing. I stood beside the bed in the magenta pink bra and pants set. I hadn't thought about it when I woke up, after all Ewan had already seen me like this last night, but now I felt self-conscious. To cover myself and get close to him I lifted the sheet and slid into the other side of the bed. The bed was so big I was miles away from him. He didn't object but, by the way he grabbed the sheet around his groin, I could see he was uneasy.

So he hadn't forgotten.

'I'm so sorry about last night, Ewan.'

'Forget it,' he snapped.

'I must have been off my face after all.'

'Oh yeah,' he laughed sarcastically.

'But also, I was shy.'

He didn't say anything to this.

'I was nervous; it's not that I didn't like your penis . . .'

This was completely the wrong thing to say. He nearly jumped out the bed. If he hadn't been naked he probably would have. He sat up rigid and held on to his bits protectively.

And then I thought of the perfect solution. I'd give him a blow job.

I wanted to prove to Ewan that I didn't think his penis was laughable. I had thought about blow jobs many times. The notion of being so horned up that you were prepared to put a penis in your mouth was fascinating to me. Especially when urine passed through it several times a day. A penis was a pipeline for raw sewage.

I had to halt this train of thought or I'd be sick while I was down there. *Dear Lisa and Lauren, Currently attempting fellatio without vomiting. Man may be unwilling. Wish you were here.*

I lay quiet and slid my hand under the sheet, slowly creeping as close as he would allow me. I heard his breathing change. After a few minutes spent in silence he moved his hand from his cock and lay back, giving me permission. My hand made contact with something warm and surprisingly hard. The skin on it was soft, like a baby's, and as I ran my fingers up and down I slowly pulled the sheet away. Ewan had a beautiful body, slim manly hips, legs that looked solid and powerful. He could have been a sculpture, but his peach-coloured skin was warm and fragrant and soft to the touch. I wanted to get closer to it. I slipped down the bed and positioned my head. I was ready to clamp my mouth around it, to fill my mouth with the size and smell and heat of it, when the bedroom door flew open and Chloe caught me with Ewan's engorged cock inches from my lips.

Chapter 13

'Well, looky, looky! What have we got here?' cried Chloe.

Ewan yanked up the sheet to cover his embarrassment.

'Chloe!' I gasped. 'My God, I thought you were coming back tomorrow.'

'Well, I was gonna, but it seems I was missing all the fun here.'

She was smiling and her tone sounded jokey, but I wasn't sure if it was sarcasm. I didn't know her well enough.

'It's a regular *ménage à trois*!' she trilled merrily, and then went out to the terrace calling to Juegita.

As soon as Chloe left the room Ewan sprang out of bed and pulled on his jeans. I caught a glimpse of his penis, dangling and even more bent-looking. He pulled on his T-shirt and stomped off to the toilet, locking the door noisily behind him. I had to sort things out with Chloe, but my clothes were on the terrace. I was wearing her bra and pants. Hanging on the back of the bedroom door was a pale pink dressing gown. I threw it on, found my flip-flops beside the couch in the living room, and went to talk to her. The dressing gown was too long for me, and trailed the ground. To stop it trailing I had to lift it and hold it out in front of me, shuffling forward like a Japanese geisha.

'Did you take Juegita out for a walk?'

I began to reply, trying to come up with something plausible, when Chloe spoke again.

'Ah, I see that you didn't,' she stated simply.

The evidence was right in front of us. Juegita had left a massive turd pile in front of the yurt. Chloe had refilled the dogs' water bowls and as she put them down Juegita and the pups rushed forward to lap from them. I should have refilled the bowls last night when I came back. That must have been why Juegita and the puppies had woken up. They didn't want my drunken kisses, they needed food and water.

I hung my head in shame.

'You've been holding out on me, Alison. You didn't tell me you had a boyfriend,' said Chloe.

'He's my brother's friend.'

'Oh, OK.' She nodded and folded her arms. 'And do you blow all your brother's friends? Is this, like, an old Scottish tradition?'

'I'm sorry. I know it looks bad but—'

'And are they all such brutes?'

'Sorry?'

'Well, come on, Alison.' She dropped her voice to a whisper and pointed towards the bedroom. 'Honey, he has red hair!'

'So?'

My own hair, a darker auburn shade, but nonetheless unmistakably red, fell across my face as I posed this question.

'Hey,' she said, holding out her hands in a none-of-my-business gesture, 'maybe you like that stuff.'

I was confused. Why was Chloe being so unpleasant about Ewan? I was the one who had neglected the dogs. This was nothing to do with him.

She was on her way to fill Juegita's food bowl.

'Nice bra,' she sniped as she passed me.

The dressing gown had fallen open enough for Chloe to catch a glimpse of magenta. I groaned, remembering the white bra and pants set. Now she'd seen me with her magenta bra, she'd no doubt link me to the disappearance of the Victoria's Secret box.

I followed her to the kitchen.

'I hope you don't mind, I needed to borrow some clothes, I had to wash all my stuff,' I said.

'So I see,' said Chloe, pulling my stuff out of the washing machine.

I'd been out all day yesterday. What with my job interview and phoning Mum and disposing of the white underwear and robbing Chloe's cash tin, I hadn't had a chance to hang up my clothes.

'It's OK, I'll get that,' I said, taking my wet jeans from her.

As I said it I heard the front door open and close again quickly. Ewan. He must have ducked out. What if he'd heard the things Chloe said about him?

'I'm sorry, Chloe, I'll be back in a minute,' I said, thrusting the jeans back into her hands and running out. I ran down the stairs, my flip-flops clacking on every step.

'Ewan! Ewan!' I wailed.

Although it was bright sunlight outside, the last flight of stairs was dark as usual. I could hardly see where I was putting my feet.

'Ewan, wait!'

As I ran I held the dressing gown up around my knees with one hand while the other skimmed the handrail. On the last flight, as I turned a corner, my right foot slid in the flip-flop and I lurched forward. Instinctively I put out both hands, let the dressing gown fall, and tripped over it. I fell three steps and cut my little toe. It bled copiously. Another bloodstained stairwell.

'Ewan!' I screamed.

He turned when he heard me. I caught up with him halfway along the street. I limped as fast as I could, and ran straight at him. Trying to keep the street dirt off my bleeding toe, I stood on one leg, a pink flamingo, buffeted by the crowds of workers and tourists moving through the narrow lane.

'I'm sorry, Ewan, what a mess. The whole thing was my fault,' I blurted. 'I was scared, first-night nerves, that's all. I've never done it before. But I'm a quick learner.'

Ewan gave a sneering laugh. 'Yeah, right,' he snorted.

'Yeah, right!' I insisted, my hand on my hip.

'Come on: you're a virgin? But you must be, what? Twenty?'

'I'm twenty-two,' I moaned.

'Jesus!' said Ewan, putting his hand to his head. He turned and began walking away. 'Look, just forget it, OK?'

'Ewan!'

He kept on walking.

'No, Ewan, don't tell me to forget it, *you* forget it!' I shouted after him.

A middle-aged couple stopped beside me.

'And you were so nearly the lucky man!' I screamed. He was far away from me now, darting through the crowd. I was losing sight of him. 'But you blew it, d'you hear me? You had your chance, Ewan, and you blew it!'

More tourists had stopped around me. They stood grinning, as if they were watching a street performance on La Rambla.

'What's wrong?' I spat at them. 'Never seen a virgin before?'

I turned and hobbled back towards the flat. The blood from my toe had splashed the pink silk dressing gown, and the stain was already turning an ugly brown colour. Even without knowing about the money and the underwear, Chloe had every right to be angry with me. Now that she was back I'd have to start looking again for somewhere to live. I needed to pick up my stuff but first I'd have to face Chloe.

Chapter 14

I chapped Chloe's door, a unobtrusive respectful chap, and waited. I wished I could limp off into the sunset and never have to face her.

I chapped again. No response.

I rattled the door harder. What was she doing in there? Everything I owned was in there: passport, clothes, money. Maybe she was going through my stuff.

I was standing on one leg, bent over, holding my cut foot, when she answered the door.

'What the hell happened to you?' she gasped.

I'd tried to protect the pink dressing gown but the damage was already done. In this heat the blood had already dried to a crusty brown stain.

'I'm so sorry, I cut my toe. I'm afraid your dressing gown got a bit dirty. I'll clean it now. If I can just give it a good scrub it'll be good as new.'

'Come,' she said, and walked into the bathroom. I followed, trying not to get blood on the floor. She plugged the bath and ran the hot water. Then without a word she walked out. I sat on the edge of the bath. The blood from my toe had thickened to a gloop that smeared the tiled floor. I had ruined everything. Chloe and I weren't going to be friends now, we wouldn't hang out and smoke dope on her roof terrace after all.

She returned and tipped a whole box of salt into the bath, then left again. Salt would be good for getting the stain out the fabric. I needed to get the dressing gown off and into the bath before the bloodstain became fixed.

Chloe came back and poured half a bottle of TCP into the bathwater. Disinfecting her clothes after I'd worn them was an unnecessary precaution. I wasn't diseased. On the other hand, it was blood. She probably thought, as she'd caught me, that a girl like me, a girl who honoured the old Scottish tradition of blowing all her brother's friends, would be hoaching with pox and disease.

'Take it off,' said Chloe.

I started to take off the dressing gown, remembering with shame the borrowed bra and pants underneath. From my position, sitting on the edge of the bath, I was having trouble getting it off without letting my toe touch the floor.

Chloe helped me. With great care she lifted the dressing gown from my shoulders. It must be worth a lot, antique silk or something. She held her forearm out for me to balance against while I lifted my bum. Gently she slid the gown from underneath me. When she had stripped me of it she rolled the expensive pink silk into a ball and, instead of dousing it in the disinfected water, threw it in a heap on the floor.

'Come on,' she said sternly, 'you have to do it. It'll sting but that's good.'

I was confused.

'Alison, put your foot in the water.'

Stupefied, I let her lift my leg and gently lower it into the bath.

It did sting.

'Ooow!'

Chloe laughed.

'That's it, now move it around, you have to get the dirt out.'

'But your dressing gown . . .'

'We'll get to that, for now just let the dirt soak out of your toe. I told you before, bugs here are different than the ones you have in Scotland. You could wind up with a serious infection. Either you're extremely accident-prone or you're on a mission to pick up every bug in Catalonia.'

'I'm accident-prone.'

'You know that's psychological, don't you?'

'No, I didn't.'

'Yup, a clear indicator of self-esteem issues,' she said cheerfully. 'And, if you have an issue,' she said, handing me the paper hankies, 'then you need a tissue.'

I was crying. I'd worn and trashed her clothes, starved and neglected her poor little dogs and yet *she* was washing *my* feet. It was all a bit biblical. I took a hanky and blew my nose.

She lifted my leg from the water and dabbed my toe with a clean towel. It was still oozing blood, some of which went on the towel. Not wanting to contaminate anything else I tried to pull my leg away, but Chloe pressed down hard, the red stain blossoming on the towel.

'At least I know now where the Band-Aids are.' She tore open the sticking plaster with her teeth and began dressing my toe. 'You can put your own clothes on now. They should be dry by now.'

'You hung up my clothes?'

'All part of the service.'

'Chloe, I'm sorry. I let you down.'

'Oh yeah,' she agreed.

'You've been so good to me and I've made such a mess of everything . . .'

'Blah blah blah. Hey, forget it.'

'I was really looking forward to us being friends and I'm sorry I've messed it all up. I wish I could make it up to you.'

I wanted to say more but there really was no more to say. Chloe had her head down but I could see a smile on her face as she gently wound the plaster round my toe and lowered my foot to the floor.

'Well, you could take me out to lunch.'

I laughed. 'Lunch? That's it?'

'Yeah, but not a sandwich, a good lunch. I know a place in the Born. It's kinda formal though, we'd have to dress.'

I knew from the guidebook that the Born was the posh end of town. Restaurants there weren't going to be cheap and the word 'formal' was even more worrying.

'Lunch, great!' I said smiling. 'We could do that.'

Chapter 15

Chloe led me across Via Laietana into the Born. The buildings seemed just as old and just as closely packed as in Gòtic, but there was a more muted atmosphere here as we passed the expensive-looking tapas bars and street cafés. I hadn't seen this part of town yet and Chloe was enjoying being my tour guide.

'And this is the other cathedral,' she said, and led me to the modern fire sculpture beside it.

'It's beautiful, what is it?' I asked her.

'It's an eternal flame, Barcelona's own memorial to Elvis Presley.'

'Really?'

The moment I said it I felt stupid.

Chloe laughed. I laughed too, to cover my embarrassment.

Five girls, teenagers, stood on the cathedral steps singing some kind of sacred music. Probably students, they were all good-looking girls. They used a straw hat with a white ribbon around it to collect donations. A small crowd had gathered to listen to their voices blending into one.

'Barcelona's memorial to the Spice Girls,' I said lamely.

Chloe laughed again. 'Ah, the Spice Girls, I loved them when I was a kid. Which one did you want to be? I always wanted to be . . .'

We both said it at the same time.

'Posh Spice.'

And then we burst out laughing.

We wove our way through the Born and came to a little restaurant which, with its ordinary appearance, gave me hope that it might charge ordinary prices. Despite having taken 200 euros out of Chloe's tin, if I was going to last here until September I was going to have to watch every centimo. When we got inside the cheapest thing on the menu was a *cubierto* at 5 euros.

'What's a *cubierto*?' I asked Chloe.

'That's the cover charge.'

The place was crowded with heavy old-fashioned furniture that the waiters had to skitter around. It was busy but the atmosphere was quiet, reverential. Most of the customers were old. Heads down, they silently tucked in.

'Jeez, it's freezing in here,' said Chloe, loud enough to be overheard. 'Check me out: my nipples are sticking out like cigar butts.'

The air conditioning was set to a low temperature, probably to preserve the flaky old oil paintings on the walls or perhaps the flaky old customers, but this was Chloe's choice. I wasn't going to criticize.

A door from the kitchen swung open and a powerful smell of fish escaped.

'This place does the best tuna,' said Chloe enthusiastically, pronouncing it toona, 'you have to try it.'

I looked it up on the menu. Toona was 35 euros. Even if I ordered the cheapest thing on the menu, I reckoned

I wouldn't get out of here without spending at least fifty. The waiter was now hovering: simpering smile, cloth-draped arm.

'*Ensalada verde*, please,' I said.

It had the word 'salad' in the middle of it and at 7 euros it was the cheapest thing on the menu.

'Sure? The *ensalada de la casa* is fabulous,' said Chloe.

'Eh . . .'

I looked at the menu again, reconsidering my choice. *Ensalada de la casa* was 9 euros. I hesitated as though weighing it up.

'Nah, I'll stick with that.'

'OK, have it your way.'

If I'd had it my way we'd have gone to Burger King. A BK meal, including fries and a drink, was less than seven euros. The thought of it got my salivary glands going.

'I'm totally gonna pig, I haven't eaten in weeks. *Bistec con salsa de Rocafort para me, por favor*,' Chloe told the waiter.

I couldn't resist looking it up on the menu. Thirty-two euros. Bloody hell.

'Oh, and let's have something fizzy to celebrate.'

Before I could stop myself I'd screwed up my face and shaken my head, no. But she didn't see me and ordered anyway, Veuve Clicquot, 52 euros. I had to fight the impulse to burst out crying.

Once the bottle was open there was no use worrying about it. I'd have to pay for it now. When the waiter filled my glass I didn't try to stop him.

'*¡Salud!*' burbled Chloe.

'Cheers,' I sighed.

Chloe's food came out first and was a fat juicy steak. A ripe pungent smell rose from the thick creamy blue-cheese sauce. Butter-glazed baby potatoes and petit pois, tiny and delicate, made the steak look even bigger. Saliva flooded my mouth. I lifted my knife and fork as I saw the waiter approach our table with another plate, my *ensalada verde*, no doubt. I couldn't wait.

A bowl of wet lettuce.

'Aw,' said Chloe, breaking off from cutting into her steak. 'They haven't brought everything. Alison, what did you order?'

'*Ensalada verde*,' I said, polishing my knife and fork with my napkin.

I could always get a BK later on La Rambla. No matter how little money I had left after Chloe's extravagances, I was going to have one last Flame-Grilled Whopper Meal before I was completely destitute.

'Yeah, but what else? Didn't you order the toona?'

'No, no, just this. Salad does me. I'm not very hungry.'

'You're gonna sit there with a bowl of lettuce? You're kidding me, right?'

'No, no. I prefer a light lunch, especially lettuce. Very refreshing. D'you think they have mayonnaise?'

Chloe hooted with laughter as I nibbled my lettuce. I had to laugh too. She was probably laughing at my eccentric Britishness. I was laughing at having got myself into such a ridiculous situation, again, and wondering if the ladies' toilet had a window big enough to escape through.

'Oh no you don't, missy,' she said, turning serious, 'I see what's happening here.'

I put down my cutlery and made an apologetic face. The game was up, she had seen through me. Thank God for that, I thought, we could either halve the bill or do a runner. Do a runner was my preferred option. Chloe put down her steak knife. She leaned across the table, clasped both my hands and searched my face.

'Alison, you don't have to lose any more weight.'

'Sorry?'

'You're round and luscious and juicy and womanly and curvy and . . . womanly.'

She said womanly twice but I let it go.

'You've lost enough, no more dieting.'

'I'm not dieting. I've never been on a diet in my life. I've lost weight recently, but how did you know?'

Chloe smiled. She lifted my left hand in the air, like the referee with the winner in a boxing match, and ran her fingers along a broken silvery line on the inside of my upper arm.

'Stretch marks. I saw them when I was wiping the blood off you after you tripped.'

I thought of Ewan kissing my arm last night. Kissing it better. He must have seen the snail trails up my arm twinkling in the moonlight. I pulled away from her and tugged down the short sleeves of my top.

'I'm sorry,' said Chloe quickly, 'I didn't mean to embarrass you. They're hardly visible.'

'*You* saw them.'

'Yeah but you have to know what to look for. Only another anorexic would notice.'

'I'm not anorexic,' I said.

'Well I sure as hell am.'

Chloe took my hand again and placed my fingers on the same stretch marks on her own arm.

'Or I used to be. I was bulimic; I used to hide little bags of vomit every which where around the house. I was really good at it, I had quite a talent.'

This stopped the conversation for a moment and we

108

returned to our plates: me, the womanly one, to my lettuce and Chloe, the anorexic, to her butter-lathered steak.

'I was so thin my head was bigger than my ass.'

'Well, it isn't now,' I said.

I'd meant it kindly but Chloe shot me a worried look.

'Not that your arse is big, it's not.' I tried to think of something positive to say. 'But it's bigger than your head, and a nicer shape.'

'Shut up!' she squealed in her Californian way. 'My ass is getting bigger every day.'

'No, but it's . . . womanly.'

I was afraid I'd overdone it and sounded insincere but Chloe laughed. Relieved that she could take a joke, I laughed too.

'Yeah, I suppose. I'm in recovery now. What about you?'

'I used to be fat. Huge.'

'Yeah? How come?'

'I don't really know, maybe I wasn't getting enough exercise. I didn't go out much. I had the usual schoolgirl diet of no breakfast, chips and Coke for lunch and whatever Mum made for dinner. Plus the occasional treat of a crisps and fish-finger sandwich before Mum came home. After she came home I ate leftover stock she brought from the bakery: custard tarts, jam doughnuts, whatever.'

'That's a typical schoolgirl diet?'

'It is in Cumbernauld.'

'No wonder you were huge.'

'Yeah, I probably was eating too much but honestly, I'm not bulimic. That's just a waste of a good doughnut.'

'So how come you're no longer huge?'

109

'I caught glandular fever, really bad. I lost three stone; I was in hospital for months, expected to die. Most of my organs are scarred, probably permanently damaged. I'm only twenty-two but if I don't choke on a coughing fit I'll probably keel over with a heart attack. Heart attacks run in our family. Believe me, there's enough serious things wrong with me.'

'Anorexia is serious,' Chloe snapped.

'Sorry, I didn't say it isn't serious.'

'You implied it. You said there are plenty of *serious* things wrong with me . . .'

'Yes but I didn't mean—'

'Anorexia kills people. I've seen some of my friends die, horribly.'

'Chloe, I'm sorry. I didn't want to . . .'

Unexpectedly, I started to cry.

'Oh God, what is it now?'

'I didn't trip,' I blurted. 'The other day when you found me, there was a dead boy on the stairs. I fell in his blood.'

I told her the whole story. She listened quietly. She reached across and held my hand again, using her napkin to wipe away my tears.

'Oh my God,' was all she said.

She didn't ask any questions or tell me I should report it to the police. She had the waiter bring us a bottle of brandy. She poured me one and put it in my hand.

'I can't pay for this,' I said quietly, 'I don't think I have enough money.'

I was tired of keeping up the pretence. If I could tell her about Bashed-Head Boy I could tell her I was broke.

'You're broke? So that's why you ordered lettuce! Here, gimme your plate.'

I didn't argue. She tipped the watery lettuce on to a side plate and scraped on to my plate all of her potatoes and peas and more than half her steak.

'Eat.'

I ate. By the third mouthful of steak and potatoes my tears had dried. I looked up and found Chloe watching me and smiling.

'I didn't bring enough money,' I sighed. 'It's stupid but it's as simple as that. My English teaching doesn't start for another two months. I'll have to go back.'

'What do you mean? Go back where?'

'To Scotland, just until my job starts.'

'No.'

'No?' I laughed, pretending not to understand.

'No. You've had a terrible experience. You're in no shape to leave town. You should stay here. Stay with me at my place.'

'But Chloe,' I said half-heartedly, 'I couldn't impose on you.'

'It's only two months; I think my allowance can cope. If not I'll ask Dad to give me more.'

Or, I thought, she could spend some of the money she had stashed in the biscuit tin. I wondered if Chloe had thought of that. If she had, she wasn't saying.

Chapter 16

In the restaurant Chloe hadn't seemed that interested but on the way back to the flat she asked me questions about the dead boy. I didn't mind going over it again, although I'd thought I would. It was good to get it out.

The last time something bad happened, I didn't tell anyone, I couldn't. The educational psychologist said this was due to the trauma I'd suffered and that my reaction, a kind of lethargic acceptance of everything, was normal. I'd come out of it in my own time, she said, but I didn't. Lethargic acceptance suited me; it made life easy, if uneventful. It wasn't trauma that made me lethargic, it was secrecy.

But this time I hadn't kept it secret. I'd told Chloe and the sky hadn't fallen in. It wasn't healthy to keep secrets, they kept burning inside you. All these years I'd been slow cooking from the inside out.

Once I'd begun telling her I couldn't stop, going over it detail by detail. Chloe was very patient and supportive. She asked if I'd touched him, or anything else at the scene, if anyone had seen me on the stairwell. I told her no, and I asked her about my bloody shoeprints.

'D'you think those might incriminate me?'

'Aw, honey, how can they? You saw a dead boy, is all. You're not to blame, you did nothing wrong. You're only a bystander, not even a useful witness. What's to incriminate? You didn't know this boy, you have no motive, how could anyone connect you to it? The best thing you can do is try to forget about it.'

'I don't know if I can forget it but I'm glad I got it off my chest.'

I stopped walking and, to stop Chloe, I put my arm out across her waist. She stood still and looked me in the eye.

'You won't tell anyone, will you?'

'Alison,' Chloe said, taking my hand and placing it on her heart, 'I swear on my mom's life that I won't tell anyone. You can tell me anything you want and I promise I'll never tell.'

I copied her gesture and took her hand and put it over my heart.

'Chloe, I feel the same, I want you to know that.'

'We're friends now, room-mates,' she said, 'we look out for each other. Deal?'

'Deal.' I smiled.

When we got back to the flat Chloe immediately set to clearing drawers for my clothes. She threw her clothes on the bed and then emptied out my rucksack.

'Hey, neat backpack,' she said, 'where'd you get it?'

'Och, you're kidding. I got this rucksack in Asda at George.'

'What, is he like, a designer?'

'It's a brand name, at Asda. Part of the Wal-Mart family.'

'You have Wal-Mart in Scotland?'

'Yes, Scotland's a far-flung outpost of the American empire.'

'I can't believe this is from Wal-Mart! Girl, you've got some style.'

'Cheers.'

She was being nice. With both our clothes piled together it was obvious which were the designer labels and which were the cheap high street copies. Chloe worked hard to put me at my ease, as if she wanted to settle me in before I changed my mind. I wasn't going to change my mind but I felt a bit uncomfortable not paying rent. Chloe also picked up the bill at lunch. Thank God she did, it was 94 euros by the time we'd had the brandy.

I wouldn't exploit her generosity though; I'd pay her back in full as soon as I started earning. I'd make myself useful around the flat and be a good friend. Another benefit of living here was that now I'd be able to return the money I'd taken. There might even be a Victoria's Secret outlet in Barcelona where I could buy a replacement set of underwear. Everything could be fixed and Chloe need never know.

I could hardly believe my luck or Chloe's generosity, but felt I understood it. She didn't want to live alone in this city any more than I did. In this strange situation, in this terrifying but amazing place, we were perfect for each other.

There was only the one enormous bed in the flat. I insisted I could sleep on the couch or even outside on the terrace, it was certainly warm enough.

'Oh yeah, it's warm enough,' she said sarcastically, 'and the mosquitoes are gonna love ya.'

I hadn't thought of that. I cast my mind back to my

first night in the hostel and the fuss the Frenchwoman made about closing the window. The mosquitoes must be bad. Before we went out for lunch Chloe had put the air conditioning on in the bedroom for the dogs, and it felt deliciously cool.

'Look, try it, there's plenty of room, we can both fit comfortably, it's fine. You lie there.'

I lay where I was told, on one side of the giant bed. Chloe lay on the other side.

'See? There's plenty of room, even when we both spread out.'

It was true, the bed was enormous.

'Well, if it's OK with you. But if your boyfriend stays over I can sleep on the couch.'

'I don't have a boyfriend.'

'Oh, I thought . . . Weren't you supposed to go to Vietnam with your dad and your boyfriend?'

'Oh yeah. No, we broke up.'

'Oh, that's a shame.'

'No it isn't. I don't want a boyfriend, I just wanna pick boys up when I want one.' She screwed up her face. 'Does that sound really bad?'

'No,' I said, my expression neutral, 'that sounds reasonable.'

We hadn't discussed Chloe walking in on Ewan and me but now we skirted around it.

'I do have one house rule,' she said, 'I don't want guys in this apartment. I don't want 'em to know where I live or anything about me.'

'That's absolutely fine,' I said, 'not a problem.'

'It's the only rule I make.'

'Honestly, it's fine by me.'

'Good,' she said with a decisive nod. 'Wanna go to the

park? We could take Juegita, she could use the exercise. You won't believe how many guys hit on you when you have a cute dog. Two hot babes like us can easily pick up a couple of Latino boys. Ever had a Latin lover, Alison?'

'No, I haven't had that pleasure.'

'Well what are we waiting for?'

I wasn't so sure. I was still stinging from Ewan's brutal rejection earlier, but I wanted to show willing.

'I'll come, but I wouldn't count on pulling boys when you're with me. They usually run in the opposite direction.'

'Oh come on, Alison!' cried Chloe, and then slyly added, 'I think you're underestimating the cuteness of the dog.'

'This bed is so comfy,' I said, 'the brandy's making me sleepy.'

'OK, let's take a siesta.' Chloe yawned. 'We can pick up boys later. Juegita! ¡*Ven aquí*!'

All the dogs scrabbled out from under the bed; Juegita, delicately ladylike despite her sagging teats, and her pups with their fat little bodies, all eager to get on the bed with us. Juegita leapt and joined us but the pups could only mewl and claw at the sides.

'OK,' Chloe groaned, leaning down and scooping them on to the bed one by one, 'let's see just how many girls this bed can take.'

Juegita snuggled into me and kept trying to lick my face. I was becoming accustomed to the doggy smell but I wasn't keen on her licking me. I tried to subtly turn my face aside whenever I saw her tongue appear. Chloe was giving me a home; I didn't want her to think I was rejecting the friendly overtures of her beloved pet.

'Chloe, you know Juegita did a jobby on the terrace?'

116

Two of the puppies were walking across her chest. Chloe had her eyes closed and held up her hand while she asked a question.

'Hold on a minute here: does did a jobby mean take a dump?'

'Sorry, yes. Exactly.'

'Hmm,' she said sleepily, 'I like that.'

'It's just that I've noticed that the puppies don't. Take a dump, that is.'

'That they don't take a jobby?'

'*Do* a jobby.'

'Whatever,' said Chloe. 'They do, but believe me, you don't wanna know. It's too gross.'

Juegita continued to lick my face and was now trying to lick my lips.

'I haven't seen any puppy-sized jobby.'

'Oh, they shit all right, but Juegita cleans it up.'

'Wow!' I said, looking at Juegita. Unfortunately this glance allowed her a direct hit, a slurp of her long tongue right across my open mouth. 'How does she manage that?' I asked.

'She eats it.'

There were three of us in the bed. Chloe, me and a guy. The guy was lying on top of Chloe. The guy didn't have a shirt on, I could see his bare skin. His head hovered over Chloe's and he was kissing her. He pushed forward an inch and moved back again. He did it again, rocking slowly forward and back. Chloe was making noises, uh and oh. They were doing it. Chloe saw me and smiled. The guy carried on, hovering on top of her, forward and back. I could only see the back of his head, his dark curly hair, but when he turned I realized that I knew him. It was him, Bashed-Head Boy. I laughed, he was alive. He smiled too but as he turned towards me I saw that there was something in his eye. He saw the horror on my face and while he continued to rock back and forth on top of Chloe, while he was fucking her and she lay smiling, he put his fingers around the twig and tugged. With a dreadful sucking sound his eye plopped out and dangled on his cheek from its stalk.

Chapter 17

I woke up. Chloe was standing over me with a concerned look on her face.

'You OK?' she asked. 'You were crying.'

'Och, just bad dreams.'

'About the boy?'

'Yeah, kind of.'

'It's just your brain processing it.'

'I suppose.'

'Come on, let's get up and do stuff. Try and get it off your mind for a while.'

Chloe was playing a CD, the music must have woken me. She sat on the edge of the bed in her bra and knickers, a small vanity mirror balanced on her knee. At first I thought she was putting on make-up but she was chopping white powder on the mirror with a credit card and singing along to the salsa music.

She smiled. *'Buenas tardes, señorita.'*

'Buenas tardes.'

She rolled a twenty-euro note and sniffed up a line. *'¡Vamos bailar!'* she yelled enthusiastically.

'Sorry?' I asked. I should have never attempted to reply

in Spanish, it was only asking for trouble. 'I don't know what that means.'

'It means let's get caned and go dancing!'

I tried to sit up but my head felt too heavy. I groaned. Chloe tapped the mirror with the rolled-up note. Some powder fell out which she quickly hoovered up through her nostril.

'This should sort you out,' she said, handing me the mirror.

There was another line on it. I had never got caned before. I wasn't sure I wanted to. I was lying in an awkward position, holding the mirror, and I couldn't lift my head.

'Oh there she is!' said Chloe, extracting a sleeping puppy that had become entangled in my hair. 'I knew there was one more.'

My head suddenly felt light and free. I sat up and held the rolled-up note tentatively to my nose, fingering both ends of it, testing for dampness.

It wasn't so much that I was scared. I knew the health risks, especially to my fragile organs, and the chances of addiction: the rest of my life spent shoplifting or selling my arse for my next hit, but that wasn't the problem. I just didn't fancy putting something which had been inside Chloe's nose, inside mine. It was way too soon to be exchanging nasal mucus.

'Are you gonna snort that line?'

'Course I am,' I said and bent my head.

'There's other ways, you know. You can put it under your tongue or rub it on your gums, I love doing that but it's sooo gonna give you gum disease.'

I had to smile; this obsession with dental health was so American.

'Roll it into a joint and smoke it if you want. Or push it

up inside you with your finger, that's nice, different. But the quickest way's to snort.'

'No, snorting's fine for me.'

I shoved the rolled note a bit further up my nose than was really necessary, making my eyes water. I closed off my other nostril and inhaled slowly. I managed to get most of it on my first attempt.

I didn't know what I was supposed to feel but it had absolutely no effect whatsoever.

Chloe handed me a glass of water. I guzzled it down in one, surprised by my thirst.

'So, whaddaya think?' she asked me.

'Yeah, nice,' I said nodding, as though I was a cocaine connoisseur. I didn't want to tell her that she'd wasted her money.

'Club Cubana will be open tonight, we could go there.'

'Oh, dancing. OK. What time is it?'

'Five after ten, we slept for hours.'

'Ten!'

'Ten's early for Barcelona,' said Chloe. 'Things don't start around here until midnight at least. We can get some dinner and then go dancing.'

'I'm not very hungry.'

'Me neither, it's the cocaine.'

Chloe and I cha-cha-chaed around the bedroom getting dressed. I first tried on my blue dress, the dress I'd arrived in Barcelona in. I could keep cool in this if we were going to be doing a lot of dancing.

'D'you think this is OK, Chloe?'

'Mmm, it's a cute colour, it really goes with your hair, but maybe it's kinda daywear?'

'Yeah, too daywear,' I agreed.

I made a mental note that in future I'd buy clothes in this colour but a different style. I next tried my short white jeans with a long lemon top. I'd never worn the top before. Chloe was reluctant to give her opinion but I insisted.

'Separately they're great, I'm just not sure they work together,' she said, 'but hell, wear whatever you want, the important thing is to feel good.'

'No, you're right, I trust your judgement, you're the artist.'

I kept with the white jeans and swapped to a strappy top in a stronger colour, a shimmering dark blue.

'That's pretty.'

She was just saying that to be nice. I could tell she didn't like this outfit either. And anyway, I didn't want to look pretty. I wanted to look sexy, like Chloe. Chloe would look sexy in a T-shirt, how could I compete?

'No,' I decided, 'I don't like it. It looks terrible. I look terrible.'

I'd run out of options. I had arrived in Barcelona with a rucksack full of drab daywear.

'Shut up! You do not look terrible!' Chloe said. 'Look, you can borrow something of mine if you want, I have a million outfits in that closet that'll look amazing on you. Take what you want. No, better yet,' she said, getting excited, 'I'm gonna give you a makeover, clothes, make-up, hair, the works. I think a Latina look could really work for you. Oh, this is gonna be great! You're gonna look like America's Next Top Model when I'm done.'

Chloe said all of this at top speed. She stood on the bed and pulled me up with her. We clasped hands and jumped, bouncing on the mattress and squealing as though we were ten years old. I was laughing because this was so ridiculously funny but also because Chloe had begun to hold herself between her legs.

'I'm gonna pee!' she shrieked.

This had the effect of making me need to pee too. I jumped off the bed and ran towards the toilet. It seemed a hilarious idea to get there before her and not let her in, but I'd forgotten her superior speed. She quickly got in front of me. In the hallway I stuck my leg out to trip her and she countered with some ruthless hair pulling, yanking my head back violently. It wasn't painful, it was exhilarating, and I realized that I liked coke, I really liked it. She made it to the bathroom ahead of me and slammed the door in my face, making us both scream with laughter. Everything went quiet as I stood with my ear against the door. I heard her sit down.

'Go away!' she yelled, still laughing. 'Go away, I can't pee when you're listening!'

I made heavy footfalls as though I was walking back to the bedroom, then I sneaked back to the bathroom door and waited silently. Chloe began to pee. It began as a delicate tinkling and quickly became a noisy torrent.

I battered on the door. 'Help! There's a horse having a piss in our bathroom!'

'You bitch!'

I felt dizzy, too much bouncing on the bed and running around. I could hear Chloe's laughter and her thunderous peeing as I slid down the door. My heart and my liver and my spleen could all pack up now if they wanted, I didn't care, I'd never laughed so hard in all my life.

Chapter 18

Dear Lisa and Lauren, My new flatmate Chloe is a scream. We've had a few lines of coke and are off out dancing. She's giving me a makeover! We'll probably pick up some hot Latino boys, who knows? The night is young . . . I suppose you'll be watching Emmerdale *tonight.*

I showered while Chloe chose potential outfits for me. When I came back, turbaned and towelled, dripping on the cold tiled floor, the bed was covered in clothes. After trying four skirts Chloe decided that the black and white gypsy one was the best option.

'Yeah, but it's slightly too long,' she said, seeing it on me, 'we're not seeing enough leg. I know . . .'

She pulled an old-fashioned brooch from a musical box on the dressing table and pinned the skirt up at the front. This showed off my new sleek thighs and definitely made the skirt more Spanish-dancer-looking.

'You look like Shakira!'

'No I don't.'

But I could see that it worked. A plain white blouse, once she had pulled it wide at the shoulders and wound a black silk scarf around my waist, completed the look.

Chloe stood back and made me twirl.

'Shakira Shakira Shakira!' she sang and clapped her hands. 'I'm liking it. I'm thinking bright red lipstick with black smoky eyes. Hair up, definitely, or maybe up at one side with a big comb and a white carnation, we can buy one on the street.'

As I sat on the edge of the bed Chloe brushed out my hair. She was gentle and I closed my eyes.

'Can you give it one hundred strokes please?' I asked. 'It's supposed to be good for it.'

'Ninety-four, ninety-five, ninety-six,' she joked, although she'd only just started.

'I'll brush yours if you want,' I offered, 'I enjoy it.'

'Sure, when I've showered you can give me a hundred lashes.'

Chloe softly drew the brush through my hair a hundred times and then gathered it and pinned it up at the back of my head. Even without the comb and the carnation, I could see how fantastically Spanish I was going to look.

'Now what the hell am I going to wear?' Chloe said. 'Crank the music up, I'm gonna hop in the shower.'

I turned it up and was practising my Shakira dancing in the mirror when my phone rang.

'Alison?'

'Hello, Ewan.'

'Is everything OK? I just phoned to see how you were.'

'Yes, I'm OK.'

'You sure? You sound a bit breathless.'

'No, I'm good, thank you.'

'What's that music I can hear? Are you in a bar?'

'No, it's a CD. I'm in Barri Gòtic, I'm still in the flat!' I laughed.

'The American didn't put you out then?'

125

'No, God no. I'm staying here. Me and Chloe are going to be sharing.'

'Really? But is it not a one-bedroom apartment?'

'Uh huh.'

'Well, that'll be cosy.'

'Yep.'

Ewan went quiet. I waited; I wasn't going to help him out.

'So, how's your toe?'

'My what?'

'Your toe. You cut it this morning, d'you not remember?'

'Oh yeah!' I laughed. 'It's fine. Chloe cleaned it and put a plaster on it. I'll live.'

'I spoke to your big brother today. Charlie sends his love.'

'That's nice.'

'He says you've to phone your mum, they're worried about you.' He hesitated before he brought up the next subject. 'They mentioned you might not have enough money. I told Charlie I could lend you some, if that would help. It would have to be short-term; I'm not exactly loaded myself.'

'Nope. I'm fine. I've got tons of money.'

'OK, good. Sorry about having to rush off like that this morning.' Ewan gave a laugh that was so obviously faked it was embarrassing. 'I was late for work,' he added lamely.

'Forget it.'

There was another silence.

'So, would you like to meet up tonight? I'm finished now. The night man has just come in.'

'Sorry. I've made other arrangements. Chloe and I are

off out salsa dancing. We're going to Club Cubana. We've had a few lines and Chloe's given me a makeover, she says I look hot.'

'Lines?'

'Of coke.'

'Right.'

'I could meet you in the bar downstairs for a quick one, I suppose.' I wanted him to see my makeover. 'We won't be going out for a while, Chloe's still in the shower.'

'No, you're all right, thanks,' said Ewan.

Why had I given him the chance to knock me back?

'And Alison? Be careful in that Club Cubana. These places can be a bit sleazy. Does your American mate know her way around? Will she look after you?'

'Well, my American mate's been pretty good to me so far. *She's* never run off and left me in the street.'

'Come on, Alison, I said I'm sorry about that. You've only just met this girl. How d'you know you can trust her?'

'I do trust her if it's any of your business, which it isn't.'

I could hear the bathroom door opening.

'Look, I have to go, Ewan. Nice talking to you, ciao.'

I barely let him get his 'ciao' in before I put the phone down.

Chloe emerged from the bathroom with Juegita running around her feet. She lifted the dog's front paws and danced with her to the salsa music.

'Should we take Juegita out for her walk now before we leave for the evening?' I asked.

'Oh, she'll be fine. She might have a shit on the terrace later but that's OK.'

'But didn't you say she needs some exercise?'

'Nope. Old Juegita's exhausted with looking after the pups. She needs rest.'

She didn't look exhausted to me. I was impressed with just how well Juegita could dance the merengue. She was enjoying it, her tail wagging happily, her teats swinging freely as she and Chloe danced around.

Chloe went and got dressed. She was gone less than five minutes. She had on a simple pink top and a white short skirt. Make-up-wise she was only wearing lipstick and a little mascara. She looked fantastic.

'I'm not overdressed for this place, am I?' I asked her.

Chapter 19

'Alison honey, you're gonna knock 'em dead,' said Chloe, and then chopped another two lines of coke. I inhaled this next one up my other nostril, but this time it wasn't a clean sweep. I left traces of the white powder on the mirror. I copied what Chloe had done and licked my finger and brushed my gums with what was left. It felt amazing and I couldn't wait to get to the club.

We got down the stairs without incident. On the last flight Chloe asked me if I was OK without the lights on and I was, I felt great. We crossed through a tight little plaza where everyone was smoking joints in the street. Kids with dreadlocks and dogs on rope leads lay around on the ground, as relaxed as though they were on sofas. A girl with long greasy hair was leaning forward at a strange angle. An ugly noise came down her nose and out of her mouth that sounded like terrible longing or terrible pain.

'Plaza Trippy,' said Chloe, 'junkies come here to trip out.'

I was glad to be out of that plaza. The streets were crowded and it took time to negotiate corners with so many people moving through. Chloe swerved and sidestepped; not wanting to lose her, I had to trot to keep up. But we were going too fast, everything was going too fast, the noise and the crowds and the traffic. Stimulation overload.

'Chloe, can we stop please?'

My heart was pounding and my whole body was quivering.

'Got the fear, haven't you?' she said.

'I don't know. I don't feel like myself. Maybe it's these clothes. I'm scared and I don't know why.'

'Hey, don't worry, it's the coke, it happens, it'll pass. You're with me, you'll be OK. If you're scared you can hold my hand.'

I immediately took her hand. 'Thanks.'

'Feel better?'

'Not yet.'

'You will.'

'¡Perdón!' Chloe yelled at an Asian woman, and then hauled me towards her.

The woman was a flower seller and she seemed amazed to have a customer voluntarily approach her. In the hubbub of the street Chloe asked her in Spanish for a carnation for my hair. The vendor quickly realized her bargaining position and insisted that it wasn't possible to buy just one carnation. They were not sold as separates. They only came in twenty-euro bunches. She was so emphatic I didn't need a translation.

'I don't have time for this haggling shit, just gimme the bunch. *Dame las flores*,' said Chloe. 'Alison, give her the money.'

'Twenty euros!' I cried. 'That's thirteen quid, for one flower?'

I really wasn't keen to spend that kind of money on a

flower for my hairdo, but Chloe wouldn't let it go.

'Honestly, Chloe, she's ripping us off,' I complained.

'Duh! I know she is, but we gotta have a carnation!'

The words *us* and *we* had been used, but Chloe was asking me to pay. It wasn't Chloe who was being ripped off. But a madly expensive hair decoration, even at 20 euros, was a lot cheaper than paying rent so, reluctantly, I handed over the money. The woman gave me the bunch. Chloe used her nails to snip a large white flower head and place it carefully in my hair above my ear.

In the flat she had spent ages doing and redoing my eye make-up. She had curled my hair and pinned it up and used half a ton of hairspray to hold each ringlet in place. The carnation was the crowning glory to her artistry.

'There,' she sighed, satisfied. 'My work is done.'

'*¡Qué guapa!*' agreed the flower lady.

Chloe handed the woman back the rest of the bunch of flowers.

'Here you go,' said Chloe cheerfully. '*Puedes venderlos otra vez.*'

The woman was as astounded as I was.

The club was free entry, which calmed me down, but every drink at the bar was 9 euros. This sent me into another flap.

'Hey, relax,' said Chloe, 'I'll get the drinks.'

She ordered us both vodkas and Diet Coke but we hardly got the chance to drink them.

'Incoming,' said Chloe sniggering, '*dos guapos* at three o'clock.'

I turned to see two boys approaching us. They were certainly *guapo*: gorgeous, dark, Latino, long-legged with small tight bums. It was difficult to decide which was the best-looking, they were both gorgeous.

131

'*Hola chicas.*'

They didn't speak any English and were amazed when Chloe told them that I wasn't an *española* but an *escocesa*.

'*¿Tienes papeles?*' one of them asked me.

I smiled and turned to Chloe for translation. She laughed.

'He wants to know if you have papers. They're from Ecuador. He's looking for a wife.'

'I don't think I do.'

'Sure you do, you're European, right?'

From what I could make out Chloe seemed to be apologizing for the fact that she was an Americana. They had a brief but intense discussion, apparently to do with politics. They were serious boys, anxious to be taken seriously.

'Ecuador's currency changed from sucre to dollars years ago. The economy was devastated.' Chloe filled me in. I smiled and nodded sympathetically in their direction. 'They don't like the US. But hey,' she shrugged, 'who does?'

Chloe did all the talking, which was a relief. She introduced everybody, telling the boys our names. She told me they were both called Juan. The one that had attached himself to Chloe was Juan Jose, Juan Jo for short, pronounced Wanho. Mine was Juan Carlos, Juan Ca for short, pronounced Wanca.

'*¡Como el rey!*' said Wanca proudly.

Both Juans laughed as though this was a great joke. 'Like the king!' said Chloe, digging me in the ribs.

We laughed politely and then they asked us to dance. Was it really as easy as this to pull men? It seemed to be. I caught sight of myself in the mirror. What would Ewan make of Charlie's little sister if he could see her now?

Other boys wanted me. To these boys I was an *española*, a *guapa*.

Chloe, unsurprisingly, was an excellent dancer. She and Wanho slithered around like greased-up snakes. People watched them dance and then when Wanca and I took the floor everyone looked at us. Our audience probably had high expectations: me in my Spanish-dancer get-up and Wanca so handsome. I was a terrible dancer. It looked easy when other people did it but although I tried my best, I clearly wasn't feeling the same rhythms as Wanca, or as anyone else on the dance floor. Uncoordinated, we were a misfiring engine. Eventually I worked out that we got on better if I didn't move. While Wanca jerked his hips in my direction I shifted my weight from one leg to the other and back again. It was boring and hard work; my thigh muscles, unused to the exercise, quickly tired. People were still looking.

I was relieved when he led me off the floor and into a dark corner. He showed me to my seat. I said 'Gracias' and smiled. Wanca spoke to me in Spanish and I smiled, my only means of communication. He put his lips to my ear so that I could hear him over the music. He spoke slowly, hypnotically, while he stroked my cheek. I smiled; the stroking was very nice. He kissed my cheek; I smiled again and offered him my lips.

He held my face in his hand, gently, as though he enjoyed the softness of my skin. He kissed my lips, light as a feather and then pressing down. His tongue brushed the inside of my lip as if knocking at the door. I was hungry to receive him and felt the thrill of his tongue in my mouth. When we stopped for a breather he held my face in his hand again and chuckled softly. I felt my cheek blush. He whispered again in my ear and I concentrated on listening to the Spanish words and pretended not to notice his hand was directly under my right breast. We kissed again, full-on snogging now, and he was touching me. I leaned into him, giving him the green light to put his hand inside my blouse. Through the kiss I moaned. There were people at a nearby table but they seemed busy talking amongst themselves.

After a few minutes Wanca stopped kissing me and removed his hand. I didn't want to stop and he smiled at my reluctance. He was teasing me. I pushed my breasts against him, mashing myself into him as he slid his hand along my thigh. I shivered and my legs parted. He could pull my knickers down and fuck me right here and I would moan with pleasure.

Except that people were looking.

My eyes flickered with the ecstasy of what he was doing and I saw that the table nearby were watching us. They weren't even pretending not to. They were openly staring. I tried to discreetly direct his attention to this. While kissing I repeatedly rolled my eyes in their direction. Mid snog Wanca gave them a cursory glance and then a dismissive shrug, all the while creeping his hand up my skirt.

I pulled away, gasping.

He tried to re-engage mouths but I managed to resist. What the hell was I thinking? I was nearly doing it, in public, with a guy I'd just met. A guy called Wanca. Had I really got so carried away?

Wanca returned to whispering in my ear. I felt my lips and my thighs ache for it, but I had to get a grip. As I batted his hand from my breast his whispering became louder and more insistent. This was pathetic; I didn't even know what he was saying. He could've been banging on about Ecuadorian currency for all I knew and I'd been ready to whip my pants off. I was pathetic. He tried to kiss me again. I stood up. I was starting to feel the fear again, I had to find Chloe but I couldn't see her on the dance floor.

'I want to dance now.'

Wanca seemed confused; he must have wondered why his sexy Spanish murmuring was no longer working.

'Shall we dance?' I shrieked.

Before he had a chance to answer I smoothed my skirt down and strode off. Chloe was nowhere to be seen, so I was forced to endure more Wanca dance moves while I scanned the floor for her. Wanca dance moves consisted of him putting his hands all over my body while he dry-humped my thigh. The people from the table were still sniggering.

At last I saw her emerge with Wanho from what seemed to be the toilets.

'Are you OK?' she asked.

'Yeah, I'm OK. That table over there have been giving me a hard time though.'

She looked them over and dismissed it.

'Oh, they're Catalan. It's not you; it's what you're wearing,' she said. 'They're Hispanophobes. They hate everything Spanish.'

As I looked around the club I noticed that all the other women were very informally dressed, much like Chloe, in short skirts and tops. I began to feel faintly ridiculous in my flamenco get-up, as though, like some old South American movie star, I should have a pile of fruit stacked on my head.

'I was looking for you for ages, were you in the toilet?'

'Yeah, I know it's nasty but there was nowhere else,' she

said. 'He offered to go down and I can never resist. It's totally mellowed me out. Anyhoo, I saw you over there in the corner with Juan Ca so I figured you were enjoying yourself.'

'Oh, I lost it a bit there but—'

'Hey, never apologize, never explain.'

Chloe had just coolly admitted to accepting oral sex in a toilet from a stranger.

'Alison, we're in Barcelona, there's nobody here to judge us, only me and you, and I won't tell if you won't.'

'I won't tell.'

'In that case, we can do anything we like, with anybody, any time and all the time. Didn't we make a deal about that?'

'Yes, we did.'

'Well all right.'

Chloe pulled me in and hugged me. I clung tight to her.

Wanca and Wanho laughed when they saw our girly hug and wanted in on the action, but it was exclusive. They stood with their arms around our waists but as we were speaking English we could safely ignore them.

'I've had enough Latino fun for one night,' said Chloe, 'have you?'

'Yeah, thanks.'

'OK, wanna lose these guys and get out of here?'

'Yeah,' I said casually as if I was used to losing guys, 'let's lose them.'

The boys' smiles were becoming tighter by the minute.

'I wanna phone my mom before she goes out for the evening,' said Chloe. 'What d'you say we go back to the apartment, smoke a joint, I'll make my call and then we can go out somewhere else?'

'Sounds good to me.'

136

I was dying to get my silly outfit off.

'Oh, I like you, Alison! You think the same way as me,' said Chloe, reaching in for another hug.

I knew at that moment how lucky I was to have Chloe; that she was the perfect friend.

Chapter 20

Back in the flat I got us glasses of water while Chloe tried to phone her mum.

'The line's busy,' she said with tired resignation, 'd'you want to call your mom while I'm waiting?'

'Oh, that's really kind of you, Chloe, but it'll cost a fortune.'

'No it won't, I have a deal for international calls. You should call your mom.'

I dialled the big long number to phone home and was surprised when there was no answer. Mum was rarely out in the evenings. She was usually in front of the telly. When she finally picked up Mum sounded terrible, as if she was ill.

'Hello?'

'Mum, what's wrong, are you OK?'

'Who is this?'

'It's me, Alison.'

'D'you know what time it is, Alison?'

'No. What time is it? It's a bit late, isn't it?'

'It's bloody two o'clock in the morning.'

'Oh God, sorry, Mum. I didn't realize. Ewan said Charlie said that you wanted me to phone.'

'Yeah, but not in the middle of the night! I've got to get up for my work in the morning.'

'OK, night night, Mum.'

'Night night, and don't bloody do that again. You frightened the life out of me.'

I put the phone down.

'Everything OK back home?' asked Chloe.

'Yeah thanks, Chloe, but it's really late. It's two o'clock in the morning in Scotland.'

'Whoa! I didn't think of that. It's six in the evening in California. I always phone my mom at this time. It's the only time I can guarantee reaching her.'

'You stay up till three every night?'

'Sure. Me and my mom love to chat, we talk for hours sometimes.'

Chloe dialled the number again and let it ring out for ages before she hung up.

'She's probably in the shower right now. She gets home and goes straight out again to dinner most nights. She's a popular lady. But come on, tell me, what happened with you and Juan Ca? Did you guys get it on right there in the club?'

'Nearly. I just managed to stop myself when I saw those people staring at me.'

'I wouldn't have let that stop me. I like people watching me.'

'Really?'

I had never had this kind of conversation before. I was discovering that talking about it was almost as exciting as doing it.

'Yeah, it makes me extra horny when someone else is there, d'you know what I mean?'

'Mmm,' I said.

139

I didn't want to lie.

'He would have been your first, huh?'

'Huh?' I felt the blood rush to my face. How could she tell I was still a virgin?

'I remember my first Latino, wow! Can't remember his name but he was a hot guy.'

I relaxed, my secret was safe.

'You should do it on the beach, when the sun's coming up. That's a Barcelona Must Do. That's one box that's gotta be ticked. Girl,' she said, redialling her mother's number, 'we gotta get you laid.'

I took the glasses into the kitchen.

'Hey, Mom!' I heard her say.

While I was in there, tidying up and trying to earn my keep, I thought about sex on the beach. It would have been exciting. Maybe I should have gone to the beach with Wanca. I'd messed up this time but I wouldn't miss my next chance. I could hear Chloe making enthusiastic noises and giggling.

'Mom! You're crazy! No! That's fantastic!'

I wasn't gone long but by the time I came back Chloe's mother was evidently about to ring off.

'Well sure, Mom, OK. No, it's fine, don't keep him waiting, I was just going to bed anyway. OK, I love you, Mom, love you. Bye, bye, bye,' she whispered.

'Guess what?' she said, excited.

'What?'

'My mom is coming to Europe! Here, to Spain!'

'Excellent!' I said and then immediately began worrying. 'When is she coming?'

'We don't know exactly yet, but pretty soon. Mom is so relaxed about all that stuff, she's always scooting around, never in one place very long. We are so similar.'

140

With a heavy heart I asked the question.

'So d'you need me to move out?'

'Huh? No, she's not coming to Barcelona. It's Madrid, she's set up an exhibition for an artist friend of hers down in Madrid.'

'Oh I see,' I said, trying to hide my relief. 'Is that her job?'

'Are you kidding? My mom's too busy for a job. She has projects. She knows everyone. She has more influence than Hillary Clinton. Believe me, when it comes to her projects, anything she wants to happen happens.'

'She sounds amazing,' I said.

'She is, although she probably got him the Madrid gig just so she can come check up on me.' Chloe giggled. 'We have to go down there, you have to meet her, you'll love her. She's gonna love you, I know it.'

'Cheers,' I said.

'What's your mom like?'

I had sensed this question coming and was embarrassed.

'Aye, she's nice.'

I would never be able to even fake that kind of adulation for my mum.

'She works in a bakery.' I shrugged. 'She's always worked there, since before I was born.'

'So did you have a nanny too?'

'Not really, my brothers and I had a childminder, Isabelle, our next-door neighbour.'

'Did you actually like your nanny?'

'Yeah, she was really nice.'

'That's sweet. Does she still live there?'

'She moved. One day I came home from school and

she'd gone. Her house was empty; all her furniture had been taken away.'

'Wow, just like that? Where did she go? Didn't you see her again?'

'I did see her once more, but it wasn't the same.'

'I know what you mean. I hated my nannies. None of them lasted more than a few months. I used to do things to 'em.'

'Like what?'

'Like glue their ass to the toilet. Once I stabbed one of 'em in the foot with an ornamental sword.' Chloe giggled. 'Yeah, Mom had to pay a lot of compensation on that one!'

'Was your dad not around?'

'Oh, him.' Chloe rolled her eyes. 'Yeah, he's always around. What about yours?'

'My dad's dead. Heart attack. It was years ago.'

'Oh I'm sorry. D'you miss him?'

'A bit.'

'That must be tough.'

'Not really. He wasn't as great as he made himself out to be.'

'I totally know what you mean,' Chloe sympathized. 'I hate my dad. Aged P, ol' golf-club Phil, is just the worst,' she told me as I nodded compassionately. 'He cheated me out of my inheritance. I'll never forgive him for that. I was supposed to get the money my grandfather left me when I was twenty-one. Aged P is the executor and when it was in probate he told the court I had "mental health issues". Bastard. I was a bad girl at school a coupla times, so what? He showed them my school reports and shit and they put all kinds of conditions on giving me my own money.'

142

'What were the conditions?'

'That I go to college.'

'That doesn't sound so bad.'

'Are you kidding?'

'But Chloe, you're American, that must be brilliant. I grew up watching *Dawson's Creek*, *The OC* and *Buffy*. In these programmes the kids always have their own cars, they drive to college with the top down. It's always sunny. And the girls live in really cool sorority houses and go to frat parties. If I was a student I'd join one of those weird clubs and major in something.'

'Alison, hello? It's not like that. A college campus is probably the most dangerous place to be in the States. And anyway, my dad can't tell me what to do. I do what I want, I'm not his bitch. He can't make me go to college. The money comes to me when I'm twenty-five anyway.'

'That must be soon.'

'Yeah, a year and three months and counting. After that he can't stop me. Until then all I get is a stinking allowance, and I don't even get that unless I jump through his goddamn hoops.'

'Hoops?'

'Dentists, gynaecologists, shrinks, whatever. He's always making appointments for me,' Chloe moaned.

'I suppose he's just trying to look after you.'

'He wants my money; it's as sad and as simple as that. He wants to control the money, how I spend it, he wants to control me. He doesn't believe anything I say, he has no faith in anything I do. I don't know why he doesn't have my fingerprints and my mugshot taken. I'm his obsession. He's the one who has mental health issues.'

She was crying now.

I came over and sat beside her. I put my arm around

her. After a while she quietened down. I led her to the bedroom and she didn't resist. She lay down on the bed and I pulled off her sandals. She still had her clothes on but she didn't seem to want to take them off. She fell asleep weeping into her pillow.

It was, for me, a surprising way to end the evening. After all, we'd had such a fun night. But the late-night crying turned out to be a regular pattern. Chloe almost always fell asleep crying. It didn't keep me awake. I grew used to the tearful sniffling, fond of it even. It reminded me of how alike we were: both fucked up, both scared. Her crying soothed me. I liked to watch Chloe's tear-stained face relax into sleep: curled on her side with her knees pulled in tight and her arms tucked under her chin, her thin shoulder gently rising and falling, her blond hair spread out on the pillow, her lips set in a childish pout. She didn't know how beautiful and how vulnerable she was, and that's when I liked her best.

Chapter 21

The next morning I sat in the yurt on the terrace. I felt rough as hell. I must have caught a cold from kissing Wanca. I was blowing my nose every few minutes, but it had been a great night out. I smiled, thinking through everything that had happened. OK, it hadn't been perfect. With hindsight my flamenco-dancer outfit was a bit embarrassing. Allowing Wanca to grope me in public was borderline shameful, but compared to my nightclubbing experience in Cumbernauld it had been a triumph.

In first year at college, during my brief but glorious reign as queen bee, it was decided that, like all the other first years, we should go clubbing. Everyone else at college was doing it.

My new girlfriends came to my house to get ready. This was the first time I'd hosted a social gathering since my tenth birthday party, when Mum was forced to invite my brothers' pals to make up the numbers. This would be different. When Lisa and Lauren arrived I ushered them straight up to my bedroom where we spent hours playing music, drinking vodka and getting dressed. It was brilliant.

The previous day we had discussed what we would wear. I was forced to admit that I didn't have anything suitable. Lisa and Lauren fell over themselves offering to lend me an outfit and, to increase their chances of becoming my Best Friend, both turned up with armloads of clothes for me to try.

I took the stuff to the bathroom to try on. Nothing fitted, some things I couldn't get past my thighs. Lisa and Lauren were like me: big girls, just not quite as big as me. But there was one nice pink skirt of Lauren's that, if I pulled it on over my head and didn't do up the top buttons, I could just about get away with. I returned to the bedroom to their squawks of approval.

'I'm sorry,' said Lauren, 'but you look fantastic.'

I looked in the mirror and felt good. This prompted me to stop pigging on the giant bag of Doritos Lisa had brought. The more we drank, the more slap we applied. The more I saw myself in the flattering pink skirt, the thinner and more confident I began to feel.

When we arrived at the club we stood in a long queue waiting to get in. A crowd of boys we recognized from college came and stood behind us. Though we didn't know them well enough to speak to, we were pleased; we were beginning to move in the right circles. This was a great idea to come here, Lisa and Lauren agreed. Even the drizzling rain couldn't dampen our expectations.

There were signs and notices outside the club, mostly prohibitive:

No Underage drinking.

Proof of age and ID required.

No alcohol to Be brought into the Premise's.

No football Colour's.

But some were playful:

Shirts and shoe's required, bras and Pantie's optional.

The sign above the door said:

Clancys Nite Spot.

Music. Dancing. Cavorting.

'When d'you think the cavorting starts?' said Lauren.

'Just as soon as we get in there,' Lisa quipped.

As the crowd moved and we neared the entrance we could hear the sounds of cavorting from within. Two burly meat-headed bouncers stood at the door. We smiled as we approached.

'Not tonight, girls,' one of them said.

He held his clipboard wide as though to bar our entry. As if to prevent us ram-raiding our way in.

'Regulars only tonight. Sorry.'

The two bouncers formed a protective semicircle, herding us out of the queue and off to the side. It was only then I grasped what he meant. They weren't letting us in.

Lauren tossed her shiny black hair and argued: we had ID proving our age. We had no alcohol with us; they could search our bags if they wanted. We weren't wearing football scarves or tops. We were appropriately shirted and shod; bra'ed and pantied to capacity. What was the problem? The bouncer gave us a weak smile, shrugged and turned back to the queue.

Lisa tugged Lauren's jacket and she finally crumpled, the three of us moving off silently, discreetly. As we walked I tried to tune out the laughter of the boys behind us. With every step my tight skirt rode up and gathered in the small of my back, making it shorter at the back than at the front. Perhaps the boys were laughing at a joke. Perhaps they were too busy laughing at the joke to even notice the three fat girls in front being turned away.

I walked off, the damp pink skirt slapping the back of my thighs – punishment for my hubris. Why did I imagine I could ever be part of this world?

We didn't care. That was the official line.

The other two went back to Lisa's house and wore themselves out with frenzied who-gives-a-fuck-anyway dancing in her bedroom. That would show them.

I never found out what Lisa and Lauren really thought; we never talked about it, ever. But they blamed me, I know they did. I was the one wearing a skirt too short for a fat girl. I was the one who skulked home to wriggle out of the wet skirt and finish off the Doritos.

Chloe was in a funny mood all that morning. I tried to cheer her up. While she was in the shower I popped down to the shops and bought nice hot bread and orange juice. I boiled eggs while she dressed; I set the breakfast table on the terrace under the shade of the yurt. She ate in silence. She ignored the pups, even Juegita. Maybe Chloe was just one of those people who took her time waking up. She was an heiress after all.

And then it happened again.

As I was munching the hot crusty bread another coughing fit crept up on me. I immediately stood up and tried to clear my throat, banging my chest a few times. The coughing got worse. I could feel my face getting red with the effort. As vigorous as the coughing was, it wasn't clearing my throat. My windpipe was getting narrower. Coughing led to dry retching, leaving little room for actual breathing. I felt my lips become numb. I staggered to the edge of the terrace, leaning over and sucking in hard, as if the space between the buildings might give me more air. I felt like I was about to pass out. I turned to look for Chloe, my mouth working like a fish.

She ignored me, chewing her breakfast and looking off into the shimmering heat. She had no idea. This one was bad, this time I was a goner, surely.

'For Chrissakes get a hold of yourself, Alison,' she said.

Chapter 22

I continued to cough and retch and struggle for breath, but it was no use. I wasn't getting any air in before I was spluttering it out again. I fell to my knees and clawed at my throat. Without oxygen I knew I wouldn't last much longer. So many times I'd cheated death but I couldn't this time.

Chloe sighed.

As I knelt bucking and heaving she daintily wiped the sides of her mouth with her napkin and then approached me. She squinted into my face and stuck two fingers against my windpipe, constricting what little breathing space I had left. She forcefully hooked her fingers in below my throat, behind my collarbone, and pressed down hard. She was going to finish me off like a wounded animal she was putting out of its misery. I flapped my hands and tried to push her away.

'Now breathe in. Slowly,' she said in a bored voice. With her hand pushed so far into my neck I didn't think I could breathe, in or out, but although my throat felt tighter, I found I could actually let air in without coughing.

'Slowly,' she said as if correcting a naughty child, 'slowly.'

I had little choice but to do as I was told.

'And out. Slowly.'

I exhaled, a long slow careful exhalation.

'And in.'

I inhaled.

'And out.'

I could breathe again. I gulped at the air.

Chloe held my eye.

'Slowly.'

I found that if I followed her instructions exactly I could breathe. After a few minutes she released the pressure and removed her fingers from my throat. Panicking, I grabbed her hand. I could breathe without her but I wanted to keep a tight hold of her hand.

'I thought I was going to die.'

I was crying now.

'You were never gonna die,' she said, unimpressed, 'don't be such a drama queen.'

'No, honestly, this isn't the first time it's happened. I have a problem with choking.'

'You have rebellious chi is all,' she said.

'But what was that thing you did?'

'It's a neat trick I learned from my acupuncturist.'

'Rebellious what?'

'Chi, spelt q. i. It's energy, spirit.'

'So that's what it is, I've got a rebellious spirit?'

'Yeah, well, you could say.'

'Cool.'

Dear Lisa and Lauren, Nearly choked to death again. Apparently I have rebellious qi! What am I like? Luckily my heiress friend is an expert in acupuncture and saved my life so I live to fight another day. Did the doctor ever get to the bottom of your candida infection?

*　　*　　*

Two weeks later Ewan phoned me again.

'Alison!' he exclaimed, delighted. 'How the hell are you?'

I was surprised, but it was good to hear a Scottish voice. We chatted, he asked me how I was settling in with Chloe; I told him things were great. He asked about our Club Cubana night out.

'Yeah, it was good,' I said.

'I spoke to your big brother again last night.'

'Yeah?'

I hadn't spoken to my family since my mum was so grumpy on the phone that night.

'Charlie says I should take you out, show you the sights. What d'you think?'

I had been here nearly three weeks and I hadn't seen anything. I needed to conserve money and it was cheaper to stay in the flat while Chloe did her artwork.

'Eh, yeah, OK then.'

I wasn't doing anything else.

I stood at the Passeig de Gràcia subway entrance waiting for him. Chloe was on the terrace working on her chimney when I left. Perhaps she'd been too engrossed in cement mixing and hadn't heard me when I'd called ciao. There was no point in worrying about it.

The last few weeks I had been really lazy. After our Club Cubana night out we'd both picked up colds, or at least that's what I'd thought. Chloe said it was the cocaine. The next day both our noses constantly dripped clear thin snot. By seven o'clock in the evening I had to go down to the shops and buy more hankies, we'd used all the toilet roll. It took days to recover.

During daylight hours, while Chloe beavered away

cementing bulges on to the corners of her chimney, I read books and cooled off in the paddling pool. I offered to help and she let me do some boring stuff but when I wanted to arrange the broken tiles and design shapes she pushed me away. The chimney was her thing.

Sometimes when she got too hot she stripped off and climbed into the pool with me. It was a tight squeeze, but it was a laugh. The rest of the time I lay back and stretched out, enjoying the cool of the water and the luxury of having the pool to myself. Once when she was moaning about the heat I teased her.

'Oh Chloe, you don't know what you're missing. It's so cool and refreshing in here. Come on in, the water's lovely.'

I had my eyes closed so I didn't see until it was too late that it wasn't Chloe but Juegita who jumped in beside me, her big tits slapping the water.

'Not you, shithead!' I screamed in fright.

Chloe laughed her head off. No doubt she'd put Juegita up to it.

When the sun went down we'd smoke joints and watch DVDs, until it was time for Chloe to phone her mum. On the nights Chloe could reach her, they'd chat and giggle for a while, then we'd smoke some more. We were too tired and too stoned to want to go out.

'¡Hola!' said Ewan cheerfully. He'd sneaked up on me and now he was kissing me. With frightening enthusiasm he gripped my arms and kissed both cheeks.

'Right, first stop Casa Batlló. This is the best house in the world.'

His enthusiasm was catching.

'The outside's like a curtain at the theatre, see? Can

153

you see the masks on the balconies there? D'you see the harlequin's hat?'

I said I thought I could. But then he was talking about bones and the sea floor as the water washed across it. I was trying to keep up but I was confused.

'See the dragon across the top of the roof?'

'Oh, yeah!' I squealed. 'I can see that!'

Ewan paid and we went inside. He was right, it was the best house in the world. We were there for hours, Ewan showing me every detail. Sometimes he took my hand and ran it over the soft curves of the plaster walls, the oak doors, the cool ceramic tiles. We went up to the roof to see the chimneys.

'Chloe's making a chimney. It's like these but hers is going to be unique. Maybe she'll become a famous artist in Barcelona too.'

'And maybe not,' said Ewan dryly.

When we came out into the busy street and the heat of the afternoon I nearly fainted. I recognized Ewan's friend Sanj talking to some tourists and pointed him out to Ewan.

'¿Qué tal, Sanj?' I asked in my best accent.

Sanj laughed. '¡Hola Esmeralda!'

'It's Alison,' I reminded him.

Ewan and Sanj laughed their heads off. I smiled tightly until Ewan explained.

'It's a joke. He's calling you Esmeralda because of your lovely green eyes.'

'Sí, los ojos, ¡qué verdes! ¡Qué guapa!'

I laughed too, and blushed with the compliment. Sanj was a sensitive guy. Probably to reassure me that he wasn't laughing at me, he asked Ewan to translate for him as he became more serious, enquiring after my health, specifically my coughing. I was embarrassed to be reminded but it was nice of him to ask.

'We're going to jump the metro down to Barceloneta. There's a good sea breeze down there today,' said Ewan in English. 'Want to come?'

Sanj declined, saying he had *muchas flores* to sell. I nodded knowingly, no longer the naive idiot who had arrived here a few weeks ago. 'Flowers' was no doubt a euphemism for maria.

When we got out of the metro the walls, like walls all over Barcelona, were covered in graffiti. In my neighbourhood, any surface, including shutters and doorways, were spray-painted with intricate original artwork. The paintings were colourful and arresting. New ones would appear overnight. It was always exciting, when I went out for bread in the morning, to turn a corner and find a new piece of art. It was like living in an art gallery.

There were also plenty of messy graffiti scrawls. These annoyed me. As they were written in Catalan or Spanish I couldn't understand them. As we walked through the apartment blocks in Barceloneta I pointed to them and asked Ewan what they said.

'They're political. This one says *We cannot separate while we continue to have separation of the classes.*'

'And this?'

'*Catalonia is not Spain.*'

'What about this?'

'*Yesterday I shit myself on the metro.*'

I laughed.

'No, really,' said Ewan, but he was laughing too, 'that's what it says. It's a protest against the lack of toilets in the metro.'

When we got to the beach there was a fresh breeze and

as we stood on the elevated promenade I lifted my face and let it blow over me.

'It's a shame we don't have our swimmies, we could have gone for a swim,' I said.

'Could we fuck,' said Ewan sourly, 'the water's manky. God knows what coal dust and radioactive muck comes down the coast from Badalona and beyond, not to mention the raw sewage.'

'Sewage? You're kidding me.'

'I'm not,' he insisted. 'I saw a big jobby floating by here this morning. Let's just say that in Barceloneta you don't swim, you just go through the motions.'

'Yeesh, that's disgusting.'

'Disgusting but true.'

'But there's loads of people swimming. The beach is mobbed. You can hardly see the sand for all the bodies.'

'Tourists,' he sneered. 'C'mon, I'll show you the fish.'

I didn't really want to see them. I pictured monstrously irradiated fish living on a diet of poo and sanitary towels, but that wasn't what he meant. Further along the beach there was a huge sculpture of a goldfish, several storeys high, its metal scales glittering and dazzling.

'It's fabulous,' I laughed.

Everything was surprising about Barcelona.

We made our way back into Barceloneta and went for a coffee in Bar Electricitat, a wee bar on the edge of the square, full of old men who randomly burst into song, and drank brandy and tiny cups of coffee. Ewan bought me a huge baguette sandwich and watched me eat it, all the while asking me questions about Chloe. Where was she from, how old was she, what did she do? I didn't give him much, I hadn't come to talk about Chloe.

When I finished my sandwich Ewan shuffled his feet and made to leave.

'Anyway, thanks for that, it was fun. I'll need to get moving, I've got Castellers practice in an hour.'

'What's Castellers?' I asked.

I could tell by the way he said it, sticking his chest out with a kind of old-soldier dignity, that he was proud. It couldn't be anything to do with the Spanish Civil War, that was years ago. Maybe it was the coastguard or fire brigade, something brave and life-saving.

'We make human castles.'

That wasn't the answer I'd been expecting.

'Like acrobats but better. Much taller. We make towers nine storeys high, standing on each other's shoulders.'

Now I understood what he meant. I'd seen pictures of the high shaky mounds of people in my guidebook, grasping at each other's shirts fifty feet in the air.

'But isn't that just for local people?'

'I am local people,' he said, offended. 'I'm a long-standing member of the *colle*. Catalan is a state of being.'

'OK,' I said.

'We have the Ascent of the Virgin Mary in la Bisbal del Penedès on the fifteenth of August, and Sant Felix in Vilafranca on the thirtieth. Then it's non-stop until the Merce in September. I haven't any holidays left so I've had to switch shifts so I'm available during the day to practise.'

'Sounds like you're going to be busy.'

'Yep,' he said cheerfully. 'You should come and see us.'

'Yeah, maybe I will,' I said.

I was scared of heights, even watching other people climb made me feel sick.

'How high up d'you go?'

'Me, not very high. I'm in the *tronc*, the weans do the high-up stuff, seventy feet or more.'

'Whoa, in the Nauld the social workers would be after you if you made your weans climb seventy feet.'

'This is Catalonia,' he said all snooty, 'it's a wee bit different.'

'Sorry,' I said.

He was such an arse.

'Right,' he said, 'I'd better shoot, I'm going to be late.'

He kissed me again, again on both cheeks. I miscalculated which cheek he was going for and we had a near miss, our lips almost colliding.

When I got back Chloe was in a funny mood. I'd stopped off and bought a bottle of orange juice for her, the kind she liked, freshly squeezed from the machine. She thanked me but otherwise she hardly said a word.

'Ewan took me to Casa Batlló,' I told her, trying to make conversation, 'it was pretty cool. I saw the chimneys but they're not as good as yours is going to be.'

She didn't respond.

'Ewan was telling me he's a Castellers, you know, where they climb up on each other's shoulders and make a big tower. He thinks he's Catalan, chu, that guy is such an arse.'

'Well you're the one who sucked him off,' she said. 'I'm going to take a bath.'

Chloe was in the bath for two hours. When I heard her bashing about in the bedroom I went in.

'I'm looking for underwear but I can't find it. I thought I'd put the box in one of those drawers. Have you seen it?' she asked me.

158

'No, sorry. What does it look like?'

'Oh, you know, bra and panties, white lace, Victoria's Secret. My mom sent them from the States, I've never worn them, they haven't been out the box.'

'Sorry, there's loads of clean underwear on the chair. I washed everything yesterday. You can pick something out of there.'

'Well, if you see them anywhere be sure to let me know, will you? My mom'll go nuts if I can't find them.'

'Of course I will,' I said.

Chapter 23

Chloe was always giving me stuff: clothes, handbags, whatever. I never asked for any of it. I only had to say once that I liked something and she gave me it. Wouldn't take no for an answer. It was embarrassing.

Every day Chloe's dad would phone and every night she'd phone her mum. Chloe would try for ages to get through, though often her calls went unanswered and she'd go to bed crying. Other times her mum would answer first time. When she hung up she'd say how much she missed her mom and then she'd be off to bed crying again.

Her daily conversations with her dad were fairly standard, Chloe being sneery and snarly with him. I didn't know why he bothered. Unless she wanted money, she dismissed him quickly.

I would always hang around and listen to her curt replies. It thrilled me to hear her be so rude to him. Knowing I was listening encouraged her to be even more rude. One day I was in the kitchen making lunch when I heard her say, 'Dad, I told you, Alison is my friend.'

My ears pricked up at this.

What was he saying about me? Had she told him how much stuff she'd given me?

'No, Dad, I came here to get away from my American friends,' she said. And then, 'Because I don't like 'em!' she yelled down the phone.

It was true; she seemed to despise other Americans. Anytime we met Americans in a bar Chloe quickly blew them off, even when they were gorgeous boys. I wanted to meet them. It was nice to meet boys that I could actually speak to for a change, instead of always hitting on South American immigrants. But Chloe had nothing but disdain for her fellow Americans. Trustifarians, she called them, rich kids partying their way through Europe before going back to the States for college, she said.

As I was tossing the salad I heard my name mentioned again.

'Alison doesn't want to, she told me already.'

I stood by, expecting Chloe to ask me to corroborate whatever story she was telling him, but she met my eyes and smiled mischievously. I returned her naughty smile; whatever she was up to sounded fun. And then she said, 'It just wouldn't be fair. Because she's educationally subnormal.'

My smile collapsed.

'I didn't tell you because you didn't ask. Daddy, I have to go now, I have to go help Alison put her socks on. Kisses, kisses, bye, bye, bye, bye.' And she put the phone down.

Chloe giggled and returned to innocently flicking through a magazine.

'Who's educationally subnormal?'

I couldn't keep the angry edge out of my voice.

'You are, apparently,' she said without even lifting her head.

'D'you want to tell me what just happened?'

161

'Oh Alison, get over yourself.'

It was true, I was slightly embarrassed by the way I'd come over all parental.

'Chloe, tell me, please.'

Eventually she sighed and relented.

'Aged P has signed me up for college. Berkeley. I told him I won't go. I've told him a gazillion times, I'm going to art school in Paris. Now he's trying to bribe me, saying if I go to Berkeley he'll pay for you to come too. He's so pathetic.'

My heart started to beat faster and I'm sure my face went red. Going to college in California?

Dear Lisa and Lauren, I have grown tired of Europe. Off to start my pre-med degree at Berkeley University in California. My heiress friend Chloe and I are roomies in a sorority house. We go to beach parties and drive-in movies and hang out with frat boys. I've had my teeth bleached. Look me up if you're ever Stateside, perhaps I can find you work as illegal nannies. Yours, Dr Alison Donaldson, MD

'I'm perfectly capable of studying for a degree,' I told her, 'I already have one from Cumbernauld College.'

'Good for you. I didn't even get my SATs.'

'I'm not subnormal.'

'I know that! I only said that to get him off my case.'

'Yes but now your dad thinks I'm—'

'What does it matter what he thinks? You're never gonna have to meet him anyway.'

'I am if we go to Berkeley.'

'That's not gonna happen.'

'Well, why not? We're not doing anything else. You could still do your art.'

'Fugeddaboutit.'

'I'm just saying . . .'

162

'Not gonna happen,' said Chloe, snapping her magazine.

But I couldn't fugeddaboutit. A girl like me from Cumbernauld didn't get chances like this every day. Chloe just needed persuading. For one thing she'd be closer to her mom, and we wouldn't have to hang out with any Americans if she didn't want to. We could do pretty much the same as we'd been doing here in Barcelona: lounging around the flat, taking drugs and picking up boys. If she didn't want to study I certainly wouldn't nag her.

But there was no rush, I knew how pig-headed she could get. I had the rest of the summer to work on her.

Chapter 24

The next time Chloe's dad called I picked it up. We were watching a movie and Chloe couldn't be bothered to lean forward and lift her phone. It was, as usual, left to me to pick it up and hand it to her. I saw it was her dad and answered it. She jumped up quick enough then and tried to grab the phone out of my hand, both of us giggling as we scuffled. Even when I'd answered she tried to silently prise the phone out of my hand, bending my fingers painfully, but I held tight.

'Yes, hello, Mr Taylor,' I said, stifling my laughter as I noiselessly fought her off.

'Hi, may I speak with Chloe please?'

'I'm sorry, Chloe's indisposed at the minute. Can I take a message?'

'Am I speaking with Alison?'

'Yes, Mr Taylor, it's me.'

'Hi, Alison, and please, call me Philip.'

I would have liked to have been allowed to call him Aged P, but Philip would have to do.

'Oh, OK, thank you. Chloe's in the bath, do you want me to . . .'

'No, that's OK,' he said hurriedly. 'She sure likes to soak in the tub, doesn't she?'

Chloe was bored with wrestling me. She had given up and was now listlessly picking toe jam from between her toes.

'Oh, yes,' I agreed, 'she's very enthusiastic about personal hygiene.'

I had to bite my cheeks not to laugh.

'Uh huh, it's about the only thing.'

I chuckled. Philip chuckled too. We enjoyed a pleasant few moments before his laughter died away.

'Er, Philip, you know yesterday when Chloe said I was educationally subnormal?'

'Oh I knew she was kidding.' He laughed. 'She's a kidder. For some reason Chloe won't go to college like any normal kid. She wants to paint chimneys or whatever it is she does, I don't know, maybe you can convince her.'

He didn't say it like a request but I responded as if it was.

'I'll do what I can to help, Philip.'

'Well,' he said, sounding surprised, 'I'd surely appreciate it, Alison. She talks about you all the time.'

When I put the phone down I knew Chloe was dying to know what he'd said, but she was never going to ask.

Philip and I understood each other. He was nice, I could talk to him. Not like my own dad, he never talked about anything. I don't remember having conversations with my dad. What would we have talked about? One week in four we lived in the same house but otherwise we were strangers.

My dad worked on the oil-rig platforms off Aberdeen: three weeks on, one week off. I'm not sure what he did

165

there, something to do with drilling. He took the job when Mum fell pregnant with me. I was a wee accident, a happy accident my mum said. On those Friday nights when Dad came home Mum made a big effort to please him. My brothers and I came home early from Isabelle's and had fish and chips in front of the TV while Mum set the table in the kitchen for her and Dad.

Mum kept everything special for those Friday nights. When she bought something new to wear, she hung it in the wardrobe until Dad was due back. She'd get off work early and have her hair done in the hairdressers. When I was about nine or ten she went through a phase of using Boots face packs. She'd smear the green paste on her face and mine and we had to wait ten or fifteen minutes until it dried and hardened. My brothers used to horse around in the living room trying to make us laugh.

'Don't move a muscle,' Mum said through unmoving lips, like a ventriloquist. When it came time to take it off she splashed cold water on her face and patted it dry. Her skin was as tight as a baby's. I always went to the mirror, smiling and grimacing, until my face cracked into a hundred lines.

'That's what you'll look like when you're old,' Mum said.

She painted my nails the same shade as hers so long as I promised to take it off before school on Monday morning. As I got older she let me do her make-up. She liked the way I did it.

One summer Friday night Mum had made all her preparations. Charlie and the twins were out playing football. She said that seeing as we were both looking so gorgeous and it was such a lovely night we should go and meet Dad off the bus. It would be a lovely surprise for him. We waited at stance 17, both of us in our pink nail polish, Mum with her new hairdo and blue dress. We stood up when the bus pulled in. All the men from the rigs got off, laughing and joking, but Dad wasn't amongst them. Mum asked but the inspector said there wasn't another bus in from Aberdeen till the morning.

Halfway through Saturday Morning CBBC, Dad came home. The boys were out playing football. Mum and I were still in our jammies having tea and toast in front of the telly. Mum's hairdo was squashed in with having slept on it. She didn't say anything to Dad. She walked into the kitchen and Dad followed her and closed the door. A while later they came back into the living room, Dad with a mug of tea.

'We went to meet you last night at the bus station, Dad,' I told him.

Dad drew Mum a fierce look and she looked away. He went into the kitchen and poured his tea down the sink. Mum went in after him. Dad was angry and shouted.

'Why do you have to involve the kids in your paranoia?'

Mum closed the door and said something quietly to Dad and then he shouted again.

'Phone the bus company if you don't believe me!'

I wanted to stick up for Mum. I went into the kitchen and asked Dad why didn't he want us to come and meet him? But he pretended not to hear. I asked him again. He turned and stared at me. I got nervous and went back to the living room and watched telly. Mum and Dad stayed in the kitchen for a while and then Dad went out and Mum went back to bed. I felt bad but I didn't know what I'd done wrong. After that I never directly asked my dad anything again. Sometimes when I heard the way Chloe spoke to her dad, teasing and ridiculing him, I wished my dad was still alive.

The marijuana plants were doing great; they had grown three or four inches. It had become my job to water them every morning and I enjoyed my task: soaking the tubs till the surface became mud, then squeezing the hose nozzle and spraying the leaves with a fine mist to keep them cool during the heat of the day.

The pups were getting bigger too. It was funny watching them learn how to sit up. From a lying-down position they walked their front paws back until they were sitting, but sometimes they pushed back too far and would keel over. One night when we were stoned Chloe and I came up with what we thought were hilarious names for them: Squaw, Conejo, Concha, Fanny, Vulva, Pussy, Tiggy and Vagina.

The pups were sleeping a lot less now and were getting everywhere. When she was doing her art Chloe didn't wear clothes, only a long baggy T-shirt to keep from getting sunburnt, no pants or bra. If she bent down or sat with her legs open I'd joke, 'I think one of the pups has got trapped between your legs.' Once one of them did get trapped, not between Chloe's legs but between the wall and a cement bag. Concha had got in behind the cement and was too fat to wriggle free. I only found her by following her high-pitched panicked yap. I asked Chloe to help me find her but she was too busy with her chimney.

When I'd first arrived in the flat Juegita used to carry the little sleeping bundles around in her mouth. She seemed to be separating those she'd already fed from those she hadn't. Then she'd carry them to the basket and lie down amongst them. Half asleep and still half blind, they would sniff out the milk and clamp on to their mother. As they got bigger their demand for milk increased and they constantly bothered her, climbing over each other to get to a teat. Poor Juegita, exhausted and with tits dragging, had little option but to let them go at her. I could see she wasn't enjoying it, who would? But even though she was sore and tired out, she let them suckle. As they got bigger she was constantly pursued by hungry puppies and spent most of her time trying to avoid them. They ran around after her, frisky and playful, jumping over each other.

At first they were too small to climb the step on the terrace which led inside the flat. Juegita was safe to lie in the cool air-conditioned bedroom and soothe her tender nipples on the cold tiles. While Chloe worked I'd watch the pups for hours. They were so cute and determined; I couldn't help but admire their puppy-dog tenacity. They tried to climb the step but it was too steep. They fell over and fell over and fell over again, but they never gave up. It was tempting to give them a helping hand up but I also felt sorry for Juegita, who needed a break from them. Inevitably one or two of the more adventurous ones learned how to climb the step and once that happened, the game was up for Juegita the Milk Machine. They were greedy little buggers. Not content with sucking their poor mother dry, the bigger ones were now beginning to delve into her food bowl. Every day I put out a little more of the dry biscuits as more of them caught on to the solid-food option. They didn't even give her peace to eat; as soon as she let her guard down they were on her. After a certain point she didn't take any nonsense. If any of the pups tried to sneak up behind her and latch on to a teat she'd growl and chase them off.

169

Juegita had, thank God, given up her disgusting habit of licking up after them. It had become my job. I preferred the more traditional cleaning method of a brush and pan but even so, it was a task that was becoming increasingly unpleasant. Every day they ate more solid food and eight little doggies' doo-doos became more like proper dog shit and difficult to keep track of.

I could hardly believe it. I'd gone to the Internet café, more for something to do than to pick up messages. The only person who emailed me was Charlie, and even then he only ever sent jokes that other people had sent him. But that day was different. I got an email from Lauren and Lisa.

It would have been better if they'd got my email address from my Friends Reunited space, that way they'd have seen the photos I posted, but they'd got it from Charlie. Apparently they'd met him in Clancy's. Lauren made a point of telling me this. She'd written CLANCY'S! as if this was hilariously funny. Anyone reading it would have thought she'd written it in an ironic way, but I knew what she was playing at. She was boasting. Other than that, the email was really friendly. I quickly scanned through the catch-up stuff about where they were working (council offices, both of them), where they were living (the same flat), and what they were doing (just chilling or clubbing at CLANCY'S!) until I got to the important bit: what they wanted from me. There was no way they'd contact me otherwise. And I was right.

Guess what? We're coming to Barcelona next weekend! We got a cheap deal in a hotel in Estartit and we're going to get the bus to Barcelona for our last night and hook up with you!

What do you say? Are you going to take us out and show us the town?

Getting the bus from Estartit. I was quite impressed. Lisa and Lauren were independent Euro travellers now.

I couldn't decide what to do so I asked Chloe.

'They were vicious bitches to me at college with all that "the Hulk" stuff, but on the other hand, I'd love them to see how I'm doing now and how much weight I've lost. That would totally sicken them, and they'd tell everyone in Cumbernauld.'

Chloe was fantastic.

'Then you gotta invite them. Tell them to come and we'll show them a night out in Barcelona they'll never forget.'

I played it cool with my email reply, giving them my mobile number and not much else, telling them to call me when they got here. I was tempted to attach the photo I'd sent Charlie to give my mum: me in a bikini on the terrace playing with the puppies, but I resisted. They'd see it all when they got here: my figure, my tan, my new designer clothes Chloe had given me. Then those two great haggises would be sorry. We'd see who was the Hulk then.

Chapter 25

We were in a hotel bedroom with a naked man. It was Hotel Museo, the posh one near the beach with the gold-fish sculpture. I hadn't wanted to come here but Chloe had insisted. She'd wanted to meet older men.

'They're way dirtier,' she said.

The hotel was pretty swish but I'd rather have been still sitting in Josep's grubby wee bar in our own barrio.

Josep was tall and broad for a Catalan, with droopy eyes and a big droopy moustache. He was always grumpy but it was an act. When I took Juegita out for a walk he would always call us in and give her a little piece of ham. His bar was like the rest of the bars on the street, a wooden-shuttered windowless cave. It was furnished with only basic wooden trestle tables and stools. It hadn't been properly cleaned in a long time. While puffing on a fat cigar Josep served hot chillies from huge jars, dried ham off the bone and thick chunks of cheese from an enormous wheel. If ash dropped off his cigar on to the food he took a big breath and blew it off. Fat sometimes dripped off the legs of ham suspended from the ceiling. The place stank but you got used to it.

Before we went to Hotel Museo we'd gone downstairs

to Josep's and had a bottle of the local hooch, *Leche de Pantera*: panther's milk. It was thick and creamy and tasted great if you shook some cinnamon powder on top of it. Josep always teased us, and no matter how much Chloe flirted with him and whispered in his ear he'd never tell us what it was actually made of. It looked like milk, tasted sweet and got you drunk, that was all I needed to know.

I always practised my Spanish on Josep. He was Catalan, but as we were his best customers he indulged me. My Spanish was coming along nicely and the words I didn't know I could get round by pulling faces and doing elaborate mimes. I'd rushed back to our table with the good news.

'Hey, Chloe, you'll never guess, Josep's just offered me a job!'

'Chu, sure,' laughed Chloe.

'He has. What, you think I can't do it? It's only bar work.'

'I think you can't speak Spanish.'

'Josep doesn't want me to speak Spanish. You know what it's like in here at the weekend with British tourists. He wants me to work Friday and Saturday. It's perfect: it's just downstairs, I get paid and my Spanish is bound to improve.'

'Honey, you don't need a job, you have a job teaching English with Señor whatever his name is.'

'Señor Valero.'

'Whatever.'

'Yeah but that's not for ages.'

'I've noticed that when we go out you never get it on with anyone. If I hadn't seen you blow the Scottish guy I'd say you were sexually dormant, Alison. That must be kinda frustrating.'

Chloe was smiling and that made me laugh.

'D'you wanna get it on with the Brit customers?' she teased me. 'Is that why you wanna work here?'

'I'm not sexually frustrated! Well, maybe a wee bit,' I laughed, 'but I want to start earning some money.'

My money was all spent. Nights out with Chloe weren't cheap. Marijuana, cocaine and Ecstasy all cost money, and Chloe often left me to do the handovers. What could I do? She was paying for everything else: the rent, the bills and food, the trips to art galleries, nightclubs and expensive restaurants. And she'd given me all those clothes. Paying for the drugs was the least I could do. Despite having taken another 200 from Chloe's tin, once again I was broke.

'Why do you need to make money? We have money.'

'Yeah, but Chloe, that's your money. I can't keep taking—'

'Don't you like living with me?' Chloe said.

Her tone had changed, now she sounded deeply hurt. I didn't know if she was still kidding.

'Don't you wanna hang out with me?'

I laughed, a wee bit uncomfortable.

'Well, don't you?' she said more aggressively. 'I can't do this alone.'

She sounded melodramatic. I couldn't take her seriously.

'Do what alone?' I laughed.

'Raise the puppies, look after the marijuana, make the chimney. And I have to decide what to do about college. Don't you wanna be a part of that?'

'Of course I do.'

'Well tell Josep thanks but no thanks.'

Josep's bar was pretty smelly. Brit lads came here at

174

the weekend to get drunk and obnoxious. I'd have to serve them and smile. Josep might try it on as well; he had that look about him, as if he might chance his arm with me. If I had a problem with him then we wouldn't be able to come in here any more. No more panther's milk.

Chloe heard me tell Josep, in my limited Spanish, that I'd think about it. But that wasn't enough to settle her. We'd done the last of the coke before we'd come out and it was making her restless.

'We're on a mission tonight and I know just where we should go,' said Chloe.

'¿Dónde?' I asked, trying to bring the jovial spirit back.

'Hotel Museo.'

'¿Porqué?'

'Porqué we need to get you laid, missy.'

'Is that the mission?' I splayed my legs. 'Should I adopt the missionary position?'

'Later, honey.'

'But why d'we have to go there?'

'Because it's full of men on conference,' said Chloe, stirring the cinnamon powder into her drink with her finger, 'doctors, lawyers, grown-ups who know how to fuck. Older guys who like it dirty.'

'Ah,' I nodded knowingly, 'we're talking about *you* now, aren't we, Chloe?'

'Shut up!' she squealed, delighted. 'I guess we are.'

'I suppose I should think it's selfish of you to put your perverted sexual needs before my frustrated ones, but I'm not that bothered.'

'That's why we get along so well, Alison.'

The hotel was unbelievably cool and trendy, a contrast

175

to Josep's hole in the wall. The walls and furniture and decor, even the flower arrangements, were on a majestic scale, and made me uncomfortable. We had both dropped two Ecstasy tablets in the taxi on the way there, and I wondered if that was what made the proportions seem so distorted. It didn't feel like Barcelona. Chloe had quickly blagged our way into some corporate function. Except for the waiting staff and us, they were all middle-aged and English, south coast posh English. We could have been in Bournemouth. They all wore a buttonhole or corsage and a name badge. The tables had been cleared of plates and the dance floor prepared. After ten minutes I came up on the Es and started to enjoy myself. Then it was great. A band played cheesy Europop covers and I danced to every one of them. Chloe danced with me for a while and then she was swept off by some handsome old silver fox. The guy was forty, at least, probably the same age as her dad but what the hell. I had got in with a sweet old couple and was jiving with both of them, one on each arm, when Chloe came back for me.

'What are you doing?' she laughed.

'I'm dancing a *ménage à trois* with these lovely people,' I told her. 'All these nice English ladies and gentlemen, don't you think they're lovely?'

'Yes, they're lovely. Come on,' she said hauling me off the floor.

We went up in the lift which had a huge mirror on one side, soft lighting and irresistible music.

'Alison, you're dancing to Musak.'

'So? It's got a good beat.'

I caught sight of us both in the mirror under the flattering lighting of the lift.

'Oh Chloe, look at you, you're so beautiful!'

176

I put my arm around her neck and pulled her round to look at her reflection.

'See?'

'Yeah, and you're beautiful too.'

'But we both know that you're more beautiful than me, much more.'

'Oh stop it. It's just the E, you're always like this on E.'

'It's a truth drug, Chloe.'

'It is with you,' she agreed. 'Are you having a good time?'

'Course I am, the music's great, isn't it? I always have a good time with you, I love you, Chloe. And that's the truth.'

I didn't want to get out of the lift. We were having a good time.

'We have everything here: music, a big mirror, we can go up, we can go down. What more do you want?'

'Are you coming or not?'

The guy was completely naked. This was the silver fox she had gone off with on the dance floor. He was strolling around the room with his cock and his balls out on display.

'Are you a nudist?' I asked.

The Silver Fox looked at Chloe.

'How come the hair on your head is silver but around your cock it's dark?'

He laughed. 'My head's where I worry about things. I don't have any worries down there,' he said, pointing.

'Alison,' Chloe said quietly, 'didn't your mother tell you it's rude to stare?'

'Sorry. Excuse me,' I said and went to the en suite bathroom to wash my face. I felt at ease with the naked man, and he wasn't bothered, but I wasn't so wasted I didn't realize how bizarre this situation was. Even if Chloe was up for it, one of us should have our wits about us.

I sluiced my face repeatedly with cold water and then spent time pushing my eyeliner and mascara back into a tidy line under my eyes. I was engrossed in this for three or four minutes, maybe more.

'Hey!' I yelled, excited. 'Have you checked out how fluffy these towels are?' I asked as I stuck my head round the bathroom door.

The Silver Fox was down on one bended knee, genuflecting between Chloe's legs. Her top was pulled up and he was squeezing her right breast. Chloe was moaning. He had his back to me. I could see his brown sac hanging between his legs, dark against his white leg.

'I'm sorry,' I said, 'I'll wait downstairs.'

I turned to leave the room and Chloe pushed the guy away.

'No. Alison, don't go.'

'Oh but . . .'

She pulled me into the bathroom, locked the door and whispered fiercely into my face. 'What are you doing? I'm about to get fucked and I need you here.'

'Why? D'you think he's dangerous?'

'No. Yes. He might be dangerous.'

'Well come on, let's just leave right now.'

'I don't want to leave, I want fucked.'

'Chloe, why d'you sleep with all these guys? Did your boyfriend cheat? Are you a scorned woman, is that it?'

Chloe shook her head and laughed. 'You come out with the craziest things at the most inappropriate times. And no, he didn't, and I'm not. I broke up with him.'

'What did he look like?'

'He was cute. Now—'

'So how come you broke up with him then?'

'He was just a kid. He was only interested in partying with his stupid friends. I was bored. Now can we get back to *this* party, please? The guy's naked, he's gonna go off the boil. Come on, let's have some fun. He'll fuck you too if you want. He knows what he's doing.'

I shook my head. 'Nah, you're all right, I'll leave it. I'm not giving my virginity away to a stranger.'

'Your virginity?'

'Shit.' I giggled.

'You're a fucking virgin?'

'No. A fucking virgin would be an oxymoron.'

'Say what?'

Embarrassed, my response was a sheepish smirk. 'I'm more of a non-fucking virgin. A virgin yet to be fucked.'

'So that's why you never get it on with anyone. Jeez!' Chloe shook her head. '*Now* she tells me. OK, whatever. But stay with me, please?'

'How about if I wait here?' I bargained. 'Then I'd be on hand if anything kicks off but I wouldn't be in your way.'

'But I need someone to watch, you know it helps get me off.'

Sometimes Chloe and I just went out to dinner and a quiet stroll around the city. On those nights we weren't interested, but other times we went out on a specific mission: to find boys, and shag them.

All those teenage years when I sat in the house watching telly and eating. All those wasted years when I was a sexless blob, a lump of a lassie no boy would look at: I was going to make up for it now, and then some. Here was the chance I'd always fantasized about, and I

179

was going to grab it with both hands. My time had finally arrived, and I was about to get dirrrty.

I always began the evening full of bravado, up for it, gagging for it, but once Chloe and I had located and contained our prey, it was a different story. Like the night with Ewan, my nerve deserted me. I couldn't help it, as the night wore on my mindset gradually moved away from rampant reckless sex on the beach or hot horny humping in a hotel room. Instead, slowly but surely, my mindset drifted towards some unwashed migrant worker rubbing their bits against mine. I wanted to be dirrrty, I really did, but I just wasn't.

It wasn't fair to ruin Chloe's night with my lacklustre lack of lust, so every time we ended up in a group-sex scenario I'd use avoidance tactics: I acted drunk and sneered aggressively; I blew thick smoke from joints to keep the poor confused boy away; once I even pretended to pass out.

But now that Chloe knew my dark secret I didn't have to pretend any more. Now I could relax, sit back and watch the show. While I watched her get jiggy with this sweaty silver-haired stranger, I tried to observe with a scientific eye. This would be research for my own future encounters.

There was something bestial about it. I stood over the bed watching them. The man was on top between her legs, her knees wide. He wasn't lying on her, he was at arm's length; the point of contact was where their groins met. Chloe dug her nails into his bum cheeks; he occasionally clutched her breasts in a way which looked painful. From where I was standing I couldn't see much of the in and out, only his bum thrusting forward at her. Chloe kept her eyes closed and squealed and moaned.

When the squealing increased in pitch and frequency she opened her eyes and reached her hand out for me.

'You're not going to put it anywhere warm and sweaty, are you?' I asked.

She shook her head. The Silver Fox ignored me. Tentatively I gave her my hand but she only held on and squeezed. She closed her eyes again and moaned. A pink blush began on her chest and travelled to her face. A second or two later the guy seemed to go into spasms, his face contorting as he pushed at her in dying waves, his damp grey hair falling over his face. I liked watching his arse pushing and grinding. It was beautiful.

In refusing the undoubted skill and know-how of the Silver Fox I'd perhaps been a little hasty. Why deny myself such obvious pleasure? At the moment of their orgasm, I'd felt a fluttering. I wanted the Silver Fox to do to me what he'd just done to Chloe.

It was a freezing cold night. My breath was steaming in front of my face. I tried to make smoke rings with it, but it didn't work. I heard the noise ahead and walked towards it. I wasn't scared, it sounded cheerful and friendly, like a dog, a puppy.

I could hardly see a thing in the thick mist. I walked with my hand out in front of me. I didn't want to walk into a tree and give myself a black eye. 'Here, boy!' I called. The noise got louder but no clearer. It sounded more and more like animals snuffling, and in a way it was.

They were standing against a big tree. He had his hands on her fat white thighs. She had her arms round his neck. They had loads of clothes on, bunched up round their necks and piled round their ankles, but their middle bits and bums were bare. They must have been cold.

I stayed still. They hadn't seen me.

'C'mon, baby.'

His white backside was clenching and unclenching, pushing forward, pulling back, like he was dancing. His head was facing into the tree; it looked like he was speaking to the tree. They were both swearing.

'Oh my love. Fuck me, my love, oof, fuck me.'

'Oof, I'm fucking you, oof, oof, I'm fucking you.'

One of her legs was hooked around him and the other was slightly bent out at the knee. Her breasts took up all of her chest, stretching down towards her waist. When he bumped forward his belly connected with them and made a slapping noise. They were grunting like pigs. That's what they were, filthy pigs.

They couldn't see me.

I took the long way round. Big soft steps. Silent breathing, until I was behind them, behind their tree, facing him. His eyes were shut, his face squashed, ugly. He didn't see me move towards him.

'Oof.'

I had a knobbly grey twig in my hand. It was sharp. He opened his eyes and saw me and closed them again quickly. But not quickly enough. He screamed. Surprised, frightened. And then he was pulling away from her, he was shoving her away and bending over. She was pulling her clothes up and around her, putting her hand on his shoulder, looking into his face, and screaming. He put his hand in front of his face.

Chapter 26

There were five dirty glasses on the bedside cabinet on Chloe's side of the bed. I tried not to think about them or look too closely at the contents. Orange juice had crystallized up the sides on some of them, or there were grey-green islands of mould floating in what had been iced coffee. Luckily the one she'd knocked over only had water in it, but the glass smashed on the ceramic floor into jaggy peaks.

'Jesus!' Chloe yelled, and then stormed off and locked the bathroom door. I heard her run a bath.

I shook my head and smiled. It was just like her to be so outraged. She was the one responsible for all this mess. She was the one who'd knocked the glass over. I said nothing but I was secretly satisfied, maybe now she'd clear the rest of them away. Although it was disgusting, I'd left them there to see how many accumulated before Chloe did something about it.

Apart from hanging up my clothes the day I moved in, Chloe didn't do housekeeping. She was not domesticated. I wasn't much better, but Chloe's slobbishness was awe-inspiring.

Neither of us had any interest in cooking. The most

we did was open a packet. We snacked on cartons of gazpacho, bread, cheese, olives, chorizo, crunchy pickled garlic, freshly squeezed orange juice, yoghurt and crisps. When the munchies hit us around midnight I'd pop out and bring back falafel, kebabs or *churros* and chocolate. Some days we'd go out for a *menú del día*. We'd pick at the food and guzzle red wine, *gaseosa* and coffee. The one and only time I cooked, as a treat and to let Chloe try it, I made us both a crisps and fish-finger sandwich. She didn't like it. She said the weather was too hot for greasy food and complained that the fishy smell made her feel sick.

She wasn't much for cleaning either. I had taken over watering the maria, feeding the dogs, removing their poo, sweeping up the dead roaches and putting down new powder. It was a small step to take on the basic household chores. Unlike her, I had a terror of cockroaches, and made a point of keeping at least the floor and kitchen surfaces clean.

Every day we saw more cockroaches in the flat. It was getting so that I wouldn't get out of bed when it was dark. I had to put the light on and wait while they scuttled into their hiding places. Chloe said it was only temporary, because it was August. The café on the ground floor next door to Josep's had closed for vacation for the whole month. The café's resident cockroach population was being starved out and was having to move upwards in search of food.

'I can hardly believe they'd climb five storeys,' I said.

'Oh yeah,' said Chloe with a laugh in her voice.

Her attitude to the roaches was different from mine. While I preferred to try to keep the place clean and prevent them from crawling all over us, Chloe enjoyed the hunt. Sometimes, while she was in the middle of doing something, painting or talking, she'd freeze. She'd have seen movement under the couch or the cooker and would lie in wait, crouching uncomfortably for as long as it took, twenty minutes, half an hour, until the cockroach emerged. Then she'd lay into it with a hammer or the heel of her shoe, mashing it to a paste. Once, when she happened to have a palette knife in her hand, she decapitated the cockroach and watched, fascinated, while the headless part continued to writhe for a few moments.

Outside on the pavement yellow powder was laid to keep them out, like garlic to keep vampires away, but it didn't work. They were already in the building, climbing up through the cracks in the walls. The old lady who lived downstairs, Señora Garcia, knocked the door and gave me another tin of powder *'para las cucarachas'*. It was much stronger, and more effective, than the organic stuff we'd been using. Chloe said it was poison and refused to touch it. This left me with sole responsibility for our roach problem.

I would've thought that someone who had so many expensive clothes might be fastidious about grooming, but Chloe rarely bothered. She was forever in the bath, but more as a leisure activity than for hygiene. She'd happily pull on a top that needed ironing or a skirt with the hem hanging down. Amongst other things, I'd blagged a freebie sewing kit from the Hotel Museo. I offered to fix her hem but she didn't care.

I regularly washed my clothes and when I did I always asked if she wanted anything put in the machine. She had no regular laundry system. A week and half after she came back from Berlin her rucksack had still not been unpacked. It was only when she was looking for something that she eventually hauled the sour-smelling clothes out the rucksack and left them thrown around the bedroom.

'You're not going to wear that top, are you?' I once asked her as we were getting dressed to go out. 'Juegita's been lying on it all week. It stinks of dog. You'll never cop off smelling like that.'

'Are you kidding me?' she said. 'Guys love it. They're beasts anyway.'

One day, a particularly hot and humid day, we came back to the flat and as soon as we got in Chloe lifted her skirt and wheeched her pants off. She rolled them down her thighs as though they were on fire. The pants came off damp with sweat and rolled in a croissant shape.

'Oh man, that feels soooo good,' she laughed.

Chloe dropped the pants where they fell and strode out on to the terrace where she lifted her skirt and wafted. I could only follow and watch in stunned admiration. The pants lay there until bedtime, when my nervousness about the cockroaches got the better of me.

And it was clear Chloe wasn't going to clear away the broken glass either. She stayed in the bath, singing. The roaches wouldn't be interested in the glass, it might even put them off, but it was still a health hazard; one of us was going to cut our feet. Even if I swept up the glass, that still left the problem of the other dirty glasses. I shivered when I thought of cockroaches coming so close to our bed.

'It's OK, Chloe, you can come out now,' I shouted at the bathroom door.

I could hear the hard edge in my voice, I knew Chloe would hear it too but I was too angry to care. While I fiercely scrubbed at the crusted-on orange juice I realized that if we were going to college together this would be the way of it: me chasing round cleaning up after her.

'I've swept up the glass that YOU BROKE. I've washed the other disgustingly manky glasses that YOU LEFT.'

'Oh Alison, you didn't have to do that,' she called sweetly as she ran the hot water and topped up the bath.

I stood at the door bawling over the noise of the running water.

'Who the fuck else was going to do it? You?'

Chloe turned off the tap but otherwise there was no reply.

I was stumped for words. I didn't know what to do; there was nothing I could do. I heard her settle back in the bath with a satisfied sigh. 'Sorry,' she said, 'I couldn't hear you there, Alison, the water was running, what did you say?'

I had two choices: kick the door in and slap her about the head, or get out of the flat for a while.

Chapter 27

Lisa and Lauren got off the bus jiggling and giggling. Chloe had insisted we met them at the station. It was polite, she said. I wanted them to be blown away by how amazingly thin and fabulous I looked, and spent hours drying my hair straight and doing my make-up. I was hoping Chloe might do me another of her makeovers, but she was too busy planning the evening.

She couldn't find the restaurant in the phone book, so she went down there when the place opened just to be sure of getting a table. I thought she'd book Taxidermista, a place on Plaza Real. I'd seen the queues standing outside for hours, but she said, 'No, better than that.' She went around the corner and booked Caracol, an old-fashioned tourist-trap restaurant. A place with a rotisserie full of flaming chickens for a window. You couldn't pass by on the narrow street without getting your face scorched.

By the time she'd come back she'd laid out a full itinerary. 'I'm thinking: we'll walk them down to Barceloneta for a couple bottles of fizz at Champaneria, back up to Gòtic, bottle of panther's milk at Josep's, then the restaurant, then Plaza Real, then that sleazy drag-queen disco Cangrejo. And I think last stop the beach. They're gonna love it. Whaddaya think?'

She was obviously very pleased with herself.

'Good plan,' I said without enthusiasm.

'Look at you!' Lisa and Lauren squealed in unison as they got off the bus and threw their arms around me.

'I'm sorry,' said Lauren, 'but you look amazing!'

Lisa agreed, giggling. 'You've lost tons of weight, you used to be huge. I can't believe it, you look amazing!'

After this, the subject of my transformation was dropped. They hadn't slimmed down, if anything they'd both put on more weight. My life and my body had changed almost beyond recognition but it wasn't mentioned again. I was a one-minute wonder.

Lisa and Lauren wasted no time bringing me up to speed with their love lives. Due to their acceptance into Clancy's they'd both recently disposed of their hymens. Lauren, for three and a half weeks, had even had a boyfriend. I prepared my sympathetic face, sure that she was about to tell us she'd been humped and dumped, but no. She had chucked him because she felt she was too young to get tied down.

'It's like this,' Lauren sagely explained, 'why run a car when there's so many taxis?'

She threw her head back and laughed. 'I'm sorry,' she added, 'but I've been taking plenty of taxis!'

I laughed too and said, 'You're right, Lauren, why run a car when you've become the town bike?'

We all laughed, Lauren more than anyone. I wasn't sure if she took it as an insult or a compliment. I didn't care how she took it.

In the restaurant Chloe went to great and unsubtle lengths to flatter Lisa and Lauren: how lovely their

190

Scottish accents were (she'd never mentioned mine), how funny they were when they described their *crazy* nights out at Clancy's. She screamed and slapped the table when they said anything vaguely amusing. How great they looked: their fashion, their hair, their tan.

What the hell was she saying? They did not look great. Fashionwise it was a case of *The Devil Wears Primark*. They both wore low-cut jeans over which spilled the muffin tops of their lardy hips and bellies. Lisa's hair colour was so obviously out of a bottle, with dods of yellow blond splodged on her head. Their tan was also out of a bottle; they had orange lines round their feet that rubbed off on their brand-new white court shoes. When they went to the toilet I asked Chloe what she was playing at.

'Relax, honey, no need to get jealous.' She put her arm around me and whispered, 'You still my bitch.'

I shrugged her off.

'It's called *winning their confidence*,' she said.

She had done that all right. She had them eating out of her hand. She kept them topped up with booze and insisted on paying for everything.

'You're our guests tonight, ladies,' she told them. 'Alison and I are picking up the tab. No argument, we invite you, it's the tradition here in Catalonia.'

Chloe was pouring the charm on by the bucketload. Except that, although we passed close by our apartment twice, she never mentioned it. I wanted Lisa and Lauren to see where I was living, the luxury I had grown accustomed to, but Chloe left them to drag their suitcases all around town, the plastic wheels on the cobbled streets clacking like trains on a track.

I liked that sound. Sometimes from our terrace above

191

I could hear tourists' suitcases in the street, arriving or leaving. It always made me feel sorry for them. Their time here was limited; sooner or later they had to go home. At least as Lisa and Lauren dragged their matching pink Primark suitcases around I knew they'd soon be gone. Their flight was at seven the next morning. Now that they could report back to Cumbernauld on how slim and gorgeous I was, they had fulfilled their function. I couldn't wait to be rid of them.

Lisa and Lauren put up a show of reluctance but they greedily accepted everything they were offered. The next time they went to the toilet, Chloe went with them and all three came back giggling, sniffing and wiping their noses. Chloe passed me the coke for a solo mission but where was the fun in that?

In Plaza Real Chloe left us, Lisa and Lauren oohing and aahing at the antics of the busking acrobats, while she spoke to a young guy. She shook his hand and although the police were standing not five feet away I had a good idea what had happened. When we got to Cangrejo, my suspicions were confirmed. Chloe produced pills. Without saying anything to the others she handed me one and we both swigged from a bottle of water. Lisa and Lauren were curious and asked Chloe to give them one.

'Well, ladies, if you're sure you can handle it,' she laughed.

They laughed too. We all laughed and as Chloe handed over the water bottle I noticed that the pills Lisa and Lauren were throwing back were different from the ones we'd just necked.

The difference showed up pretty quickly.

We'd only been dancing twenty minutes or so when Lisa and Lauren started to go gaga.

'What did you give them?' I asked Chloe.

'*Ketamina*.'

I'd never tried ketamine, and I couldn't believe the effect it had. Lisa and Lauren were still smiling but they had gone floppy and began stumbling around.

'Let's get them outta here,' said Chloe. 'Lauren, you forgot your suitcase,' she reminded her.

Lisa and Lauren, staggering from the drink and the coke and the ketamine, held their suitcase handles and each other and giggled uncontrollably. 'This is the best night out we've ever had,' said Lisa, kissing me and pulling me into their girly huddle.

We picked up a taxi on La Rambla.

'Get in,' I barked at them.

They did as they were told in their awkward bendy way. It was like being in charge of two toddlers. We spoke about them as though they weren't there, they were too monged to even be offended.

'Let's take 'em to the beach,' said Chloe.

'No, let's just send them to the airport,' I remonstrated. The Ecstasy I'd taken had kicked in and it always made me speak my mind. 'I don't want you to be friends with them. You're my friend, Chloe. Their flight leaves in three hours anyway, they can sober up before they get on the plane. I'm sick of them. I don't want them missing their flight.'

'Who wants a party on the beach?' Chloe asked.

'Woohooo, midnight swim!' yelled Lisa.

'Skinny dipping!' yelled Lauren, and started to pull her top off.

'Chloe, please, let's just get rid of them, they're no fun now anyway.'

'You think?' asked Chloe.

She looked Lauren and Lisa up and down as though they were sides of beef.

'Nah,' she said, 'the fun's just starting. Let the partying begin!'

Chapter 28

When we tumbled out of the taxi Chloe insisted that we go and sit under the lifeguard's lookout post. We had to help Lisa and Lauren drag their suitcases along the sand, tripping over and steering the heavy luggage around groups of boys and girls sprawling on blankets. Although Lisa and Lauren had only come for a long weekend, they had made sure to stuff in as many cheap tops as their pink suitcases could hold.

In Barceloneta the beach was almost as crowded at four a.m. as it was during the sunlit tourist hours. Because they lived with their parents, Catalans came to the beach when the bars closed to smoke dope, swim, and have uncomfortable chafing sex. Or at least that's what Chloe had told me. I'd yet to know the delights of having gritty imported sand worked between the cheeks of my bum. It was the quintessential Barcelona experience, she'd assured me: the stars twinkling above, the waves lapping the shore, the buttock-grazing friction burns. I could hardly wait.

'Come on, girls,' said Chloe, hustling us along.

'Are we there yet?' I asked petulantly.

'Not quite.'

'We haven't got time to go all the way along the beach, these two have a plane to catch. Why don't we just stop here? There's tons of space here.'

'Just a little further, nearly there,' Chloe soothed.

'Nearly where?' I moaned.

'Here.'

We'd come to an abrupt stop under the lifeguard's lookout post. The clusters of beach parties had thinned out this far along the beach, and now we were quite isolated. Chloe was up to something. I glanced at her but she was giving nothing away.

Lisa and Lauren were grateful to slump down in the sand and they immediately began clawing at their clothes.

'Wanna swim,' Lauren mumbled.

If they went swimming there was every chance that they might drown, which was no bad thing in my book, but as the responsible adult I had to say, 'I don't think that's a good idea.'

'Oh, loosen up, will ya?' Chloe sneered. 'They're on vacation. You do what you want on vacation, right, Lauren?'

'Right,' Lauren slurred.

She had begun to haul her top off but halfway through she'd lost momentum. Trapped inside the top, her arms dangled above her head, her head and shoulders bound like a mummy. Her breasts toppled over the rim of her bra and an avalanche of loose flab lay piled below.

Chloe helped Lauren off with her top and then, without being asked, gently eased Lisa out of hers.

'There you go, honey,' she said mildly. 'My, you're both such big girls.'

She said this in an admiring tone and Lauren and Lisa,

accustomed now to her flattery, laughed and accepted it as such.

'I mean, Lauren, you are a whole lotta woman! You gotta be, what, a hundred and ninety pounds? And Lisa, you can't be far behind.'

Lisa and Lauren giggled uncomfortably at this change in direction.

'Now, help me out here, girls, I can't remember. Which is which? Lisa, are you the Hump or the Hulk?'

A look passed between them and then there was a shamefaced glance from Lisa directed towards me.

I kept my head down.

'Yep,' said Chloe, 'it's a puzzler. What say we keep it simple, huh? Lauren, you be . . . well, which is it, the Hulk or the Hump?'

Lauren looked to Lisa, then to me and finally to Chloe.

'The Hulk?' she whispered.

'That's my girl! Which makes things nice and easy for you, Lisa. You're the . . .'

'Hump,' said Lisa with her head on her chest.

'That's what I'm talking about!' said Chloe gleefully. 'Whaddaya think, Alison, think the names are a good match?'

I looked at them: both bulging out of their clothes, stupid, sweaty, shameful.

'Whatever.'

Chloe laughed. No one else did and there were no more glances. We had nowhere to look but out to sea. Lisa and Lauren sat quiet and cowed, stupefied by drugs or shame or both. But Chloe wasn't finished with them.

'Hey, come on, girls, I'm only fucking with you,' she said, producing a small bottle of absinthe from her bag.

197

'What d'you say we kiss and make up and have a little drink?'

I ignored her, continuing to watch the water.

Lisa and Lauren looked at each other and then to Chloe, smiling their relief at being let off the hook.

'Come and get it, girls,' said Chloe, pouring absinthe into the bottle cap, 'come to Mama.'

Lisa fell forward on to all fours and laughed a throaty laugh as though she was doing something really naughty. She began to crawl heavily across the sand towards Chloe, who was holding out the capful of absinthe like a carrot on a stick. Lauren laughed too and began crawling, making it a race. They lumbered towards her, their breasts hanging like overstretched dough from their bras, and slurped the absinthe like slavering dogs.

When Chloe had fed them three or four capfuls each and they couldn't drink any more they rolled in the sand and laughed and gasped and stared into the sky. I sat rigid, scanning the shore.

'Look at Alison,' said Chloe, 'she's so slim and beautiful. Isn't she just the cutest little Scottish girl in the world?'

'¡Hola chicas!' said a male voice.

Two boys had approached us. They stood over us, black shapes outlined against the full moon. Chloe spoke to them, or rather she spoke to one of them, the same one she'd spoken to in Plaza Real. I *knew* she was up to something. This was no coincidence. That's why we'd had to schlep all the way to the lifeguard's post; she must have arranged to meet here.

Chloe and the guy spoke too fast for me to make out much. I didn't want to ask in front of Lisa and Lauren. Since they'd arrived Chloe and I'd been putting on a pretty good show of me speaking Spanish. I'd ordered all the food and drinks and, with discreet nods and pinches from Chloe under the table, I was able to answer the waiter *claro que sí* or *no* when he asked a question. But even my apparent fluency in Spanish didn't much impress Lisa and Lauren.

Chloe and the guy were talking seriously and intensely while the rest of us sat silently. In amongst lots of other stuff I didn't understand I heard Chloe emphatically repeat the phrase *'nada de nada'* – nothing of nothing, what did that mean?

With a command from the lead guy, the other one sat down beside Lisa and Lauren. They were handsome boys in that generic dark-haired, dark-eyed Latino way, and they were smooth operators. Lisa and Lauren were too wasted to properly introduce themselves, lurching forward and giggling at everything. One of them stroked Lauren's face and within minutes had begun kissing her, running his hands across her rippling love handles. Once this action kicked off Lisa obviously didn't feel the need to stand on ceremony either. She hauled the other one down on top of her and pushed her face into his, kissing and fondling the boy before he knew where he was.

'I need a beer,' Chloe announced. 'Why are there never any vendors when you need 'em? I'm gonna get a beer. Who wants one?'

Lauren surfaced briefly and said, 'Cheers, Chloe, I'll take one,' before redoubling her efforts to suck the face off the guy. Lisa, her tongue too far down the other guy's throat, couldn't reply.

'Come on, Alison, help me get the beers in,' Chloe said as she moved off.

Going for beer was a good excuse to get away from Lisa

and Lauren for a while. I just wanted to go back to the flat, lock the bathroom door and lie in a hot bath. But I knew I shouldn't leave them. I sat hugging my knees and trying to think. Chloe called over her shoulder.

'Are you coming?'

Chapter 29

We found a beer vendor within a few minutes. The man, an old Asian guy, was rummaging in the sand when we came upon him. He'd buried a cache of beer stubbies and was disinterring some of them. He was very edgy, probably worried that now we knew where his treasure was, we'd steal it when he left.

'*Dos cervezas por favor*,' said Chloe.

'*Tres*,' I corrected her, 'Lisa wants one as well.'

'*Dos*,' she repeated.

I shrugged, too tired to argue.

Chloe paid for the beers and continued walking away from the beach. We strolled to the boardwalk and then upstairs on to the promenade. It was quiet up here and there was a fresh breeze. Chloe found a bench, we cracked open our beers and sat in a mellow silence. This was the nicest time I'd had all night.

I'd got so used to it being just me and Chloe. We knew where we were with each other. When it was just the two of us she was a different person, a real person.

'Ringside seats,' she said with a smile.

'Eh?'

'Can you see them, down there?'

I peered and below the lifeguard's post I could just about make out two writhing bundles.

'Yes, unfortunately,' I grumped. 'It's not fair, those two lumps of gristle are getting the sand between their cheeks. They're having the fucking quintessential experience before I am!'

'I think you mean the quintessential *fucking* experience.'

'You know what I mean.'

'Hey, it's not my fault you're a virgin. Nobody's fault but your own. You've had every opportunity.' Chloe held her hand up as if to give testimony. 'God knows I've done my best.'

'I know,' I said quietly and thought about it for a while. 'I know you have.'

'Anyhow, how come you're still a virgin? I thought you did it with that guy Ewan. You looked pretty cosy when I came in.'

'Yeah but we hadn't done it. I wanted to, I wanted him to be my first. Wanca and the Silver Fox and those other guys, I don't know, I really wanted it but . . . maybe there's something wrong with me.'

'Easy, tiger. There's nothing wrong with you, nothing wrong with being a virgin. I wasn't judging. I was just surprised. I haven't met any twenty-two-year-old virgins unless they're Christian. Even then they've usually just fessed up and rebranded.'

'Well, I am. I wish I wasn't. Lisa and Lauren don't seem to be having that dilemma, they're getting stuck in. Look, Lisa's sitting on him, look at the way she's bouncing on his balls. Ooow! That's got to hurt.'

We giggled and swigged from our beer cans until Chloe turned back to watch them again.

'We should have got popcorn,' she said.

'God, you can't take your eyes off them, can you?'

'Euuw, that is so gross, Alison! Why would you say that?'

'Eh,' I paused for effect, 'because it's true?'

'Shut up! I don't want to watch, I like to *be* watched, it's totally different.'

'Well *excuse me*, I'd hate to suggest that you're any kind of sexual deviant.'

'Why, thank you kindly,' said Chloe with a coy Southern-belle-type nod before dismissing me with her usual hand wave. 'Anyway, this is just the overture. The show hasn't started yet.'

'What else is going to happen? Remember, they have to be on a plane in two hours' time, otherwise we'll never get rid of them.'

'Watch. It's gonna be fun, and you know what they say. The show ain't over till . . .' she said, squinting towards the beach, 'and boy, are these fat ladies gonna sing.'

We returned to quietly sipping beer. It was slowly beginning to get light, the dark blue of the sky becoming paler, but still there wasn't much to see.

'But you shouldn't have told them,' I said.

'Shouldn't have told them what?'

'You know what: about the Hulk. I understand why you did it, and cheers and all that, but I didn't want that.'

'They had to know. It's part of the plan.'

'What plan?' I asked, but Chloe didn't answer, she was too busy watching what was happening below.

Further along the beach, with dawn approaching, other groups started to pack up and head home. Those that stayed pulled their blankets around them and settled down to sleep. It had been a long night. I had started to nod off, my beer can tipping at an angle, when Chloe dug me in the ribs.

Lisa and Lauren and the two boys were standing now, all four of them naked from what I could see. The boys dashed towards the water, and Lisa and Lauren followed squealing and giggling, their breasts thudding their ribcages with every step.

A post-coital swim – something else I hadn't done yet.

They were having great fun, young people cavorting the way nature intended: uninhibited, breasts and penises dangling free. The boys would run and then stop, almost letting Lisa and Lauren catch them, before running away again. This pointless playground-style chase went on for a good ten minutes. My eyes were tired and were beginning to close again. It was obvious that Lisa and Lauren were never going to catch them, the boys were far too fast. They still half-heartedly ran towards them but they had lost pace.

The boys stood at the water's edge. The low tide had uncovered a huge expanse of smooth sand. This time they held out their arms to beckon them and let the knackered girls reach them. Almost. Suddenly the two lads darted past them back up the beach. The girls laughed and turned back. And then I saw what was really going on.

The boys ran to where Lisa and Lauren had left their stuff: their suitcases, their handbags, their clothes. The boys hastily pulled on their jeans, stuffed the girls' clothes in the handbags, lifted the suitcases clear of the sand and ran with them above their heads. They ran fast, like experienced coolies, as though they weren't holding aloft twenty kilos of Primark size-eighteen leisurewear.

Lisa and Lauren squealed with laughter and ran after them. It was no use. The boys sprinted to the boardwalk, up the stairs past our bench, ran across the road and disappeared into the backstreets of Barceloneta. Lisa and Lauren hadn't even made it back to the lifeguard's post yet.

'Get down, they're looking this way!' Chloe hissed.

We hunched forward on the bench and stayed still.

Naked and stranded, Lisa and Lauren weren't laughing any more. To pursue the boys meant leaving the beach and coming up on to the street. With no clothes on. We lost sight of them as they headed towards the stairs.

'You think they'll come up here?' Chloe asked.

As a precautionary measure we crouched down behind a dumpster and lucky we did, because seconds later we heard them puff up the stairs. They were crying now. They weren't making any sense, I could only make out garbled words through the sobbing: passports, tickets, purse. Being naked seemed to be the least of their problems.

Chloe could barely restrain her glee. She had to ram her hand over her mouth to hold it in. They were arguing now, blaming each other. Chloe's eyes scrunched up with hilarity when Lisa and Lauren lumbered off in the wrong direction, away from Barceloneta.

I wanted to come out from behind the bin. *They went thataway!* I wanted to shout but I knew I couldn't. This was theft, a particularly heartless theft, and I was implicated. It was so obviously revenge for calling me the Hulk. Who'd believe it wasn't set up by me, but on my behalf by my loyal but crazy friend?

Anyway, what good would it do? Lisa and Lauren couldn't catch them on the beach; they'd never catch them in the backstreets. Those guys would be miles away. They'd have taken the money and dumped the cases.

'C'mon, Chloe,' I said, as soon as Lisa and Lauren were safely out of sight. 'We have to find those cases. They'll have taken the cash and thrown everything else away. If we're lucky they'll have left the passports and tickets. There's still time for Lisa and Lauren to make their flight.'

'You gotta be kidding.'

'Look, if we find the cases at the very least they'll get their clothes back. We can make out we found them while we were trying to buy beer. They might believe that.'

I was a hundred yards ahead before I turned and saw Chloe reluctantly following me. With the sun peeking over the horizon we entered Barceloneta, Chloe dragging her feet and me striding ahead, searching every corner and doorway for a glimpse of pink suitcase.

Chapter 30

I found the suitcases outside the Barceloneta market hall, led there by an enticing trail of what Lauren had been wearing: skirt, top, outsize bra and less than fresh panties. The suitcases were dumped between two big metal bins the market traders used for their rubbish. The cases were intact but the handbags and what was left of their contents were strewn around the street. There was no sign of passports or tickets.

'Why would those guys take the plane tickets?' I said, more to myself than as a direct question to Chloe. 'They're hardly likely to fly to Glasgow.'

'Because, dumbass, I told them to.'

She had never spoken to me like that before.

'Chloe, I can't believe . . . You really have no . . . Not only have you left them *naked*, but they've no money, no way of getting home and . . .' I said, floundering around for something that would adequately express my disbelief and outrage, 'they're fucking *naked*!'

'And your point is?'

'My point is . . .'

'They're naked, yeah, you said.'

I was back to being dumb again.

Chloe struggled to pull a tightly wedged case out from between the bins.

'I told them the stuff was to disappear. What if Miss Hulk and Miss Hump had come this way, huh?'

'Chloe, we can't leave them like this, it's not right.'

'Oh yes, sweetheart, we can.'

'We have to give them their clothes back.'

'No, we don't. Look at you, all concerned for them. It's sweet that you Scottish girls stick together.'

I turned away, trying to pretend I wasn't part of this vicious trick.

I watched the traders unload their vans and receive their deliveries. People came in and out of the modern market building with trolleys loaded with boxes of fruit and veg, crates of fish and meat. An old lady carried a big sack of onions into the hall. The sack looked heavier than she was. I half expected her to fall over but she continued past slowly and stoically. I wanted to look at anything other than Chloe or the suitcases.

Even while she was wining and dining Lisa and Lauren, laughing at their pathetic jokes, praising their pitiful fashion sense, I'd probably known all along that Chloe was planning something. Maybe I hadn't realized that she'd be quite this heartless but still and all, I'd led my fat gormless ex-friends into the trap and let it happen. I was still letting it happen.

A trader passed with a huge tray of whole fish, tails flapping over the edge, the fresh sea smell filling my nostrils. From the corner of my eye I heard and saw Chloe unzip the suitcase and toss the contents: a mixture of neatly folded unworn clothes, and rumpled worn clothes, on the ground. Wrapped in a pair of jeans, a toiletries bag fell and tinkled as its contents smashed. A strong chemical smell of perfume leaked out, obliterating the natural fish whiff from the market. Chloe picked up the bag and opened it.

'Hey, check this out,' she said.

Despite myself I turned and looked. She was wiping off a bundle of foil packets of pills.

'Eca Stack Xtreme! Man, you can't get these in the States any more!'

'What are they?' I asked, worried. 'Medication?'

'What are they? They're slimming pills. The best. Ephedrine, caffeine and aspirin, high dose, you can drop ten pounds in a few days with these bad boys.'

'I wonder which of them is taking slimming pills?'

'Maybe both of them,' reasoned Chloe. 'Jesus! How fat were they before they took 'em?'

When we'd met them at the station Lisa and Lauren had acknowledged how much weight I'd lost, and all the while one of them was taking diet pills.

'Hey,' said Chloe, animated, 'maybe there's more in the other suitcase.'

She now hauled the other case out and dug through the clothes until she found the toilet bag.

'Oh yeah,' she confirmed, 'that's what I'm talking about!'

Chloe handed me another foil packet. I could just make out the small type: *Sildenafil Citrate 100 mg.*

'So now we know,' she said soberly.

'More slimming pills?' I asked. I'd never heard of sildenafil.

'It's Viagra!'

'Shut up!' I said, borrowing Chloe's usual expression of disbelief.

'I'm telling you, Alison. Those two probably slip it in guys' drinks.'

'You think?'

'Well, how else are those munsters gonna get laid?'

Chloe was laughing her head off.

'No wonder she was bouncing so hard on his balls,' I giggled.

It was funny. When I stopped laughing I realized I hardly knew these two girls. Lisa and Lauren had probably spent a lot of money on these pills, a lot of hope. And yet they were still enormous. And unattractive. And currently naked. I suddenly felt a bittersweet tenderness for their poor vulnerable Scottish flesh.

While Chloe was still counting the packets of pills I gathered up clothes and stuffed them back in the suitcase.

'What are you doing?'

'You know what I'm doing. I'm going to find them and give them back their clothes.'

As I turned to pick up some more Chloe threw out what I'd just packed. We began what might have looked to anyone else like a ridiculous game: me trying to pack clothes and Chloe throwing them out again, a petulant child throwing her toys out of her pram. This was silly. But although we were both laughing I was serious.

I was knackered but determined: I'd last longer than her. I couldn't stop her throwing the stuff out, but I could keep picking it up until she lost interest. She had to eventually. Chloe had a short attention span. She didn't care about Lisa and Lauren. She made out like she had exacted this terrible revenge because they had insulted me, but the whole thing had really only been a bit of sport for her, an evening's entertainment. I guarded the clothes I'd lifted and we began to elbow each other out of the way to get at the suitcase.

Things were escalating, we weren't laughing any more. I had secured the stuff that lay around our feet, but to get to the more widely scattered clothes I had to leave my post for a second. This was a mistake. Chloe took her opportunity and heaved the case right into the big market bin. As I reached to recover it she hoisted the other case up and into the bin.

I'd been temporarily outflanked but I wasn't giving up. What I lacked in speed I could make up for in bloody-minded commitment. I was prepared, if necessary, to climb into the bin to get the cases, a step I was sure Chloe would be unwilling to take. As I prepared to clamber up the fish trader came past again, this time with his tray filled with offal from the fish he'd just gutted. Blood dripped off the tray and flies buzzed around it, the smell from it like a punch on the nose. The fish man completely ignored us, behaving as though we were invisible; as though two girls tussling over a ragbag of dirty clothes at five a.m. was normal. He pushed past us and tipped the lot into the bin, then walked back to the market hall shaking his head. I stood on my tiptoes to see inside the high-sided bin. Chloe poked her head over too. The fish skeletons and blood, the foul-smelling eyeballs and innards had spread in a slimy mess over Lisa and Lauren's clothes.

Chapter 31

We walked back to the flat without a word between us. As soon as we got in Chloe called her mum. She'd been trying to reach her for a few days to make arrangements for us to go down to Madrid.

'Aw, well, when are you coming?' I heard Chloe moan.

I went straight into the bathroom, locked the door and ran the bath. I'd only just got in and begun to sink sleepily under the water when Juegita came scratching at the door. Oh shit, I thought, the dogs hadn't been fed or watered. Chloe wasn't likely to do it. She wouldn't even think of it; no matter how much Juegita pestered her she'd chat on the phone, then she'd go to bed and cry herself to sleep. That was why I'd locked myself in the bathroom. I had no sympathy to offer Chloe tonight, or rather this morning. But I had to feed the dogs.

I got out the bath and unlocked the terrace door to let them out. The puppies gambolled around me, not least because both their water bowls, the one in the kitchen and the one on the terrace, were completely empty. It was going to be another scorching day. I took the bowl to the kitchen and filled it before sorting out their food. They were all on the solid food now, although they still chased poor old Juegita for milk. She needed water more than any of the pups, but this morning she wasn't demanding a drink. She seemed quiet and a bit depressed, probably dehydrated.

They all dived in at it as soon as I put the bowl down. Except Juegita, who kept whining and wandering off across the terrace and coming back again.

'Are you OK, Gita darling? What's wrong?'

Though the pups were supping it up like there was no tomorrow, Juegita didn't touch the water.

Not all the girls were here. I couldn't see Fanny. I called her and had a rummage in the yurt, but she wasn't there. She was probably inside the flat snoozing in her favourite place, under the bed, the coolest place when the AC was on. She had been the first, the most daring and determined to work out how to get into the flat.

Something was definitely wrong with Juegita. She walked off again and this time looked back as though she wanted me to come with her. I followed as she skulked across the terrace. Before we even got there, before I saw, I knew. I could hear Chloe giggling at something her mother had said. Gita stood with her shoulders hunched forward and her head hung low.

'I'm so sorry, Gita,' I said, putting my arms around her neck, crying for us poor things.

Fanny was in the paddling pool, her soft puppy-dog fur wafting in the water, her sweet little paws splayed and relaxed, her head immersed in the nine-inch puddle and her cute little bum and tail sticking up. Poor drowned little Fanny.

I cried. Not just for Fanny. I cried for Juegita's terrible loss, and for Chloe who clung so desperately to her mother, and for those other sad puppies, Lisa and

Lauren, we had treated so shamefully. And for myself. I cried hardest when I thought of poor me.

I lifted Fanny out the water and laid her beside Juegita. She was such a tiny wee thing. Yesterday I'd yelled at her for sniffing my sandwich. If I hadn't caught her when I did she would have dragged it off to some corner, fought off the rest of them, and eaten it all by herself. Now she lay curled and still on the ground, a bedraggled brown lump, like nothing more than a squeezed-out tea bag.

We had caused this, or I had. As I'd gradually become responsible for their feeding, Chloe took less and less notice of the pups. She hardly even gave Juegita the time of day any more. I was the one who'd shut the terrace door. Last night I was so busy primping myself for Lisa and Lauren's benefit, I'd left Fanny on the terrace all night and half the morning without water. I'd never considered the paddling pool to be a hazard. The pups were far too small to scale its smooth rigid sides. She must have been dying of thirst. How she'd managed to get in was a complete mystery. And having got in, there was no way she could have got out. I'd heard that dogs were natural swimmers. How long had she paddled round and round? If we'd come back at a reasonable hour, three a.m. like we usually did, Fanny would probably still be alive.

It was me. I was cursed. Death followed me, and no one, not even an innocent little puppy, was safe.

The other pups came and nosed around but Juegita nipped at them, trying to corral them, to keep them away from Fanny's body.

'Come on, girls,' I called with my enthusiastic voice, still wiping away tears, 'come and get your breakfast!'

I went into the flat to fill the food bowl, the only thing I could do to help. Thankfully they all followed, all except Juegita who stood guard over Fanny's body. Once I'd fed the pups I closed the terrace door and came back with a polythene bag.

We wanted to bury her in Ciutadella Park under a tree near the lake, but we couldn't leave the flat yet. Lisa and Lauren might still be lurking somewhere in the city. Wrapped inside four poly bags and a heavy blanket, Fanny's body lay at the furthest edge of the terrace. I wanted to keep her in the fridge but Chloe wouldn't let me.

'Eeuuw,' she shuddered.

Chloe shed no tears, all cried out after speaking with her mum, but she seemed depressed by the news. She even stopped working on the chimney for a while.

Juegita was off her food. She rarely spent time in the same room as me and when she did, she looked at me with sad reproachful eyes.

I felt awful. Too many late nights and drugs, too much alcohol. I had dark shadows under my eyes and my skin was a sickly yellow colour. I only wanted to sleep or watch films; I didn't have the energy for anything else.

Chloe dug out a DVD of *Trainspotting* and put it on, trying to cheer me up. I watched it three times and cried buckets every time.

Chloe shook her head. 'They're just a bunch of loser junkies.'

But it wasn't the sad Edinburgh drug addicts I pined for, it was the Scottish accents, the Scottish scenery, the Scottish food they were eating, the Scottish drinks they were drinking, the Scottish jokes they were making. She didn't understand. She couldn't even understand what they were saying until she switched the Spanish subtitles

215

on. We slobbed around on the couch watching movies for three days. It wasn't relaxing. Too paranoid to touch the maria, we didn't even smoke. For those three days we were too nervous to leave the flat. And then Charlie phoned.

'What the fuck d'you think you're playing at?' he bawled at me.

It was a relief. The fact that my brother was shouting meant that Lisa and Lauren had made it back to Cumbernauld. It was nice to hear his voice; it reminded me of Mum and our house and everything I was missing. I cried silently while my big brother harangued me. I signalled a thumbs up to Chloe everything was now OK, but Charlie was so loud she could hear him anyway.

I feigned innocence and disbelief. The official line was that we'd gone to get beer and when we'd returned Lisa and Lauren had disappeared. But Charlie knew better.

'They were picked up by the police, found wandering the streets bollock naked.'

'*Bollock* naked?'

'You know what I mean. They were left without a stitch. They said the guys you set them up with stole their stuff. They suffered traumatic stress and they're seeing a counsellor. They're blaming you. It's all over the *Cumbernauld News*.'

'Really?'

I'd had my name in the paper before, when I was thirteen, but this time was different. This time I wasn't the injured party.

'The British consulate bailed them out. They got them clothes and shit and repatriated them but they had to agree to pay back two grand.'

'Wow!'

'Each. They're just daft wee lassies, Alison. Why did you do that to them?'

'Charlie, I didn't do anything. We took them out in town, we left them to get a beer and when we—'

'Ewan says you're taking drugs.'

I exploded. 'What the hell has Ewan got to do with anything?'

'I phoned him five minutes ago to find out what he knows. He says that weirdo American girl you're staying with is getting you into drugs. I told him the Lisa and Lauren story. He's worried.'

Chloe heard every word Charlie said, and made a face when she heard the bit about the weirdo American girl.

'You had no right to discuss this with him, you don't know—'

'Listen, I've got every right! You've got us worried sick. Mum's upset at the things they've said about you in the paper.'

'Tell Mum it's not true. We lost them, that's all that happened. Make sure and tell her that, Charlie, please.'

'Tell her yourself,' he shouted. 'And come back home before you get yourself into any more trouble. Alison, you're recovering from a major illness. Taking drugs is the worst thing you can do, your vital organs'll pack up and then where will you be, eh? Now listen to me, I've looked up the Internet. There's a Globespan flight tomorrow afternoon, three hundred euros. Just get yourself on it. Mum's right, you should be here, with your family, before something worse happens.'

Chloe squeezed my hand and in reply I squeezed back. It was strange to find our roles reversed. Normally she was the one fighting or pleading with her family, I was usually the one comforting and supporting her.

'Alison, I mean it, you're to get a flight home tomorrow, d'you understand me?'

Chapter 32

No sooner had I put the phone down than it rang again.

'Alison? I've just spoken to Charlie.'

'Hello, Ewan, yeah, I know.' My voice was cold. 'He just called.'

'Is it true? Were your friends robbed and left bare naked?'

'Apparently. Don't know for sure. Wasn't there. Can't help you, mate. Sorry.'

'Alison, is something wrong? Why are you being like this?'

'Why did you tell Charlie that Chloe was getting me into drugs?'

'I didn't say that exactly. Charlie told me it'll be months, maybe a year before you're completely recovered from the glandular fever. I just said maybe—'

'Did you tell him you gave his wee sister her first joint? And wanted to fuck her? And to get her to suck your cock the next morning? Did you tell him that, Ewan?'

There was only his shocked inhalation in my ear.

'No, I didn't think so,' I said grimly.

Once I'd hung up on him Chloe smiled and asked if I wanted a cup of tea.

'You know Lisa and Lauren have to pay two thousand pounds each for being repatriated?' I asked.

'No,' said Chloe dispassionately, 'I did not know that.'

Dear Lisa and Lauren, I'm so sorry about the dreadful mix-up. I hear you had a bit of an adventure! Not to worry, all's well that ends well. I'm sure you'll look back on it and laugh. Hope you're both fine and see you soon, lots of love, Alison xxx

Chloe brought me my tea.

'So: now that we know they've left town, why don't we go out for lunch to celebrate?' she said. 'We can go anywhere, your call, my treat. Let's go somewhere delicious. Where d'you wanna go?'

'I can't be bothered going out.'

It wasn't like me not to go along with Chloe's wishes. She was as surprised as I was and put up a strong argument.

'But we gotta go out!' she yelled, almost stamping her feet. 'We've been holed up here for days. There's nothing left to eat and I'm starving.'

'You go. I'm not hungry.'

'We have to get out of this apartment, it's driving me crazy. I can't stand it any longer with that fucking dead dog on the terrace. I'm getting cabin fever, I have to get out of here.'

'Then go out, but I'm staying.'

To stop any further argument I went to the bedroom and lay on the bed. A few minutes later I heard the front door slam hard, but I was too tired and too fed up to worry about Chloe.

When I woke up later she still wasn't back. I lay dozing and fretting, trying to get things into proportion. It wasn't so bad. No one had died – unusual where I was involved – and Lisa and Lauren had been taught a lesson. But I still felt guilty.

Chloe hadn't got me into drugs. I wanted to get into them. I wanted to be the same, to do the same things as everyone else my age. I liked smoking maria, I liked the giggles we had when we'd had a joint and the nice relaxed way I felt and the great sleep I always got. I loved cocaine. Careful to use it only occasionally, I was far from being addicted, but I loved the way coke made me feel so confident. Ecstasy was probably my favourite. I loved the way Ecstasy made me fall in love with everybody, the way it made me just say what I felt. It did make me blurt out things occasionally, like telling Chloe I was a virgin, but that was fine, she was OK about it. Whenever I'd had Ecstasy I always liked getting stuff off my chest, not having to keep it in like it was a secret.

But it was true that the drugs weren't good for my health. I didn't tell Chloe but sometimes, the day after we'd had a few lines, I felt really ill. I'd seen the adverts on telly; I knew what it was doing to my system, especially my heart.

I got out of bed. I was going to do it, I knew I was. I'd known for a while; there was no point in worrying about it or putting it off any longer.

I put my hand into the back of the cupboard. The tin was still there. Including the last time I'd visited it, my debt was now running at 700 euros. Chloe had already been so generous, she'd never asked for a penny in rent and she'd given me all those fabulous clothes. Nine times out of ten she paid for everything. That tenth time however, when I paid, was a killer. Even occasionally funding this lifestyle meant I was now broke again. I couldn't keep this up. Sooner or later she'd find out.

Being a habitual drug user and a thief wasn't good for my nerves or my health.

The contents looked the same, thank God, untouched since I'd last been here. I teased out another three hundred euro notes from the bundle. Now I'd taken a nice round figure, a thousand.

As I was closing the tin I heard movement in the corridor outside the flat. Chloe had come back. There wasn't time to get the tin back in the cupboard. She was going to walk in on me. I shut my eyes tight. As I waited for the door to open I broke out in a sweat and my heart battered my ribs.

But nothing happened.

There were a few more sounds, coming from further down the stairwell; it must be Mrs Garcia washing the stairs.

I ran all the way to the travel agency. There was a queue. Four people ahead of me, only two desks staffed. There was the usual too-hot-to-hurry attitude in the customers and staff. I had a panic about whether or not I'd brought my passport. I rifled through every compartment of my bag, twice, until I found it. I *had* brought it, I knew I had. The queue took ages. After twenty minutes I thought about leaving and trying another place. One of the agents spoke English: I heard her make a leisurely paced reservation on the phone. If I went somewhere else they might not speak English. I didn't know all the words in Spanish. I'd have to stay here. Finally I got to the desk. There were still seats available. The ticket would be 315 euros.

'But it's three hundred, my brother looked it up an hour ago,' I wailed.

'This is Internet price,' she smilingly explained, 'in shop is three hundred and fifteen.'

I had a ten-euro note in my purse, four fifty-centimo pieces and another twenty-four cents in fives, tens and ones. The girl smiled again, apologetically this time. I tipped my bag out on the floor and knelt down sorting through it. I found a two-euro coin. It wasn't enough.

'Yes,' the girl said, 'is OK.'

I had to get back to the flat before Chloe came home. If I got back before her I could get back into bed and pretend to have slept all day.

As I left the travel agents I braced myself against the possibility of running into her outside. What the hell would I say? Luckily the coast was clear. The day was hot, in the thirties. Everyone in the street moved in slow motion, not wanting to sweat into their clothes. My clothes were already soaked; my face felt red and my hair clung to my neck. The underarms of my pink top had turned a deep maroon, embarrassing, but that was the least of my problems. Dodging the slowcoaches, I had to run all the way back to the flat.

As I ran I heaved for every breath, sucking at the damp Barcelona air, and made it back home in under ten minutes. I ran up the stairs a flight at a time, gasping on every landing, getting my breath back and rushing at the next flight. This place was falling apart. All the time I'd lived here no one had ever come to even look at the broken lift, never mind fix it. My head was throbbing with the pressure and the heat and the stress.

I might as well have strolled back. As I put my key in the lock I realized that Chloe was already there.

Chapter 33

I couldn't believe my rotten luck. I'd only been gone about an hour.

'Hey, Alison! Where've you been?' she called from the kitchen.

She sounded friendly enough, but that didn't mean anything.

'Sorry Chloe, I'm absolutely bursting!' I called.

I rushed into the bathroom and locked the door. I stood behind it, holding my breath and listening. I heard her in the kitchen: plates and glasses being moved around, the fridge door opening and closing. Based on these noises, it was difficult to read her mood.

I couldn't let her see me puffed out like this; she'd know right away something was wrong. I looked at myself in the mirror and nearly laughed. What a state. My cheeks were purple and my eyes were bulging. My hair was clamped to my head. I looked as if I was about to burst a blood vessel. I ran the cold tap and stuck my head under it. I had to get my breath back and cool down. I concentrated on taking deep breaths and slowing my heart. Then I had a truly horrible thought.

I couldn't remember if I'd put the biscuit tin back in the

cupboard. Covering your tracks was a pretty important part of theft; surely I would've made it a priority? But I had no memory of doing it. Perhaps in my rush to get the ticket I'd left it lying on the bedroom floor.

But maybe Chloe hadn't been in the bedroom yet. Maybe she'd gone straight to the kitchen to fix something to eat; that was why she sounded cheerful.

After five minutes I was still red-faced and breathing too fast, but I had to come out of the bathroom. She'd notice if I stayed in there too long. And anyway, if I could get to the bedroom before her, maybe I could hide the tin. I listened again at the door. She was still in the kitchen, still pottering.

I turned the key silently. Slowly and carefully I pulled the handle down and opened the door.

'Alison!' Chloe cried, rushing at me with her arms raised.

She meant to hit me. I flinched, trying to protect my face. But she threw her arms around me and kissed my hot cheek.

'Oh, I'm so glad you came back. I thought you'd gone to the airport.'

'The airport?'

'To fly to Scotland.'

'No, I . . .' I wasn't sure what I was going to say.

'Look, I picked up the mail. Aged P sent the prospectus for Berkeley. You were right; they do have an art faculty! There's arts foundation, fine arts degree and all kinds of postgraduate. Listen to this: "Recent fine-art graduates have exhibited throughout the United States and Europe."'

While she was reading I shuffled from one foot to the other.

'Yeah, I know, that's what I thought, but wait till you hear this: "Gozie Joe Adigwe enhanced her reputation with her award-winning exhibit at the Venice Biennale while Marcus Blair has won the esteemed New York New Talent award. These and others are scheduled to exhibit next year in the Guggenheim gallery in Bilbao." I mean: the Guggenheim!'

I wasn't sure what she was talking about, I was only half listening. Maybe I'd missed a bit, but I could tell from the way she said 'Guggenheim' what kind of reaction she expected.

'Wow!' I said.

'So, whattaya say?' Chloe dug me in the ribs playfully.

'Eh, I don't know.'

'Shut up!'

Chloe launched herself at me, tickling under my arms. At least she was in a good mood, if a bit manic.

'I *know* you wanna! You and my dad have been plotting the whole summer long. You're the one that suggested the art course. So OK, you win, we'll go. If you still want to. Do you? Tell me you still want to come to Berkeley.'

'Yeah, OK.'

'Then tell me. Say it.'

'I want to come to Berkeley.'

Chloe flew at me again. She grabbed both my hands and jumped up and down on the spot.

'It's gonna be so great! We'll get an apartment on campus and a car, we need a car in California, and we can go visit my mom on the weekends, and, and it's gonna be so great!'

We both jumped up and down. Chloe tugged on my arm. 'Come and see what I bought,' she said, excited, hauling me towards the living room.

'I'll come in a minute,' I said vaguely. The last thing I wanted was her following me into the bedroom. 'I just want to change my top.'

Chloe trotted off happily to the living room.

'So where did you go?' she called.

'I just went out for a walk.'

As soon as I'd said it I realized how false this sounded. I'd never once taken a walk without the dog. I waited for the inevitable question, scouring my mind for a likely explanation as to why I hadn't taken Juegita, but the question never came.

In the bedroom the tin was nowhere in sight. Either she'd found it or I had remembered to put it away. For the sake of my sanity I'd have to go with the latter. I quickly hid my plane ticket at the back of my underwear drawer, changed my top, looked in the mirror, and took a deep breath before I had to go back to the living room.

I could have a place at university in America: an apartment, a car, a career, a future in the Sunshine State.

But I'd just bought my ticket back to Scotland.

Things were changing faster than I was able to process and Chloe was about to hit me with another bombshell.

The living-room floor was strewn with stuff.

'I figure that now we can leave the flat without being stalked by naked people,' said Chloe, 'and before the dog actually explodes, we bury her. Tonight.'

Chapter 34

'OK,' I said.

I was glad to have something other than my Scotland/California dilemma to think about. A lavish funeral for a dead puppy, that was certainly new.

'I've been all over the city and I've found some great stuff to decorate the grave, see?'

Laid out on the floor were ten little votive candles in red glasses, a bag of beautiful seashells and a four-foot-tall potted rose bush.

'It doesn't have flowers yet, but when they come out they'll be sweet little white ones. Look,' she said, showing me the card attached, 'that's what they'll look like. I thought white was appropriate, respectful.'

'Yes,' I said, nodding my approval.

'And for a casket, I thought this.'

Chloe pointed to an ornately carved wooden box.

'It's a jewellery box, but if you take out the liners it's quite a good size. Think Fanny'll fit in there?'

'Och yeah, I think so, if she's not bloated up too much.'

'Eeuw, shut up, Alison.'

'Sorry. No, I think it's a lovely gesture.'

I started to cry. Chloe rushed to hug me.

'Oh, come on now, we'll give Fanny a nice send-off, huh?'

I sniffled and nodded. I couldn't tell her I wasn't crying about Fanny.

'You're such a kind person, Chloe. I don't deserve a friend as good as you.'

'Sure you do,' she laughed and rocked me in her arms while I sobbed. 'Everybody deserves a good friend.'

This made me cry even harder.

'I know what'll cheer you up. After I got the prospectus I got kinda excited and needed a sugar hit. I think I went a bit crazy but you're soooo gonna love the goodies I got.'

We went into the kitchen. I thought she was talking about drugs. I wasn't in the mood. But the goodies turned out to be sweet and savoury snacks, loads of them.

'How the hell did you get all this lot up the stairs?'

'I tipped the cab driver to help me bring it up.'

There was a huge round pastry coated in fine sugar, an *ensaymada*, in a box from a posh bakery, and a grease-spotted bag of pastries, nut-laden, fruit-filled, sugar-coated. There were *churros*: long sugar doughnuts, chocolate-filled or chocolate-coated. There were crisps, three giant bags.

'And look!' she said, pulling open the icebox in the fridge and producing a packet of frozen fish fingers.

I nearly started crying again. No one had ever tried so hard to please me.

'Here, knock yourself out,' she said, and pushed a *churro* into my mouth.

The sweet greasy smell was making me feel sick, but I had to eat something after all the trouble Chloe had gone to. The chance of a lifetime had just been offered to me but I only felt guilty and miserable. Feeding my misery, I nibbled my way through the chocolate *churro*, half a packet of crisps and an almond slice.

'Anyway,' I said, beginning to feel better, 'I thought you were anorexic.'

'Bulimic,' she corrected me, 'but I told you, I'm in recovery. I still pig out occasionally, I just don't sick up any more.'

'And that's progress?'

It was too hot to go on to the terrace and anyway, Fanny was out there. Inside the AC was turned all the way up. We moved the snacks through to the living room and put on one of the latest romcom DVDs Chloe had brought from the hire shop. With the snacks within easy reach we lay sprawled on the couch.

After all the stress of the day, watching a movie was just what I needed. Absently munching my way through bags of crisps felt like being back in Cumbernauld: safe, comforting. It felt like home.

We'd have to wait until it got dark before we could start the funeral, anyway.

'Do we have spades?'

'Yeah,' said Chloe, engrossed in the movie, pointing distractedly to another polythene bag. I reached over and pulled it towards me. Inside were two kiddies' bright yellow beach spades. I didn't say anything. We were at an important scene in the film.

Because it had been such a hot cloudless day it took a long time to get dark. We were halfway through the next movie when Chloe decided it was time to go.

'Oh, let's wait until this one's finished,' I moaned, 'or even better, we could set the alarm clock, get up early, say five or six, and do it in the morning.'

'Set the alarm clock?' said Chloe, incredulous.

'Yeah, I know it's a new concept, but we'd have the advantage of it being light.'

'And the disadvantage of witnesses. I don't think it's legal to bury dogs in public parks. Why do I feel you're not with me on this, Alison?'

'I am, but . . .'

'Well come on then, look, you can borrow this skirt and wear it with my black Versace top.'

'What are you wearing?'

'Black Versace dress.'

'So, let me get this straight: we're taking all this stuff to the park, the candles, the shells, the enormous rose bush—'

'And Fanny,' Chloe interjected.

'And Fanny. We're sneaking into the park in the dead of night and digging a hole with plastic spades, and, *and*,' I stopped to make sure she was following, 'we're doing it in Versace.'

'Versace widow's weeds. Pretty cool, huh?'

'Can we do it tomorrow? Please?'

'No, we do it now. I'm sick of that rotting corpse on my terrace. There's all kinds of gases and shit building up there, if we leave it any longer the thing's gonna explode.'

'Honestly, Chloe, I don't feel very well, I've eaten too much.'

'Barf then.'

'I can't, I've never made myself sick, I wouldn't know how.'

'It's easy. Put your toothbrush down your throat, I'll show you. I'll do it for you if you want.'

'Thanks,' I said sarcastically. 'You're a real pal.'

Chloe was serious. She went immediately to the bathroom and came back with my toothbrush.

'No, I can't. Even the idea of it makes me feel sick. Anyway, that way lies bulimia. I don't want to end up like you.'

'Hey!' said Chloe and rushed out the room again. She came back with the foil packet of pills. 'Eca Stacks! A few of these babies'll burn it off real quick.' She popped a handful out of the foil, necked them and swigged from her Coke can. 'Here you go.'

She passed me four tablets and I studied them in my hand. Taking these had to be better than sicking up. They hadn't done Lisa and Lauren any harm. While Chloe got changed I swallowed the pills one by one and watched the movie to the end. She came back in her tight black Versace number, chopping coke on her wee vanity mirror.

'This'll get you up and at 'em,' she said, passing me the line she'd made.

I didn't think so. The sore head I'd had all day was still a background thud in my brain. The rubbish I'd stuffed myself with was nice at the time, but the sugar rush had passed. Now I only felt the Versace skirt uncomfortably tight and my belly full of gas. As I held the plastic straw to my nose and inhaled, I felt the familiar tingle I loved so much. My lungs opened and my body felt light and strong. I could do anything.

If I went to California I'd have a wonderful time with Chloe. I'd see a doctor and get my glandular fever checked over. They had great doctors in America. I'd explain to Chloe that I had to stop taking drugs, just until I'd recovered. She'd understand.

If I decided to go back to Scotland, I'd pack my bag and

sneak out tomorrow morning while she was sleeping. I'd send back every centimo I owed her. She'd be cool about me taking it, she'd understand. We'd still be friends.

Whatever I did, it was going to be OK. Chloe wasn't going to find out about the money. My vital organs weren't going to pack up. Everything was going to be OK.

Chapter 35

We took a taxi to the park, we had to, there was too much stuff to carry.

'You're carrying the dog,' said Chloe.

'No, I'm not,' I countered, 'you're the guy who wants the fancy funeral.'

'Hey, you're the guy who killed it.'

I carried it. I sneaked the body off the terrace while Juegita was snoozing under the bed. She'd lost interest by now, anyway. She had the other pups to take care of, life went on, but she still wasn't speaking to me.

I had to sit with the body on my knee in the taxi. It wasn't heavy but it was totally unpleasant. It felt squidgy. Some sort of fluid had leaked out and got between the polythene layers.

The taxi dropped us at the side of the park near the railway station.

'Oh, that's a shame, the gates are locked,' I said, relieved.

Now we could go home and Chloe could call her mum and while she was on the phone I could secretly pack. But Chloe wasn't giving up that easily. She knew a place where we could climb the fence. We walked around the perimeter for fifteen minutes through the heat of the night air.

'This is it,' she whispered.

'But it's the same height here as it is round the front,' I complained, 'we've walked all that way for nothing.'

'Yeah, but no one can see us here,' she whispered. Chloe laid down her black bin bag full of stuff and clasped her fingers to make a basket. 'OK, I'll give you a leg-up.'

'Why do I have to go first?' I moaned.

'Jeez, Alison, what's with the attitude?' said Chloe, no longer whispering. 'You're smaller than me and I can give you a hand up from this side, that's all. Stop being so paranoid!'

'Sorry,' I said, laying down my bag of dead dog in preparation.

'Forget it,' said Chloe and, nimble as Spider-Man's girl-friend, scaled the fence. From the other side she issued the next instructions.

'OK, climb up and drop me down the stuff.'

It would have made more sense for me to go first, but it was too late. Now I had to clamber unassisted up the fence. I could only hold on with one hand, which was slippery with sweat. My other hand held her poly bag which I was to lift over the fence and drop down to her. The bag was heavy.

'We'll have to do it a piece at a time,' said Chloe.

Getting the rose bush, the wooden box and the dog's body over the fence was hard work and tricky.

'Are you ready?' I asked.

'Yes!' she hissed impatiently.

She caught the rose bush and the box but she wasn't ready, or she was too squeamish, for the last one.

'Eeuuw!' she squealed as she let Fanny splatter to the ground.

I prayed the bag hadn't burst.

Eventually I hauled myself over the fence and we trudged towards the lake. When we passed through a well-lit area Chloe insisted that we run and creep in and out of the shadows. It was too hot for running.

As we came past the sculpture of the hairy mammoth I spotted a hole in the fence and pointed it out to Chloe. All that fence climbing, bag throwing and corpse splitting was for nothing, we could've crawled through the fence right here.

'But this is more fun,' she giggled, 'like *Mission Impossible.'*

I smiled, too exhausted to laugh.

'The rose bush won't take the heat,' said Chloe. 'We'll have to plant it in the shade. Those big trees over there, nice spot, huh?'

I didn't answer.

'Lemme see, the rose needs to go down two and a half feet and the casket is eighteen inches deep. It goes underneath. We need space between them, something for the roots to cling to. Also a wild animal might dig it all up if it's not deep enough. That wouldn't be good. It'd kill the rose bush.'

The first hole we dug, we got down about three feet before we hit the tree roots. It wasn't easy. The plastic kiddy spades were probably excellent for shifting sand but they were hopeless for hacking through sunbaked earth.

I was sweating heavily into Chloe's Versace top. I hadn't known a hotter night in Barcelona. Wet patches weren't so obvious on black, at least until the sweat dried and appeared in white salt rings underneath the armholes.

'It's no use, Chloe, there's tree roots everywhere here. We'd be better off out on the grass.'

Chloe pulled her chin in. 'It has to be here, for the rose. It's a symbol, of Fanny's life, of her not having died in vain, her little body nurturing new life in the form of those tiny roses. It needs to be here.'

Her bottom lip was starting to wobble.

'OK, let's try in the middle, furthest away from any of the trees. There should be fewer roots there.'

'Thank you, Alison. I love that you understand what I'm trying to do.'

My heart was pounding and my head was bursting. It wasn't like Chloe wasn't working, she was doing her fair share of the digging, more if I was honest, but she didn't seem to find it as hard work as I did. My breathing was becoming laboured.

'Are you OK, Alison? You look like shit.'

Chloe sounded genuinely concerned. I took a break from digging to answer her.

'I think it's indigestion, I shouldn't have eaten all that crap.'

'Is indigestion meant to make you sweat like that? Come on, honey, sit down, take a break, you don't look so good.'

Sweat was dripping into my eyes. Despite the sweating I felt cold. I noticed that I'd begun to shiver. My heart was pounding in my ears and I felt a restrictive tightness across my chest. Everybody knew what chest tightness meant. As I lifted my head I was overwhelmed by a dizzy turn and felt myself fall forward, into the freshly dug grave.

He was driving when it happened. A heart attack, a small one, not fatal, but enough to make him crash. He felt it coming, gasped and clutched at his chest and then flopped unconscious over the steering wheel. He was a hazard, a menace on the road. For perhaps a minute the car continued on a straight path with him lolled over the wheel. It didn't lose speed but increased as it careened down the hill. Then the road curved. The car crashed through the barriers and down the embankment. The first thing it hit was an oak tree. The tree had been there a long time and didn't take kindly to being so roughly jostled. By way of protest it punched its branches through the windshield and knocked the little car sideways. This caused the car to flip over and plough upside down through a nursery of baby trees. It stopped, still upside down, thirty feet below, at the bottom of the gully. It didn't burst into flames. It lay there smoking and cooling in the freezing night air.

He was not dead. He'd been so angry when he got in the car that he hadn't put his seat belt on. He was thrown around the inside of the car and seriously injured, but he landed on something warm and soft. He lay unconscious for twenty minutes, though it seemed much longer, but he was alive. It

238

was extremely cold and another fifteen minutes before the fire brigade would reach this remote spot. The cold woke him. He tried to move and moaned in pain when he found he could not. He cried thick tears. He cried and prayed. He asked forgiveness and that his secret would be kept. A dying wish. With a clearer understanding of his situation he became aware that, as well as his other problems, he had something in his eye. It was the shock of this that made his heart stop for the third and final time.

Chapter 36

I was scared, pissed off and depressed all at the same time. I was about to die. This was so unfair. I hadn't wanted to go to hospital, I'd had enough of hospitals for one lifetime. I knew exactly how deathly dull they were.

I told Chloe I wanted to sit under the tree and close my eyes for a while. I thought that if I could just keep still, the sweats and chest tightness would pass. Then I'd get up, shake her warmly by the hand and catch my flight back to Scotland.

'Just keep breathing,' said Chloe.

What frightened me was her reaction. That time I lay on the terrace gasping for my last breath she hardly blinked. Now she couldn't keep her eyes off me, watching me breathe in, watching me breathe out. She spoke slowly and carefully as if I was an idiot, as if having a heart attack had made me mentally deficient. Educationally subnormal.

The taxi dropped us at the wrong door and, despite Chloe throwing a tantrum, the staff made us walk out and round the side of the building to the Accident and Emergency department. In Hospital del Mar a heart attack, even in someone my age, impressed nobody. We had to stand in a queue at a wee glass window. The boy in front of us had blood running down his neck and was nursing what looked to be a broken arm. He was a biker, obvious by his leather jacket and boots, and waited his turn in silence, probably in shock.

When we got to the window Chloe blurted it all out in a rush of Spanish and the nurse made her say it again, bit by bit. I understood very little but it was better I stayed out of it. That way I wouldn't say the wrong thing and drop us in it when they asked awkward questions about drugs. The nurse directed us to a cubicle with a trolley bed in it. I was grateful to get out of the queue and lie down. I was still sweating a lot but I was grateful for the blanket Chloe pulled over me. Once I lay down the dizziness came back and I passed out a few times, for seconds at a time.

We were in the cubicle a while. Nobody came. I knew this would happen, hospital was always like this.

'Chloe?'

'Shhh, Alison, don't try to speak. I'm right here.'

'I know you are, I haven't gone blind.'

'Everything's going to be OK.'

'Chloe, can you do me a favour please?'

'Of course.'

'Can you phone Ewan?'

Chloe looked incredulous. 'Ewan?'

'Here, his number's on my phone.'

I held out my phone to her with my hand shaking.

'I can't, honey,' she said sadly, 'not in a hospital, it interferes with the equipment. I'd have to go outside.'

She said this as if it was a reason not to.

'Then would you go out and call him for me?'

'I don't want to leave you.'

'Chloe, please. I'm fine here.'

She wasn't keen to go, obviously scared she'd miss something. I didn't want to die alone while she was outside making the call, but at the same time I didn't want to die without someone from home. I wanted my mum; I wanted Charlie and the twins but they were miles away. Ewan was here. He was from Cumbernauld, a family friend, a witness. He would make the arrangements.

Chloe gave me a long sulky look. She swiped the phone from my hand and flounced out. I concentrated on keeping breathing.

I don't know how long she was gone. Time seemed to be slowing down and speeding up and it was difficult to keep track. I lay quietly in my cubicle, screened from view and from the action, but I heard everything. I didn't understand the words, I didn't have to. I understood the embarrassed mumblings, frightened shouts, the soft or noisy grief, the bored workaday voices of the staff. People were dying here.

Nurses walked or ran past my cubicle, making the curtain gently billow. I was still here. If I died I wouldn't die alone. I was surrounded. We'd abandoned poor Fanny and all the gubbins. It would've been interesting to see what the park keepers made of it in the morning: the grave, the box and the rose bush, the candles and the putrefying puppy. They'd probably think it was some kind of devil-worshipping cult. But, unless my departing spirit happened to fly over it, I'd never know. If I died now I'd never know anything again. Never work for Señor Valero, never learn Spanish, never have the quintessential Barcelona experience, or any experiences.

I thought of Isabelle and wondered where she was now, if she was still attending spiritualist meetings and receiving messages from her husband. I wondered if she ever received messages from my dad. Every time I came close to death I thought about meeting my dad on the other side and how unbearable it was going to be. He was the only person I knew there.

A nurse came to me at last. She spoke and when I didn't answer she gave an exaggerated comedy shrug and said 'Inglesa!' as if to say, what can you do? She carried on speaking to me in Catalan while she took my blood pressure. Then she stuck wee round plastic things on my chest and took a printout from the machine they were attached to. I tried not to look at her, concentrating on my heart rate, but she didn't even notice, keeping up her professional smiling and talking. This insincere chatter distressed me. I was dying, I had more important things to worry about, but the fact that I couldn't understand her made me feel scared, out of control. I had to focus on keeping my heart ticking.

The nurse took the things off my chest. As she was packing up the machine Chloe came in.

'Thanks for coming back, Chloe, I was scared.'

Chloe ignored me and began interrogating the nurse. The nurse appeared vague, out of her depth, and whatever replies she gave seemed only to annoy Chloe. The nurse moved quicker now, folding away equipment, dismissing Chloe's next round of questions with quick negative replies. She had stopped chatting and smiling.

'You have insurance, right?' Chloe asked me, her face inches from mine.

'I think so,' I replied lamely.

'You *think* so?'

'Well I'm an EU citizen, I should be covered.'

Chloe turned her attention back to the nurse and she

243

was now shouting and rummaging in her bag until she produced her Visa card, the platinum one. There was another quick exchange and the nurse was gone.

'Chloe, what's going on? The nurse took a printout from that machine, what did she tell you?'

'They need to do more tests, decide if they need to operate.'

'Operate?'

'Don't worry, I promise I won't leave you again.'

'Did you speak to Ewan?'

As if apologetic, Chloe shook her head and bit her lip.

'Chloe, you have to, I need to—'

'I did call him. He's out of town.'

Now I remembered, he said he was going on tour with his Castellers group.

'And . . .' she began and then tailed off.

'Yeah, and?' I insisted.

'And he said he doesn't want to see you. He said it's over, no point, it's not going anywhere, blah blah. The guy's a waste of time.'

'Did you tell him I'm in hospital and . . .'

Chloe nodded ruefully.

The nurse came back with a handsome young doctor. He gave me a quick smile and then turned his attention to Chloe. After a few minutes of discussion and another flash of the credit card, the doctor gave the nurse a nod. She grasped my trolley and started to haul me away.

I would have screamed but I didn't want to put a strain on my heart.

'What are they doing?' I whispered to Chloe as the nurse wheeled me past.

'Don't worry, honey, they're gonna do their best, and I'll be right here. Everything's gonna be OK.'

'Chloe, Chloe!'

I wanted to come clean, to tell her everything and ask her forgiveness, but there wasn't time. For such an unwieldy trolley the nurse had quickly established a fair pace and Chloe was forced to jog alongside.

'Thanks for everything you've done for me. You've been the best friend I've ever had.'

Tears were streaming down my face. Chloe was crying too. As the foot of the trolley battered through the swing doors and she was forced to leave me she mouthed, 'I love you, Alison.'

Chapter 37

I spent the next six hours being shoved in and out of machines. I felt like a well-fired roll. It was only when that was over that I found out, when Chloe told me, that I would be allowed to go home.

'So they're not going to operate?'

Despite Chloe's platinum credit card, they didn't send us home in an ambulance. Chloe had to go outside and hail a cab. A nurse walked me to the front door, and not in a good way. It was as if she were seeing an unwelcome guest off the premises.

So as not to put a strain on my heart, we came up the stairs really slowly, one at a time, like pensioners. I could have probably moved faster, but I was scared. Chloe was gently encouraging: 'Easy does it, honey. Thattagirl. There you go.'

I was crying before we reached the flat.

As soon as we got in Chloe bundled me into bed and brought me a glass of water and two tablets.

'What are they?'

'Hell, I don't know. Your prescription, from the hospital. The very best that medical science has to offer.'

'Were they expensive? How much did all that treatment cost, Chloe?'

'You don't have to worry about that. Your job is to concentrate on getting well. Now be a good girl, and take 'em.'

I was a good girl and swallowed the pills. Then I grabbed her hand.

'Chloe, why are you so kind to me?' I blubbered.

'Shut up!' said Chloe softly. 'Listen to me, you're gonna get well, OK? Everything's gonna be fine.'

I nodded vigorously, the only thing I could manage vigorously.

'I'm not going to die.'

'No, honey, you're not gonna die.'

'No, it wasn't a question.'

'That's my girl,' she said and hugged me. 'Listen, you gotta get well for starting college. We're gonna be busy. We'll have to find an apartment and pick out a car. Aged P says no soft tops but screw him.'

'I can't drive.'

'You can learn. You'll take lessons. It's not like here, everybody drives in California.'

It was a nice idea but I'd never really believed we'd go to college. Why would Chloe's dad agree to pay college fees for a complete stranger? And even if he did, Chloe was fickle. If she was excited about this art course, she'd change her mind again soon. I didn't trust her not to. There was something else that made me suspicious. It was too much of a coincidence that Chloe suddenly wanted us to go to college the day my brother ordered me home. She knew how bad I felt about everything that had happened. She knew how homesick I was. Maybe she'd used the promise of college to make me stay.

'Chloe, are you serious about college?'

'Yep.'

'Are you absolutely sure you won't change your mind?'

'Nope.'

'And we're both going?' I asked.

My flight was this afternoon. If I was going to catch it, I'd have to get packed now. I'd have to tell her.

'D'you swear on your mum's life?'

'Yes. I swear on my mom's life. Jeez, Alison, what do you want from me?'

Chloe stormed out of the bedroom. She came back a second later with the UC Berkeley prospectus.

'You already have a degree, right? Well if my dad can get me in – with my school record – he can sure as hell get you in. Quit worrying. This is only the Arts Practice faculty programme but it'll give you an idea. Check out the studios. Cool, huh?'

I nodded.

'We are going to Berkeley, me and you, and we are gonna have the time of our lives. My mom has a little beach house she never uses. We can go there on weekends, we can barbecue and swim and read our college books and sit and listen to the ocean. It's gonna happen. I'm serious, OK?'

'OK,' I whispered. I tried to maintain my dignity, I couldn't stop the tears but at least I kept them silent. Chloe wiped them away and kissed my wet cheek.

'And I'm gonna take the best care of you. You'll probably feel sleepy right about now so I'm gonna go out and get food.'

'Chloe, don't leave me. I'm really not hungry and anyway, we've got food. We've still got loads of cake and crisps from last night.'

'I mean real food. That stuff's going in the garbage. No more crap. Chicken soup, that's what you need.'

There was no talking her out of it. And she was right, I did feel tired. It was great to be off the hospital gurneys and back in our own bed. I was nodding off when I heard her leave the flat. Things weren't so bad, I was still alive.

When I woke up Chloe was back, I could hear the television in the living room. I lay dozing, woozy, unable to properly wake up, until she came in to check on me.

'Oh, you're awake. Want your soup now?'

I didn't, but I didn't want to disappoint her. The soup was home-made, from scratch. 'Free-range chicken,' she assured me. It tasted like it too.

Chloe had brought her bowl and perched on the edge of the bed, both of us slurping noisily.

'I didn't know you were such a good cook,' I said.

'There's plenty of things you don't know about me.'

'Oh God, this is so good. My mum sometimes makes soup like this.'

'Are you still missing your mom?'

'Not really,' I lied. 'And I'm not going to tell them about the hospital. No chance. Mum and the boys would be all, "We warned you. We told you to come home." Thank God I didn't die, Charlie would have been so smug.'

'Shut up!' Chloe laughed.

'No, I'll phone in a few weeks, once the Lisa and Lauren dust has settled, once I'm working. If I leave it till then they'll be grateful to hear from me and they won't give me such a hard time.'

After the soup Chloe let Juegita and the pups visit me for a while. They romped around the bed and when they walked over me I noticed how heavy they were getting, how much steadier on their feet. We'd only been gone overnight but the pups seemed so much more grown-up. Juegita seemed pleased to see me too, she had forgiven me and I hugged her neck in gratitude.

'Did you fill their bowls?' I asked Chloe.

'Duh! Of course.'

'Sorry, just checking.'

'Yeah well, I think I can be trusted to look after my own dogs. I managed pretty well before you got here, remember?'

I hung my head.

'No, hey, my bad. I didn't mean that. That was a cheap shot. I'm just tired, with all the running around and all.'

Chloe had been up all night and all day too. While I was being wheeled around the hospital from one machine to another she was by my side. I'd been asleep all day while she'd bought food, made soup and took care of the pups. No wonder she was exhausted.

'Chloe, you need to get some sleep. Come on, lie down. Oh, and have you got my phone?'

'I thought you weren't going to call your mom.'

'I'm going to phone Ewan, ask him not to tell Charlie about me being in hospital.'

'Yeah well, whatever,' Chloe said reluctantly. 'I'll get it.'

She rummaged through all her jeans pockets, all her clothes in the wardrobe and then the bedroom drawers. I kept up a hopeful expression but my heart sank when she started crying.

'It's like we're cursed. Nothing ever goes right. Everything we do turns to shit.'

'It's OK.'

'No, it's not OK, I can't find it anywhere. The last place

I remember having it was at the hospital. I've lost it, or it was stolen, I don't know, I feel like a dumbass idiot.'

'You're not a dumbass idiot. Come here.'

It was my turn to wipe her tears away.

'For God's sake, it's nothing, it's only a phone.'

'Yeah but it's *your* phone, and *I* lost it. I'm one of the few people who've never been robbed in this city. I've been here five months, that's a record. Now I feel stupid. I hate that!'

'You're not stupid. Shut up. You were busy, it happens.'

'Yeah, but I should've—'

'You've been busy looking after a friend in hospital, a very grateful friend.'

She stopped crying.

'Let's just forget about it, will we?'

Chloe sniffed. I changed the subject and asked her all the questions I'd wanted to ask earlier.

'What did they say was wrong with me? Was it a heart attack?'

She nodded solemnly.

'What else did they say?'

She shrugged.

'Not much. The tests were inconclusive. They might have to do them again. They're gonna send a letter. For now it's just medication and bed rest.'

'Och jeezo, not bed rest! I had enough of that with glandular fever.'

I'd had a good sleep, despite my heart-attack ordeal I felt quite refreshed. My fear of dying had become a bit more rational. I wanted to get up, the dogs would need feeding again soon and the kitchen would be a mess. Left like this, roaches would be climbing the walls within days.

'It better not be for long. I'm going to be starting work with Señor Valero soon. Did they say how long I had to stay in bed?'

'Nope,' said Chloe, 'they didn't. They just said they'll send a letter. So until then I'm afraid you're legally required to lie back and relax.'

Chapter 38

I was in bed waiting for the letter from the hospital. Chloe would only allow me to get up to go to the toilet. Every night, when it was cool, usually after she'd tried again to reach her mother on the phone, she'd walk me round the terrace.

'The chimney's coming along,' I enthused. She had tiled it nearly to the top. 'It must be hard working up those ladders all day.'

She took my arm and made me walk slowly, as if I were an invalid. It was ridiculous. I felt fine. I read and slept a lot; the medication was making me sleepy. Apart from that I felt as strong and frisky as a racehorse. But I was fed up.

Chloe was brilliant, or at least she was to begin with. The first few days she went out to the market and brought back fresh meat and vegetables, and made soup and nourishing stews. The weather was too hot for stews, but the bedroom was air-conditioned and I was so bored that I welcomed the diversion. When my appetite did finally flag she even made me a crisps and fish-finger sandwich.

She was so good to me. She brushed my hair every morning, 100 strokes, and then again later in the day.

'Your hair is so great, Alison, it's an amazing colour.'

'It's the same colour as a Highland cow,' I told her. 'Moo.'

'I feel like I wanna do something with it, put big fancy ribbons in it or something.'

'When I was wee, Isabelle used to put my hair up with ribbons, in bunches or a ponytail,' I said.

'I could buy ribbons in Corte Inglés, they have amazing colours, purple and lilac, or maybe yellow.'

'Yeah, all the Highland cows are wearing ribbons this season, it's a good look.'

'Shut up! You don't look like a cow.'

'No?'

'No. Anyway, cows are kinda cute. You're more like a buffalo.'

'Watch it, pal. Just brush the hair,' I said, closing my eyes.

Chloe looked after the dogs too. Twice she took Juegita out for a walk and a poo in the park. After my pill I'd fall asleep for a few hours and when I woke Chloe would have cleaned the flat and cooked something wonderful. She'd bring the food to the bedroom and after we ate she'd read to me.

I told her she didn't have to, I was quite capable of reading for myself, but she wanted to so I let her get on with it. It was very comforting being read to, like being a kid again, like having Isabelle read *Harry Potter* to me, the two differences being that Chloe had a Californian accent and Isabelle had a Cumbernauld one; Harry Potter was a boy wizard and Belle de Jour was a prostitute. While Chloe read out kinky sex I dropped off to sleep.

It didn't last. She quickly got bored. She stopped taking

Juegita out, saying she was at a critical stage with the chimney. The pups were annoying her too, getting under her feet. Once she locked them out on the terrace and hid the key. In this baking hot weather the dogs hated the terrace. At first they pawed at the door and cried to get back in. After a while they must have given up and slunk off to find whatever shade they could, lying with their tongues hanging out, panting heavily. I had to plead with her before she finally relented.

And still no letter came from the hospital.

I was frustrated, so was Chloe, but for a different reason. She tried at all times of the day to phone her mum, but her mum was never at home. In desperation she even phoned her dad to see if he knew where her mum was. He didn't, and he only wanted to argue with her for maxing out her credit card.

'It was a fucking emergency, Dad!' she screamed.

It was my fault, she'd used her card to pay for my treatment, all the tests, and the medication from the hospital, but she never once reproached me with it.

'Yeah,' she snarled at her dad, her voice dripping with sarcasm, 'that's why they're called *credit* cards!'

On the next call she skilfully segued from sarcasm into rage. 'Of course I understand that it's an appreciable amount of money, Dad, and I really hope *you* can understand that I DON'T GIVE A SHIT!'

Next time it was a soft voice, almost kindly. 'I totally do not give a shit.'

After that she refused to speak to him at all. When he called I had to answer. All communication now came through me. At first it was awkward, but it gave me a certain amount of power. Philip was scrupulously polite to me at all times. Seeing as Chloe had spent the money on my healthcare, he never brought the subject up again.

Chloe was getting frazzled, not so much with the contact from her dad but with the complete lack of contact from her mum.

I didn't say anything when she stopped making the stews. I was getting fed up with stew anyway. We went back to our more usual diet of cartons of gazpacho and takeout kebabs. The flat began to suffer. I noticed on my frequent trips to the bathroom, the highlight of my day, that the sink had acquired a greasy tidemark. I locked the door and got busy with the bottle of Cif I kept in the cupboard. If she noticed she never mentioned it, and I kept up my daily cleaning of the bathroom. It gave me something to do. But if the bathroom was this dirty, what state was the kitchen in? I pictured the roaches crawling across the work surfaces.

She stopped hanging out in the bedroom with me so much. She worked on her chimney or tried to get through to her mum. I spent my time reading. I'd read every book in the flat and had started rereading the ones I'd enjoyed. After three days I asked Chloe if the letter from the hospital had arrived yet.

'No, not yet. It's probably stuck in a mail room or admin centre or something, it'll probably take a while.'

After five days I asked again, but her reply was a curt 'no' this time. I was hurt. It wasn't as though I had pestered her, I'd only asked twice.

I hadn't been able to sleep. I couldn't contain my frustration any longer and early on the morning of the sixth day I nudged Chloe awake and asked her if she thought the letter had got lost.

'What am I,' she sneered, still half asleep, 'Postmaster General? How the hell do I know?'

I chose to ignore her tone.

'Well, I think it has. In fact, I'm sure it has.'

'Well good for you.'

'I can't lie here for ever. I'm going to get dressed and go to the hospital and find out what's going on.'

'Whoa, tiger! You are gonna do no such thing.'

I slid my legs to the side and began to haul myself out of bed.

'Yes I am.'

'Alison, wait up. Think about it, you don't speak Catalan or even Spanish, and besides, you'll never make it down there.'

'I'll take a taxi.'

'OK, you want to have another attack? Is that what you want? Cos that's what'll happen.'

'I'll take my chances.'

I made to stand up.

'Come on, Alison,' Chloe said in a much sweeter voice. 'OK, if it means so much to you I'll go down there.'

Halfway up I felt dizzy and had to sit back down again.

'But how will you get it?' I asked.

'You remember Dr Fernandes, the Portuguese guy? No? He's your doctor. I'll find him and he can tell me what's going on.'

'But they said they'd send a letter. It has to be a letter.'

'OK, I'll get him to give me the letter, or write a new one, will that make you happy? It'll probably cost another couple of hundred bucks but it'll be worth it to get you off my back.'

I lay back in the bed. Another couple of hundred

bucks. Chloe had already spent so much. But I needed the letter. I didn't actually know for sure what was wrong with me. I didn't know what the pills I was taking were or what they were for – as far as I could see they just made me sleepy. Of course I wouldn't be able to read the letter, it would be in Catalan or Spanish, or both, but Chloe could translate and I could always ask Ewan for a second opinion.

'If you can speak to Dr Fernandes I'll pay for it.'

I was going to have to visit the biscuit tin again.

'OK, OK, I'll go. Just let me get dressed.'

'Thanks, Chloe, you don't know what this means to me. You're the best pal I've ever had.'

'Yeah yeah,' she said, 'whatever.'

Chloe, as usual, didn't bother with breakfast. She brushed on two thick layers of mascara and then started pulling things out of the drawers, looking for something to wear. She tried on two blue tops before settling on a green one, all the while going on about how hot Dr Fernandes was: how she was glad she had an excuse to go down there and see him again. I didn't say anything, I wasn't required to, but actually I was struck dumb by the sight of one of the pups attempting to take a dump, right in front of us, in Chloe's designer shoe.

Conejo had her bum in the air and was straining. So far Chloe hadn't noticed. I pulled myself up again. I had to get to the shoe before the dog dropped the turd or Chloe saw what was happening. But it was too late. As I was still heaving myself out of bed Chloe let out a hideous shriek. She had blindly plunged her foot inside the shoe. The shit squidged over the sides and on to the floor.

Conejo, having no concept of having done anything wrong, didn't bolt under the bed. Chloe grabbed her by the neck and, with the shit still oozing from her shoe, marched out of the bedroom.

Suddenly I found the strength to move quickly.

'It was an accident,' I yelled as I followed her, 'she didn't mean it, she's only a pup.'

It was as if Chloe didn't even hear me. She stomped on through the living room and stopped for a moment to unlock the terrace door.

'I'll clean your shoe, it's not a problem, honestly,' I whined. 'Please, Chloe, don't leave her out there. Not all alone.'

I hated to think of another little wooden box.

But I had read the situation wrong. Chloe didn't intend to leave Conejo on the terrace. By the sporty style with which she dropped Conejo on to her waiting foot, I now realized she was about to drop-kick the puppy off the roof.

Chapter 39

'No!' I yelled and threw myself in front of Chloe. Conejo was propelled with tremendous force not off the terrace but against a solid surface: my head and shoulders.

The puppy yelped and hit the terrace floor with a sickening thud. I thought her back must be broken, but miraculously she quickly found her feet and ran away. My forehead, having taken most of the force, was stinging.

'For fuck's sake, Chloe! You shouldn't play around like that, you could've killed her!'

'Who says I was playing?' she screamed.

Chloe was pulling the dirty shoe off with her fingertips. When her foot emerged it was stained brown. There were little parcels of soft turd deposited between her toes.

'If I thought for one minute—'

'If you thought *what*?' She shook her head violently on the word 'what'. 'If you thought for one minute, it'd be a whole lot longer than you usually spend thinking,' she sneered.

Chloe was getting good at sneering. She'd had plenty of practice lately. It was becoming her default facial expression, but when she shot me one of her super-sneers I realized she was actually mirroring my expression.

'It's not you,' I said defensively, 'it's the dog poo, it's disgusting, it's grossing me out.'

'Oh!' she fired into my face. 'You too, huh?'

'You weren't really going to do it, were you?'

Chloe hopped across the terrace towards the maria where the hose was.

'Tell me you weren't going to boot a puppy off the roof!' I yelled. 'Tell me!'

Despite being on one leg, she turned on me, all attitude: eyes blazing, chin jutting, dog shit oozing between her toes.

'The dog's OK, no harm no foul. I'm the one whose foot is covered in it and whose five-hundred-dollar shoes are ruined!'

'No foul? You kicked her; you deliberately dropped her and kicked her, hard. I saw you. For God's sake, she's only a baby!'

Chloe put her head down and concentrated on washing the shit off. She held her foot over the drain and hosed water across it. We watched the shit break up and slide into the drain. Then she turned to rinsing out the shoe. On hearing the running water Conejo came out of hiding, looking for a drink. Chloe filled the dogs' bowl from the hose. The puppy stood beside Chloe waiting for the bowl to be filled, and then happily lapped the water. Chloe stroked Conejo, who didn't seem to mind.

'I know, I know,' whispered Chloe. 'Yeah, I know.'

She sniffed and wiped her cheek.

'What can I say? I was angry, I do crazy things sometimes, I can't help it. Cooped up too much in this apartment, it's not good. I'm a bad person.'

'You're a crazy bitch,' I said sadly.

'Yup, I know.'

Conejo turned away from the water and licked Chloe's hand. This made Chloe cry harder.

I felt exhausted. I stumbled back to bed and left them on the terrace.

Chloe came into the bedroom and shook me awake.

'Alison. I'm gonna go get your letter now.'

Eyes half shut, I squinted at her but didn't say anything.

'I'll get the letter, OK?'

'OK.'

I turned away and pulled the sheet over my head. I didn't want to see her.

I was glad when she left the flat. I needed a bath, I felt dirty, like I smelled bad. While I was running the bath there was a knock at the front door and my heart sank. It must be Chloe, she must have forgotten something, her keys most likely.

It was Señora Garcia from downstairs.

'*Eres* Donaldson?' she asked me.

She was holding an envelope. I was only wearing a T-shirt, which I pulled down over my legs as best I could. Señora Garcia smiled shyly. We were both embarrassed at my state of undress and our lack of communication. Gradually I understood that she had received this envelope, my envelope, in her mailbox.

'*Sí*, Donaldson!' I said enthusiastically, pointing to myself, '*muchas gracias, señora, muchas gracias.*'

When I closed the door the first thing I checked was the postmark. It had only been sent out yesterday.

Chloe had been right; it probably had been processed through a mail room. In the last few days I'd begun to harbour some uncharitable, perhaps even paranoid thoughts. I'd begun to think that Chloe was withholding my letter. Once or twice I'd come close to actually accusing her. I blushed at the memory. Thank God I hadn't.

The letter was headed EAC. Despite telling them nothing, the doctors were on to us. Those pills we took, that's what they were called. I went and found the pills to check but I was wrong, they were called ECA. As I read the letter closely EAC seemed to refer to *enfermedad de la arteria coronaria*. Coronary was heart, wasn't it? They said things in American films like *he had a coronary*, didn't they? There were four paragraphs that meant nothing to me but near the bottom of the page the last paragraph had my name in it, Señorita Donaldson, and other medical-looking terms, some I recognized, some I didn't. *Estrés psicológico* – that sounded psychological. *Isquemia silenciosa* – no idea what that meant. *Angina de pecho* – some kind of angina, obviously. Angina, was that serious?

The last and final medical term jumped off the page and slapped me so hard I gasped: *infarto de miocardio*.

I knew that one: myocardial infarction, it had to be, it was too close for it not to be. *Infarto de miocardio/* myocardial infarction was nothing less than a heart attack, I knew that for certain. I knew because that's what it said on my dad's death certificate.

So I really did have a heart attack. Until I actually saw it written down I'd never quite believed it. It was another thing, in my bored and paranoid bedridden state, I'd thought Chloe had invented. Nobody at the hospital told me I'd had a heart attack, I'd only Chloe's word for it. Thank God I'd managed to restrain myself from blurting out any of these crazy suspicions.

Now I felt guilty. Everything Chloe did was to make me happy. Even now she was running around trying to find Dr Fernandes and spending hundreds of bucks for my benefit. She'd given me her home, her money, her clothes, a shoulder to cry on. She was the only friend I had in this city. She had looked after me and never complained once. OK, the cooking and cleaning had fallen off a wee bit and the thing with the dog, well that showed the kind of stress she was under.

Lying in bed all day, somewhere between waking and sleeping, had done strange things to my mind. Earlier that morning I'd nearly asked Chloe if she'd lied about the heart attack. She'd have had every right to throw me out in the street there and then. No more Barcelona penthouse apartment for me. No Berkeley. I'd come seriously close to misjudging Chloe. I wouldn't make that mistake again.

Chapter 40

By the time Chloe got back I'd cleaned the kitchen and baked an apple pie to welcome her home. It felt good to be on my feet again. I'd wanted to cook a nice meal for her, but the only things left over from her healthy-eating shopping frenzy were some wrinkled apples. I didn't feel strong enough to go out shopping, the stairs were a bit daunting, so I improvised. The pie looked fantastic, really American, but Chloe didn't even see it. She was too busy screaming about the article in *Metro*.

'She was here!'

Chloe threw the newspaper at me. *Metro* was a free newspaper, the same as they had on the Cumbernauld buses, except this was in Spanish. It was open at the arts section and I scoured the page, looking for a clue as to what she was ranting about. The main feature seemed to be about the guy in the photo with the paintings behind him.

'I went to find Dr Fernandes but they told me he's on vacation and on the way back I saw this: that's him, Rafael Gomez, that's her boyfriend!'

Chloe viciously stabbed her finger at the man in the picture.

'Sorry, Chloe, I'm not getting it.'

'My mom's boyfriend, she came to Madrid with him for the opening of his new exhibition. She set it up.'

'Well, that's good, isn't it?'

'Read it. The show opened to the public on Friday night. Rafael Gomez flew back to LA on Saturday, it says so right there.'

'Sorry, I—'

'Well, has she called? Has she called me? Has she? She flew all the way to Europe, she was in the same country, a few hundred miles away, and did she call? Did she?'

'Maybe she's still in Spain; maybe she's coming to Barcelona to surprise you.'

'Oh yeah?'

Chloe pulled out her phone and pressed number one, the speed dial for her mum's home number.

'Let's test that theory then, huh?'

She put it on loudspeaker and we listened to the phone ring. She let it ring for ages, I counted thirty-two. Normally it activated the answering machine after ten rings, but for the last week her mum's phone had just been ringing out. We were up to forty-six.

'She's not there, Chloe.'

'Hello?' said Chloe's mother's sleepy jet-lagged voice.

'You fucking whore,' Chloe snarled.

'Chloe?'

'I know you were in Madrid, I read it in the news.'

'Oh honey, it was such a hectic schedule, I didn't have a minute. It was crazy . . .' She tailed off. Chloe's mum didn't sound like she was even convincing herself.

'I hate you,' said Chloe, still in her psycho voice.

'No you don't, darling, you're just upset. I'm so sorry you're disappointed.'

266

Chloe dropped the phone and flopped down on to the couch. She was snivelling and mushing her face so hard with the heel of her hand that she made black mascara circles around her eyes.

'Chloe?'

Chloe looked at the phone as if she didn't understand the noise coming out of it, as if she'd forgotten who this disembodied voice belonged to.

'Chloe, are you still there? Speak to me, you're scaring me now, honey.'

I picked the phone up. I looked to Chloe for instruction but she wouldn't look at me.

'Chloe doesn't want to speak to you at the moment.'

There was a little acid in my tone, I couldn't help it.

'Oh, OK. It's Alison, right?'

'Right.'

'Well thank you, Alison, I'll call her later, when she's feeling better.'

'Yeah, you be sure to do that,' I said stiffly, and cut her off.

I sat beside Chloe on the couch and rubbed her back. Comforting each other was all we seemed to do these days. I was keen to have her translate my letter but I had to let her cry it out. After a while she stopped crying.

'I've got something that'll cheer you up.'

She didn't respond. I went and got it anyway.

'Ta da!'

I presented the apple pie with a flourish and put it down on the coffee table in front of her. I went back to the kitchen for plates. When I came back she seemed to have perked up a bit. She was examining the pie.

'Nice work.'

'I made it as a thank-you for looking after me so well.'

'Aren't you supposed to be in bed?'

'Well, maybe you can tell me. The letter came today.'

'Huh?'

I showed her it.

'I don't know what all this stuff here is, hopefully you do, but I know what *infarto de miocardio* means.'

'Yeah?' Chloe took the letter from me and scanned through it.

'Yeah, myocardial infarction, it's how my dad died.'

Chloe finished the letter and put it down.

'So? What does it say? Do I have to continue with the bed rest?'

Chloe picked it up and read it again. I could see her mind was not on it, but I had to know.

'Yeah, no more bed rest. It doesn't say much, it's just for your records, it says you should give it to your regular doctor.'

'But no more bed rest?'

'Uh, no.'

Chloe didn't seem entirely sure. Her answer seemed too pat. I wondered if she was telling me what she thought I wanted to hear.

'You're sure? I'm supposed to start work soon. It might be dangerous if I—'

'I'm sure!' she yelled.

'And what about the medication?'

'I don't know. I'm not your doctor. It says you're to give the letter to your doctor. Stop bugging me, will you?'

'Excuse me, I was only asking.'

Neither of us spoke for a few minutes. Chloe broke the silence.

'Nice-looking pie,' she said.

It was the nearest I was going to get to an apology. There

was no point in keeping up the huff. I didn't have to stay in bed any more, which was something to celebrate. I was going to be able to start my new job after all, that could only be a good thing. When she was in a better mood I'd ask her to help me find a regular doctor here in Barcelona. I'd just have to wait till then. Everything, it seemed, even my health, had to depend on Chloe being in a good mood. I had to keep smiling.

'Cheers.'

I handed Chloe the knife to cut the pie.

'You can do the honours.'

'Every kid loves apple pie, momma's apple pie. My mom never baked a pie,' Chloe moaned, 'she wouldn't know how.'

I thought it was the beginning of another self-pitying rant against her mum, but she went quiet. She'd progressed immediately to the sulky stage. Chloe pricked the middle of the pie crust and a little steam escaped. She pricked it again and more came out. Slowly and methodically she began pricking holes all over the top of my nice pie, ruining the look of it. Then she began randomly thrusting the knife sideways into it and pulling upwards, making a mess.

I shouted, I couldn't help myself. 'For God's sake! You're making my apple pie into a dog's dinner!'

This only made things worse. She started angrily hacking at the pie now, chopping it to pieces. She treated me to her new psycho stare and, with the ghoulish mascara rings around her eyes, it was pretty convincing.

'Chloe,' I said, serious and grown-up, 'give me the knife.'

She threw it petulantly towards me. It landed on the floor and dripped apple-pie gunge. Juegita, always the opportunist, came into the room and sniffed at it, but even she turned up her nose.

'I'm sorry about the thing with your mum, but you didn't have to destroy my pie. You're twenty-three, Chloe, you don't need your mum.'

'I do,' she wept.

'No you don't,' I said softly but firmly. 'Remember when Juegita first had the pups? Remember how she constantly fed them, letting them suck at her day and night? Because they were tiny babies and they needed her. When they got bigger they could eat solid food but they still wanted milk, remember? But she wouldn't give them any more. She growled and bit them and chased them away. She had to, so that they'd learn to fend for themselves. That's her job. D'you understand?'

I smiled at Chloe. I thought that had gone rather well. I'd just made it up on the spur of the moment, but I'd surprised myself with such wise insight.

'Thanks for that, Alison,' Chloe said quietly.

'It's my pleasure.'

'Thanks for that charming parable . . .'

Her tone wasn't clear, was she being sarcastic?

'That pearl of doggy wisdom, that sentimental baloney.'

She *was* taking the piss.

'You have no fucking idea,' she said.

Chloe jumped up off the couch and stood over me. I didn't like the way she was trying to intimidate me, so I stood up too and faced her down. She quickly gave in. She lifted the pie and started to walk away. Before I had time to congratulate myself on standing up to her bullying, she turned and launched the pie straight at me. As it flew through the air I just managed to dodge it. It hit the wall behind me and slid down. As it slid it left a slimy trail of pale yellow, the colour of vomit, down the wall. Some of it lodged in a giant crack in the plaster as it passed.

'Good one, Chloe, that'll be a treat for the fucking cockroaches!' I screamed. 'I spent hours making that pie. Well, I'm not cleaning it up. You threw it, you can clean it,' I yelled.

'You know what?' Chloe said. 'I've had it with this shit.'

She rushed into the kitchen and started banging about. She came back with a black poly bag and began stuffing the dogs' bowls and toys into it.

'Oh jeezo,' I said, 'what are you playing at now?'

'I gave that dog a home, her and her pups, all pissing shitting eight of them. Well you're right: a time comes when they have to fend for themselves.'

'You know I wasn't talking about the dogs.'

'Sure you were. They can fend for themselves on their own fucking time, down on the street. Let's see how long they last.'

'Look, calm down. We'll have to find homes for the pups in a few weeks' time, we've talked about that, but not yet, they're not ready, you know that.'

Chloe clipped Juegita's lead on to her collar and the dog danced with glee at the prospect of being taken out. The puppies caught their mother's mood and joined in.

Even at this stage, although I could see she was furious, I hoped I could jolly her along, cajole her out of her rage. Cajoling had become my method of managing Chloe.

'Come on, you're overreacting. You love Juegita, I know you do.'

'Love?' Chloe spat in my face. 'I don't love anything. Anything or anyone.'

'Chloe, no more drama, please? We've had enough for today. It's too exhausting.'

'Don't fucking tell me what I've had enough of!' Spittle flew out of her mouth as she screamed. 'I know what I've had enough of! You can take your cutesy doggy lecture and blow it outta your ass!'

'Listen to yourself. You're behaving like a spoiled brat.'

'Shut the fuck up and stop telling me how to run my life. Like you know any better.'

'I know better than to kick dogs.'

'I'm taking these dogs: my dogs! Not yours! I'm taking them and I'm dumping them, the same way I'm dumping you. This is my apartment, missy, and when I get back I want you and your cheap nasty little Wal-Mart backpack outta here!'

'Oh! Nasty! Nasty, is it? You weren't saying that when you were so desperate for me to move in,' I shouted. 'Poor little Chloe all alone in Barcelona, desperate for a friend. But you don't know the first thing about friendship. You torment people for your own sick twisted fun.'

'What people?' Chloe scoffed.

'People! My friends for starters; my friends and a defenceless wee puppy. People and dogs. Dogs are people too. I'm sick of your petty cruelties, Chloe. You're a heartless, selfish bitch. You're fucking dangerous, you are. You and all your carry-on and all the grief you give me. You're what caused my heart attack!'

'I wish you'd had a fatal heart attack, I wish you'd had a massive coronary and your face had turned blue, because right about now you'd be where you should be: in a box in the cargo hold on a plane back to fucking Scotchland!'

'Well, that's nice. And by the way, you're not dumping

me, I'm dumping you,' I shouted, hurling my keys at her. 'I can't stick it any longer. I'm sick of your neediness and your constant bleating. "Oh, Mommy doesn't love me!"' I put my hand to my brow and struck a melodramatic pose. '"Oh I'm an artist don't you know, that's why I'm such a nutcase, I suffer for my art!" Art which, by the way, is SHITE! A five-year-old mongoloid could do better. Well I'm not your fucking therapist. I'm sick of your tantrums, I've had it and I'm leaving. I'm dumping you, Chloe, just like Mommy did!'

Chloe picked up the keys I'd thrown at her and put them in her pocket. She stood in the doorway with Juegita straining at the leash to get out and heaved the poly bag over her shoulder. She'd obviously not seen a mirror recently. With her eyes still ringed in black mascara, she looked like a zombie. Ordinarily I wouldn't have let her leave the flat like that, but fuck her. Her face reflected her mental state. She was mental. I hoped the *mossos*, the local police, would catch and physically restrain the psychotic bitch.

'You think because you're rich and spoiled and your mummy doesn't love you,' I told her, 'you think that makes it OK for you to hurt people. Well it doesn't. You can't play with people's lives, Chloe.'

'Really?' she said, lowering her voice. 'I think you'll find I can.'

With all the shouting the dogs had become excited. In the mayhem of howling and barking and eight wagging tails rushing out the door, Chloe, with her zombie eyes blazing, screamed at me, 'Now get the fuck outta my apartment!'

273

Chapter 41

Go back to Scotchland, that was rich. A week ago I'd had a valid ticket back to Scotchland. Even after the heart attack I could still have made the flight if I wasn't so doped-up on the medication. The plane ticket had been non-transferable non-returnable. Three hundred euros down the drain.

The medication wasn't the only thing that had stopped me catching that flight. I'd had the opportunity of an all-expenses-paid education at one of America's top universities. Who wouldn't have been enticed? I'd spent much of my existence watching TV shows where people enjoyed just such an idyllic Californian lifestyle. The irony was that now Chloe would go, and I, who'd subtly sold her the idea, wouldn't. I'd have to leave Barcelona, leave my nutcase friend, give up my hopes for Berkeley. I'd have to crawl back under my stone; settle for a Cumbernauld lifestyle.

But with such an unstable character as Chloe, how could I have expected things to turn out any different? She was right about one thing: I had to get out of here. We were driving each other crazy. If I stayed, one of us would end up dead. It was a lovely flat and all that, but it wasn't worth this amount of grief.

I began packing by attacking the bundle of clean laundry that was stacked on the bedroom chair. For as long as I'd been here there'd always been laundry on that chair, my pants and bras mixed with Chloe's. I washed her clothes; I wasn't going to put them away for her. Hers never made it back into the drawers. She just dipped into the bundle whenever she needed clean stuff, taking mine when she ran out of her own. Our clothes had become interchangeable.

Choosing what to take was a confusing task and, for some reason, made me cry. I sat down on the bed. Another 300 euros. That would bring the total debt to 1,300. How the hell was I going to pay that back? If I didn't, Chloe would have the moral high ground. There was no way I'd give her that satisfaction. I'd save it up and send it to her. If she refused to accept it I'd come to America and find her and throw it in her face. Then she'd be sorry. She'd have lost the best friend she ever had.

The tin was still at the back of the cupboard. It looked like it hadn't been touched since the last time I'd opened it. I slid out another 300. The last ticket had cost more than that. It was 315. I found a bundle with tens and fives and took one of each. I'd need to get myself and my luggage to the airport, but I still had a few journeys left on my metro ticket. I'd manage.

It was still very hot. Down in the bowels of the metro system it was a lot hotter. Lugging my heavy rucksack on and off the underground trains might be too much. I could overexert myself. I didn't want to have another heart attack while I was stuck in a subway. I might not survive the next one. They didn't have defibrillation

275

machines down there. It could take them ages to get me out and to the hospital, and by then it might be too late. They'd call Chloe and she'd have to identify my body. Then she'd have something to cry about.

My imagination was working overtime. A taxi cost 30 euros. I peeled off another three tens. And I might need a hotel. If I couldn't get a flight today I'd need to spend the night somewhere. I didn't know where there were cheap hostels except in Raval, and I wasn't going there. I had already taken 1,345, I might as well round it up to 1,500.

I pulled a 100-euro note out and then another one. I was replacing the smaller notes in their original bundles when I heard a noise. A clicking noise.

How long had she been gone? She'd said I had to be out of here by the time she came back. She was going to go ballistic. She might even think I was hanging around hoping she'd changed her mind. She'd think a lot worse if she found me with the tin opened and her money all over the floor.

Chloe had caught me once before in a compromising situation: with Ewan's equipment in my mouth, or very nearly. And now, unless I could get the money back in the tin and the tin back in the cupboard before she made it to the bedroom, she was going to catch me again.

I jumped off the bed and scrambled across the floor. It was too late. Chloe burst in and found me shoving bundles of notes back in the tin.

'I knew it, I knew you wouldn't be able to resist putting your hand in the cookie jar!' she squealed.

She was laughing. She seemed to be in excellent spirits. And she was alone.

'Where's Juegita and the pups?' I asked.

276

'None of your business. Why are you still in my apartment?'

'I was just leaving.'

'No you weren't,' she said chirpily.

Chloe flopped down on to the bed. She lay on her
stomach. She propped her chin on her hand and swung
her legs lazily up and down.

'But actually I'm much more interested to know: why
are you stealing my money?'

'I'm not. I'm . . .'

What could I say?

'I wasn't going to take it all.'

'I can see that.'

Chloe had found the 100-euro notes I'd left on the bed
and was counting through them with great glee.

'Three, four, five hundred. Well well, quite a haul.'

I couldn't deny it.

'Keep it,' she said, lobbing it gently to me where I knelt
on the floor, 'you'll need it.'

I threw it back at her.

'I don't need anything from you.'

'Oh really? And how are you gonna live? I assume
you're staying on in Barcelona?'

I didn't say anything.

'So you'll need money. You don't have any of your own
money left.'

'How do you know that?'

'But Meester Bond,' said Chloe, affecting an accent, 'I
know everytheeng about you!'

She laughed. She laughed and made eye contact with
me, trying to make me laugh. It was a good joke, but I
wasn't giving in.

Chloe rolled to the edge of the bed, pulled out a fat

bundle from the tin and, with her arm outstretched, offered it to me.

'You're gonna need more than five hundred.'

I put my hands behind my back to indicate my refusal to take it.

'Now come on, Alison, say you get a room in an apartment for, I don't know, four fifty. Let's say five hundred for some place decent, and five hundred deposit. That brings you up to a grand. Even when you start work, it's gonna be a month before you get paid. You have to eat and probably have to pay for transport.'

'You don't even know how much money's in that tin, do you?' I asked her.

'It doesn't matter. I don't want you to be short on money. I don't like to think of you wandering the streets cold and hungry.'

'Like Juegita and the pups, you mean? I'm not your pet, Chloe. I can look after myself.'

'Oh yeah? How? You gonna sell your ass like the girls in Raval? Because, honey, you're not gonna get much.'

This did make me laugh. Not laugh exactly but smile. She was so cheeky. She could never take anything seriously.

'It'll be better than staying here with you, you mad bitch.'

'Hey, did I ask you to stay?' She was smiling. 'I don't want you here.'

She did want me there. Obviously she did. I had to smile.

'Good, because I'm not staying.'

'Look,' said Chloe, suddenly sounding exasperated, 'I just want you to take the money and get a room in a decent apartment.'

This confused me.

'Really?'

'Yes!' She was losing her patience now.

'Chloe, I said some terrible things. I didn't mean them.'

'I know.'

'I'm sorry.'

She nodded but otherwise ignored my attempt to apologize.

'Maybe you can get somewhere close by,' she continued. 'I could help you find a place. We'd be neighbours. Maybe we could visit.'

She did want me out.

'What about Berkeley?' I asked.

'What about it?'

Now wasn't the time to ask about Berkeley.

Maybe I *could* get a room in a flat. It might rescue our relationship. We'd still have all the good times together, and none of the disadvantages.

'Would you like me to live nearby?'

'Yes.'

'Really?'

'You know we're gonna drive each other crazy if we both stay here. It's better this way. This way we can still be friends.'

'OK,' I said quietly.

'There's no rush,' Chloe said soothingly. 'We can start looking tomorrow.'

'OK,' I nodded. 'But there's something I have to tell you.'

I weighed up the risk I was about to take, but I had to tell her.

'I've already taken money out of here. A thousand euros.'

'I know.'

'You know?' I gasped. 'How do you know?'

'Well, I didn't know how much but I knew you had no money left, so I figured you had to be getting it outta here. It's OK.'

'But why d'you keep it in a tin?'

'It's just whatever's left in my account at the end of the month. I take it out the bank and put it in the tin. If I don't take it Aged P just tops up my allowance. Mean bastard. It's my money.'

Still on my knees on the floor, I leaned forward and grasped her hands.

'I swear to you I'll pay you back every penny. We've got a second chance and I promise I'll never lie, I'll never do anything behind your back again. We're a team, Chloe. From now on you can rely on me one hundred per cent.'

'OK, cool. And you can rely on me one hundred per cent too.'

'Right.'

'So, just so that I can close the case: the underwear. The Victoria's Secret pantie set. You took 'em, right?'

I covered my face with my hands.

'How did you know?'

Chloe smiled.

'Meester Bond, I know everytheeng.'

We spent the rest of the day quietly. Instead of working on her chimney Chloe cleaned the flat. She gave it a very thorough going-over. As if all these months I'd been cleaning it I hadn't cleaned it properly. As if she was showing me she was going to get along fine without me. I didn't say anything. For lunch I cooked pasta with a pesto and cream sauce. She said how much she enjoyed it, but I wondered if she was just being polite.

'What did you really do with Juegita and the pups?' I asked her.

'They're with Josep. I gave him fifty to babysit them for the day. It's kinda nice without them, isn't it?'

'Yeah,' I said, 'but it's a bit weird. I miss them.'

'So do I,' she agreed.

Later we were out on the terrace watching the sun set over the hills behind the city. The air was cooling and we could hear the evening buzz from the street. Any other night Chloe or I would have suggested going out. Instead we sat in silence, avoiding each other's glance.

'Kinda weird atmosphere, huh?'

I didn't want to hear this but I was forced to nod agreement. Acknowledging the rift between us seemed to make it real and make it worse. I dropped my head and fought back tears. Nothing was going to be the same between us ever again.

'If we were a couple we'd have make-up sex,' joked Chloe.

I lifted my head.

'We still could.'

'I don't think—'

'Not with each other, with a boy. We could go out, pick up a boy and have great make-up sex. We should do that. I don't have to stay in bed any more. Why don't we go out? We haven't been out on the town for ages.'

'Are you sure you're well enough?'

'I'm fine.'

'But if we're gonna find you a new apartment tomorrow . . .'

'Oh, right.'

I couldn't hide my disappointment. I didn't want to find a new apartment.

281

'But hey,' said Chloe, 'you're right; we haven't had any fun for ages. Maybe that's what we need.'

This encouraged me.

'C'mon, let's go somewhere nice for dinner and see if we can find a nice-looking young man.'

'Yeah, but you always say that. You're always hot to trot and then you don't do anything.'

'I wasn't ready. I am now. I admit it; I've been a bit slow on the uptake. Remember, Chloe, I'm from Cumbernauld, I'm not used to good things coming my way, I've missed too many opportunities. I almost died a week ago. I hadn't planned on dying a virgin. From now on I take every chance for experience and pleasure that comes my way.'

'OK,' she said, 'we could go out tonight, see what happens.'

'OK.'

Later, as she applied her mascara, Chloe said, 'You know, you don't have to find an apartment tomorrow. We could leave it a few days. There's no rush.'

I smiled.

'Chu. Sex with each other,' I scoffed, 'as if.'

Chapter 42

Never had sausage and beans tasted so good. The restaurant was lovely, a Catalan place where they served the best *butifarra* and *habas* in Barcelona. I felt so relaxed, enjoying the calm after the storm. I no longer had to worry about the money I'd taken, or the underwear, or anything. Everything was sorted now.

'Wine?' said Chloe, holding out the expensive bottle.

'I don't know if I should.'

'It's red, good for your heart.'

'Oh, go on then,' I said, holding out my outsize glass.

Chloe tipped the bottle almost upside down and let the wine gush in.

'Yeah, Chloe, a *glass* of wine, not half a litre.'

We both laughed. I had a sip and then a mouthful. I hadn't had a drink in more than a week. It tasted wonderful.

I felt fine. It was hard to believe that a week ago I'd suffered a heart attack. But I was young and, as Dr Collins had once said, had a tremendous life force. I'd made a terrific recovery from the glandular fever, so long as I took it easy my heart would be fine. A drop of wine, quality wine like this, would probably do me the world of good.

'Damn, this wine is good,' said Chloe, swigging a mouthful and wiping *butifarra* grease from her mouth with the back of her hand.

I had to smile. The concept of moderation simply did not exist for Chloe.

'What?'

'You'll never grow up, will you?'

'What does that mean?' she said, mock-offended.

'You'll always be crazy, extravagant, hopelessly impractical, wildly generous, and fucking infuriating.'

'I hope so,' she said and winked.

'Here's to the best flatmate ever,' I said, ceremoniously raising my glass. 'To Chloe: mad, bad and dangerous to know!'

'Quite an accolade, I thank you. To Chloe,' she said, toasting herself. 'Cheers!'

We clinked glasses and glugged down the wine but we didn't look each other in the eye the way we usually did, both embarrassed by my slip into such naked sentimentality.

The conversation moved on. Chloe told me she'd finally tracked down a craftsman who would make the ceramic crowns she'd designed for her chimney project. She was very excited about it and I let her chatter. I was relieved that the bitter rowing was now forgotten, sluiced away by the wine.

'Oh yeah but the Aged P had to have something to say about it. He's going crazy saying he won't pay for them because I can't take 'em with me back to California.'

It was interesting that when she talked of returning to California she said can't take them with *me* instead of can't take them with *us*, but I didn't comment.

'I don't remember that, when did he say that?'

'When I spoke to him yesterday. You were asleep.'

I wasn't quick enough to hide my disappointment; when Philip called I usually answered Chloe's phone. Chloe left it unanswered if I was asleep. She hadn't even mentioned he'd called until now. This was the way things were going. I was out of the loop.

'He called yesterday to inform me of his state visit.'

'State visit? You mean he's coming here?'

'Yeah, unfortunately. He's gonna be in town on business,' said Chloe, between mouthfuls of beans. 'Only for two days, thank God, just passing through. He wants to meet you.'

'Really? Tell me,' I said, 'what does he look like?'

'Huh? Whaddaya wanna know that for?'

'Well, you have loads of photographs around the flat of your mum but I haven't seen any of your dad. I've spoken to him so many times now, I feel like I know him but I've no idea—'

'You *don't* know him.'

'No, of course but . . .'

'Yeah, you like old Phil, don't you?' she said in a teasing voice.

'He seems very nice,' I said carefully.

We both loaded our forks and filled our mouths. Time out while we chewed this one over.

'S'pose it's natural,' said Chloe, breaking the silence, 'you probably miss your own dad, don't you?'

'Not really.'

'Why not? Weren't you a kid when he died?'

'Yeah but he was never around much anyway. He worked on the oil rigs, for an American company. He earned good money but he was away most of the time. I only ever got to spend time with him after his heart attack.'

'Didn't you say he died of a heart attack?'

'Yeah, but not the first time. It was a minor one, a warning. He got sent home from the rigs on sick leave during Christmas holidays; Mum was at the bakery so I was at home all day with him, but we didn't really speak. We didn't have anything to talk about.'

'That's tough.'

'Not really. I hardly knew him. We'd never done the father-and-daughter bonding thing. He'd always worked on the rigs since before I was born. I never understood the way girls at school were so in love with their dads.'

'Yeeesh, daughters and dads, it's disgusting. It was the same at my school. I know what you mean.'

'No, I don't think you do.'

Chloe stopped with her fork halfway to her mouth. 'Oh yeah? What don't I know?'

'That I killed him.'

'You didn't kill your dad. How could you kill your dad? You were just a kid. What were you, fourteen?'

'I was thirteen and OK, I didn't directly kill him, but it was my fault he died.'

'Shut up! This I've got to hear. What happened?'

'I've never told anyone. Before he died he made me promise not to. I couldn't talk about it, I had a kind of mental block. Eventually people stopped asking me.'

'Well, I'm asking,' she said gently, 'if you want to tell me.'

I found that I did want to tell her. I'd told her all the other stuff, about Bashed-Head Boy and nearly doing it with Wanca in front of people. Even when I admitted I'd taken the money and the underwear Chloe was fine about it.

'OK, well, first of all, Mum and Dad didn't get on.

286

That's probably why he worked on the rigs. Mum was always crying and it was all long silences and bad atmospheres. You know the way.'

'Oh yeah, I know it.'

'But when he came home for such a long time on sick leave they just fought constantly. I was sick of it. My brothers were out playing football most of the time so they hardly noticed the arguments, but I didn't go out much. I was stuck trying to watch *Coronation Street* while my parents had whispered rows in the kitchen. One night I couldn't stand the tension any more and asked if I could go out. There was a youth club in Abronhill. I didn't have a friend to go with but I decided that I'd go alone, it was better than watching them glare at each other.

'Mum asked Dad to drive me to the youth club; it was a cold night and the club was on the other side of Cumbernauld. At first he refused but then when he heard it was in Abronhill he changed his mind. All the way there in the car, he never spoke to me once.

'He was sending texts on his phone. Instead of watching the road he kept sending texts, and then reading the replies. I was scared. I offered to type the text in for him, but he ignored me. I asked him to stop. I pleaded with him. I was scared he was going to crash. I knew it was going to happen, I just felt it. It was a horrible feeling, as if I was seeing it before it happened. And it did happen!'

'He crashed?'

'Yes! He crashed the car down an embankment.'

'But I thought he died of a heart attack.'

'He did. He had terrible injuries but they said he'd have survived if his heart hadn't given out.'

'What happened to you?'

'Broken arm and punctured lung. Not much, considering the car fell thirty feet. The newspaper said it was a miracle. But he died before the fire brigade could get to us.'

'Oh honey, it must have been awful.'

'It was cold. And heavy. He was trapped on top of me. A twig from a tree branch was stuck in his right eyeball. The liquid from inside his eye was dripping on me, on my face.'

'Oh,' said Chloe, putting down her cutlery, 'gross.'

'Before he died he was crying and pleading with me not to tell Mum. He said it had to be a secret.'

'I would've definitely told my mom. Reading stupid text messages while he was driving? No wonder he crashed. It wasn't your fault, Alison, you didn't kill him.'

'No, that's not what I meant.'

'Stupid bastard, he had his kid in the car, he could have gotten you both killed!'

'No,' I laughed, 'sorry. I'm getting the story all mixed up now. We've jumped ahead. He didn't crash while he was texting, it was later, on the way back, after the youth club. That wasn't the secret.'

'Well what the hell was? Stop teasing me and get to the point. What's the big secret, Alison?'

'Buy a flower for the lady?'

A young Asian guy stood at our table. He held out a large bunch of roses and grinned at me.

'¡*Hola* Esmeralda!' he said.

'¡*Hola* Sanj,' I replied.

For a moment I thought Ewan had sent him. Sending flowers to apologize for what he'd told Charlie. But how did Sanj know to find me here? Then I realized it was just a coincidence. The flowers weren't from Ewan. Sanj was selling them to loved-up, splatter-cash tourists.

'Please to see you *otra vez*, Esmeralda.'

'You too, Sanj,' I smiled. I'd forgotten what a nice guy he was.

'You two know each other?' said Chloe.

She was smiling, oozing charm towards Sanj, but I could tell she was annoyed. This was a friend of mine that she had never met and knew nothing about.

'Esmeralda?' she said pointedly.

'Eyes,' I said, my finger pointing to my eyes. 'Esmeralda because they're—'

'Green. Yeah, I got that. What I don't get is why you're not introducing me.'

'Sorry. Chloe, this is Sanj. He's a flower seller . . .'

'Evidently,' she said with a gracious nod towards Sanj's massive bouquet.

'And a friend of Ewan's. Sanj, this is Chloe, my flatmate and very good friend.'

We were still flatmates.

'Please to meet you,' said Sanj.

'*Encantado*,' Chloe replied.

After the introductions there was an awkward moment when we all ran out of things to say. Chloe smiled up at Sanj and he smiled down at us. I'd already mentioned Ewan. I wasn't going to do it again. I wasn't going to ask after his health. Sanj rescued us by enquiring after my health, specifically my cough.

'Oh yeah, it's totally gone,' I reassured him. I didn't mention my heart attack.

'I'd like a rose for my friend please, Sanj,' Chloe said, stretching down to find her handbag under the table.

'*Por favor, un regalo*,' he said, choosing the best roses and handing us one each. He refused to take the money.

'Thank you, Sanj, you're very kind,' Chloe smirked.

'But you won't do good business if you give your roses away every time you see a pretty lady.'

Sanj's English wasn't really up to a reply so he switched to Spanish, the gist of which was that there weren't two ladies in Barcelona as pretty as us.

'Your friend's a charmer,' said Chloe, trying to sound cynical, but I could see that Sanj had already charmed the pants off her. It wasn't only what he said, which sounded pretty cheesy to me, it was that it was in Spanish. Chloe always preferred when we were chatting to boys that she did all the talking. I was always her dumb friend.

Sanj apologized for interrupting our meal, excused himself and went round the other tables.

Chloe's eyes followed him. 'Impeccable manners,' she said, 'I like that, and so good-looking. You kept quiet about him, you sly dog.'

'I'm sure I told you about Ewan's friend Sanj.'

'Whatever, I don't remember. Anyhoo, I think we've found our guy for tonight.'

'Chloe, no. Not him, he's a friend.'

'What's wrong with getting a little friendlier? It's kinda romantic, him selling flowers and all. It suits him. He looks like a sensitive guy. His place is probably full of flowers.'

'He's a vendor. His place is more likely to be full of drugs.'

'Yeah,' she said, ignoring me, carried away by her idea, 'and his bed's probably filled with fragrant rose petals, dark red ones.'

I rolled my eyes.

'What? It's my artistic temperament. That and I've never had an Asian guy go down on me.'

This had us both hooting with laughter. Sanj heard

us and looked over, smiling his big innocent smile. I felt sorry for him. He had no idea what he was in for. While Chloe signed the bill and tipped the waiter I had one last stab at putting her off.

'Don't be fooled by those big liquid eyes. He's a gangster.'

'No way. He's too cute.'

'I'm telling you. His uncle runs all the drug vendors in the city.'

'Wow! How cool is that? I've always wanted to be connected. I think I'd make a great gangster's moll.'

'I don't really think Sanj wants us to go back to his place. He's not like that, he's a really nice boy.'

'Oh I'm pretty sure he wants us. He's an eager little beaver. Here he comes.'

Chloe welcomed him back in Spanish. I realized that apart from his tourist sales pitch, Sanj didn't speak English, but he was kind enough to include me in his smiles. I pretty much knew the script anyway. Chloe did her usual ear-whispering thing. She always pressed her breasts against their arm and her lips to their cheek and ear, but lightly, light as a kiss. I heard her say the word *cocaína*.

'*Aquí no, lo siento*,' Sanj whispered.

There was no need for apologies. That was exactly what Chloe wanted to hear.

When she suggested going back to his place Sanj at first appeared reluctant. I didn't look directly at Chloe. I didn't want her to think I was being superior. Clearly embarrassed, Sanj said he had to sell his flowers before he could go home for the night. He'd promised Tío Mahmood, his uncle, he'd sell them all. He was emphatic about this.

'*En este caso, quiero comprar todas las floras,*' Chloe said expansively.

Sanj appeared not to understand and stood grinning.

'Chloe, buying his flowers is like buying him. He's a friend, it's not right. We can go to a club and find Latino guys for free.'

'Hey, it was your idea to come out tonight. I want this guy.'

She spoke to Sanj again, making her proposition more direct, and this time he understood. His reaction was businesslike.

'*Trescientos, por favor,*' he said, discreetly palming the notes. '*Muchas gracias.*'

I kept my eyes on the table, smoothing out my napkin, taking care that it was very smooth.

'This guy's not cheap,' said Chloe, laughing. 'I kinda like that. And this way we get petals on the bed.'

Chapter 43

Before we left the restaurant I went to the toilet. After a while Chloe came in looking for me.

'Come on, we're waiting for you!'

'I think I'm just going to head back to the flat. I'm not feeling great but I'm sure you and Sanj will have a great time.'

'It's because he's Ewan's friend, isn't it?'

'No, well yeah, there is that, but fuck it. Ewan didn't want to see me when I was in hospital so who gives a shit what he thinks?'

'Thattagirl.'

'No but Chloe, it's something else.'

'What?' she yelled. 'He's waiting for us.' She gestured madly towards the door.

'I can't go to Sanj's place. He lives in Raval.'

I said this slowly so she would understand its significance. She thought for a moment. I nodded. She was getting there.

'So?'

She hadn't got the significance. The most important thing that had happened to me while I'd been in Barcelona, and she'd forgotten all about it.

'Bashed-Head Boy?' I said, giving her a clue.

'Oh you're not still obsessed with that, are you? For Chrissakes, Alison, that was months ago.'

'Yeah but there could be people down there looking for me: the police, the killer. Those Asian guys, they all got a good look at me.'

'And *I'm* supposed to be the drama queen! Look, the police are too busy taking bribes and scratching their asses to give a shit about one dead tourist. If anything was gonna happen it would've happened by now. Nobody gives a shit. That's Barcelona, honey.'

'Och, you're probably right but, I don't know . . . Raval just gives me the creeps.'

'Come on,' she said, dragging me by the arm. 'We'll go straight to his apartment. It's dark, no one will even see us.'

Sanj lived alone. On the second floor of a neglected building in a run-down street in Raval, his place wasn't the gangster's paradise I'd imagined. The tenement stairs, like our own, were poorly lit, with lights broken or unlit on some of the landings. But his flat wasn't bad.

It was a long room that ran the length of the building and had balconies on either side, through which a fresh breeze blew. Natural air conditioning. It was a studio, more like a warehouse loft than an apartment, metal brackets still bolted to the ceiling, no doubt from some previous industrial use, but it was nicely laid out. The living-room space was at the front, the kitchenette and bathroom in the middle, and the bed towards the back of the room. It was newly decorated. Sparsely furnished, the few bits of furniture looked tiny in the vast vanilla-coloured space, and for a guy's flat, it was remarkably tidy. There were no dirty dishes in the sink, no clothes or trainers lying around the floor. At the front near the open balcony two easy chairs faced a TV and DVD player. It was here that Sanj directed us to sit while he buzzed around getting things. A pile of *Bizarre* magazines were neatly stacked on the coffee table, and there was a vase of fresh flowers. Chloe had been right; he did have a flat full of flowers. Three buckets of roses and chrysanthemums stood by the door, competing with the smell of curry. The smell of flowers always reminded me of Dad's funeral; I preferred the delicious curry aroma. I directed my nose towards the kitchenette and breathed deeply.

Barcelona was great but the food in the Indian restaurants was disappointing: bland curries cooked to suit Catalan tastes. I missed a good spicy curry, a proper curry. Although we'd only just eaten I hoped Sanj would offer us food, maybe a wee samosa or something.

Instead he offered us cocaine. After he'd lit two low-wattage lamps and docked his iPod to play Arabic chill-out music, he got out the coke. Sanj went to the kitchen counter and chopped up two generous lines on a shaving mirror before standing over me like a waiter and offering it. I declined. I was all for new experiences but after my heart attack I was finished with coke for evermore. He passed it to Chloe, who hoovered up a line in one slick move.

'¿No quieres?' she asked him.

Sanj didn't want any either. He was quick to remove it.

'That is so mean!' she whispered as Sanj tidied it away in the kitchenette.

He dug out a bottle of wine from the back of a kitchen cabinet and again Chloe was the only one who wanted any. Sanj offered me bottled water, which I accepted, and he poured a glass for himself. As soon as the coke took effect Chloe began to chatter away in Spanish about how fab the flat was, how she liked the minimalist feel of it. Sanj seemed uncomfortable, probably embarrassed at the lack of seating. In an attempt to look relaxed he folded his arms and leaned against the wall nearby, listening politely while Chloe gassed on. This struck me as ridiculous but I didn't want to giggle and embarrass him more. I stood up and offered him my chair, moving over towards Chloe, indicating that I could share with her.

Sanj flapped his arms, telling me no, but Chloe had another idea. If we all three moved to the bed then we'd be quite comfortable.

Sanj was not averse to this idea.

'No, you're all right, I'm quite happy here thanks, you two go,' I said.

This didn't suit either of them.

'Pero no,' said Sanj, in that long-drawn-out Spanish way, as if I were being unreasonable.

They both put pressure on me, Sanj cajoling me out of my churlishness, Chloe making malicious gestures towards me behind his back. I could see that, short of leaving, there was no way out of it. I couldn't leave. I was too scared to walk the streets of Raval on my own. Earlier today I'd flung my keys at Chloe. Later it hadn't seemed appropriate to ask her for the keys back and she hadn't offered. She put her hands together in a pleading gesture and mouthed 'make-up sex'. I was going to have to go along with it.

'You're a pervert, you know that, don't you?' I whispered as we crossed the room.

'Oh yes indeedy,' she said, handing me her wine-glass while she plumped up the pillows.

I meekly stood holding her glass as she made herself comfortable sitting up in bed, legs crossed demurely. Once she was settled she held out her hand to receive her wine. Sanj went round the other side and joined her on the bed in the same position. I perched on the edge with my back to them. A few seconds later I heard the inevitable sucking sounds of kissing. I took a sip of water and stared into space.

Between kisses I could hear Sanj and Chloe breathe. I missed kissing. The gaps between Sanj and Chloe's kisses were getting longer. Now I could hear clothing being rumpled. I didn't have to imagine Chloe's naked body, I'd seen it so often I was as familiar and bored with hers as I was with my own, but Sanj was a different ball game. I imagined his beautiful toffee-coloured skin against Chloe's California tan. She'd be going home with damp knickers and a big grin.

While I was thinking these thoughts a hand hooked itself round my arm and pulled me gently but firmly down into a lying position.

Chapter 44

It had been Chloe, surprise surprise, who'd pulled me down. She pushed my head towards Sanj's, my lips towards his. He seemed eager. We snogged and, compared to Ewan, Wanca and other lads I'd kissed, it was certainly different. When I'd kissed the others it had just been the standard two-person thing. There hadn't been anyone else with us, never mind physically between us. As I had to lean over Chloe, her knees were digging me in the ribs. I couldn't decide if it was the snogging that was so good or the weird situation, but whatever it was, it was pretty exciting.

I wanted to feel every part of Sanj's bod, to rumple his clothes, howk his shirt over his head and wheech his trousers to the floor, but I was shy. I made do with rubbing my hand across his back in what I hoped was an erotic way. I moved my fingers, light as feathers, up and down and in sexy circles across his back until I realized that this might seem like I was trying to get him to burp. And anyway, wasn't the man supposed to make the first move? I wasn't sure. Maybe the rules were different with a threesome.

Sanj did finally make a move, or, more accurately, a

move was made that resulted in Sanj's hand cupping my breast. I had my eyes closed at the time so I couldn't be certain, but I would have expected to feel some kind of creeping groping movement. Instead the hand was plonked down on my boob, placed there perhaps by my good friend Chloe. When this thought struck me I opened my eyes. I wasn't comfortable being a puppet in Chloe's sex games.

Sanj was now, all by himself, kneading my breast in a pleasant way. I let him continue. By closing my eyes, wriggling against his hand and moaning 'Oh yes', I actively encouraged it. It was surprising just how dirrrty I was getting. Maybe once I got started I'd turn out to be even dirrrtier than Chloe. She wouldn't like that. Did this kneading mean that I should now fondle him? I wanted to. I slid my hand towards Sanj's crotch and found something warm and hard: Chloe's hand, she'd got there before me.

I opened my eyes and watched as she reached into his pants and teased out his cock. Sanj's cock was no different from Ewan's or the Silver Fox's. In terms of colour and size they were all much of a muchness. The only thing different was that Sanj's was soft.

Chloe shot me an accusing look, implying that Sanj's squidgy cock was my fault. She moved sideways in towards him, pushing his hand off my breast and me further from the action; the expert taking over from the apprentice.

'Let the dog see the rabbit,' she said slyly and smiled.

'I'm falling off the bed here,' I complained.

'OK,' said Chloe, 'get over there, on the other side of him.'

Rather than clamber over them I got off the bed, but

the minute my feet touched the floor Chloe issued another order.

'Hey, while you're up, could you fix me another glass of wine?'

I sighed and stomped off to the kitchenette. I pulled two glasses from the cupboard and filled them to the brim with wine; if she was having a drink, so was I. I needed one. This was too exciting not to drink. I brought her glass and she sat up and took a break from touching Sanj.

'*Salud*,' she said chirpily.

I moved to the opposite side of the bed where Sanj, despite his soft cock, smiled up at me.

'*Salud*,' I said and necked the wine greedily.

If there had been a fireplace I would have thrown my glass in it.

'This is so depraved, isn't it?' I said. 'I'm loving it.'

I pushed myself at Sanj and snogged him again fiercely. With Chloe as a rival, if I was going to get a look-in I'd have to really want it.

And I did. I was greedy for wine and kisses and getting my tits touched and everything else that was to come. I lifted Sanj's hand and clamped it to my breast, where he began squeezing. I put my glass down and, panting and moaning, concentrated on getting properly sexed-up again.

Chloe let me take over feeling him up. I copied what she'd done, running my hand up and down his cock and then pumping it up and down. I'd been doing it for a good ten minutes, maybe more, but there was nothing happening.

Chloe leaned over and looked intently into Sanj's face.

'Is there something else you'd like?' she said kindly, like a nurse to a patient.

I stopped chugging and smiled at him too, offering support. Sanj shyly turned his head away from us, embarrassed at his lack of erection.

'Maybe you want to sniff my shoe or something?' said Chloe.

Sanj turned back to us, apparently encouraged.

'Although I think Alison's shoe would probably be more potent.'

Chloe and I laughed and Sanj, perhaps not quite understanding the joke, smiled and nodded.

'You know, Chloe, maybe it's the two-girl thing, maybe that's freaking him out.'

'No, I don't think it's that,' she said analytically. 'He's into kissing both of us, it must be something else.'

Chloe switched to asking him in Spanish.

'¿Digame, cariño, qué prefieres?'

This seemed to do the trick. At last we were getting somewhere.

'¡Por favor, átame!' Sanj whispered.

I looked to Chloe for a translation.

'Me gusta atar,' Sanj whined.

I didn't get it. Sanj said it again, this time more loudly when we didn't understand. And then I realized by Chloe's expression that she had understood. She just wasn't keen.

'What does he want? What the hell is it?' I asked, thrilled and scared at the same time.

'He wants us to tie him up,' she said, rolling her eyes.

'¡Átame! ¡Átame!' begged Sanj, as he mimed his hands bound together.

Chapter 45

Chloe and I went into a huddle to discuss it.

'Don't you think this kinky stuff sucks?' said Chloe.

'Each to his own,' I shrugged.

I actually thought it was a bit rich of Chloe to turn her nose up at other people's perversions when she was such a renowned deviant, but I didn't say anything. I knew one thing, I wouldn't be giving my virginity away tonight after all. I wasn't sure if I was disappointed or relieved.

'I gave him three hundred euros,' she said indignantly.

'That was for the flowers.'

'Chu! That was for the sex. I'd kinda like to get my money's worth. Did you see where he put the coke?' she whispered.

'In the kitchenette somewhere, I didn't really notice.'

'Here's the thing: if we're gonna do this I'll need to be totally caned. OK,' she sighed, 'let's tie him up. But he has to go down on me. This is too weird,' she moaned. 'I don't think I'll get off unless he goes down.'

Sanj had wasted no time. He'd opened a drawer in the bedside cabinet and was pulling out black PVC underwear and bondage equipment.

Chloe and I looked at each other.

He'd already pulled on a black netting vest and was now scrambling into a pair of latticework PVC panties. The pants were decorative rather than functional, covering very little, and, as he either had no pubes or had shaved them, we were able to get a good view of his package. The pants did seem tight, his bits were bulging and oozing out of the lattice, but he obviously liked them that way.

On the bed there was a box that hadn't been opened. I looked at it, surprised to find the details of what was inside written in English.

'Look, Chloe, it's an S&M starter kit.'

'You have gotta be kidding me.'

'I'm honestly not,' I laughed, 'look what it says here. "This kit has everything you need to get you started on your S&M fantasy and all in black leather – whip, gag, handcuffs and ankle cuffs."'

'Sounds fantastic,' she said sarcastically.

Sanj burst open the box and attached himself to the ends of the bed with the ankle cuffs. He popped the black-rubber-ball gag into his mouth and then locked the handcuffs on his right wrist and held his hands out in front asking us to chain him up. As swift as an arresting officer, Chloe pulled his arms behind his back and locked the handcuffs. It looked really uncomfortable, his chest was pushed out unnaturally, but he seemed to like it.

'¿Mejor?' Chloe asked him.

Nodding enthusiastically Sanj agreed, smiling through his rubber-ball gag.

She patted him on the head and then tried to take the gag out of his mouth. Sanj shook his head no, and when she persisted he jerked his head from side to side to avoid her. The gag was supposed to fasten behind his head and the ends flicked around, smacking his face and leaving a red mark.

'Look, he's whipping himself!' Chloe laughed.

Whenever she was quick enough to get her hand on his face Sanj snarled like a dog. He was enjoying his role as the puppy with the rubber toy, refusing to give it up. The gag was wedged tightly behind his teeth, alarmingly far back in his mouth.

'D'you think he'll swallow it?' I asked.

'Nah, they design them this size so you can't swallow 'em.'

'That's quite clever I suppose.'

Chloe wasn't having much success in getting the gag out of his mouth. To help out I approached him from the other side and began trying to touch his face. Now we had him cornered. We were getting close to taking it from him and this made him snarl all the more. The more Sanj snarled the more we laughed until Chloe said, 'OK, I'm bored with this shit now. You get up behind him and hold his head.'

I stood on the bed and the next time he whipped around I was ready for him. I held him in a tight head-lock while Chloe worked her fingers into his mouth. I was glad she was doing this, not me. I'd have been scared to put my fingers in his mouth in case he took the fantasy too far and bit me.

He moaned when she prised his jaws apart, whether in pleasure or pain I wasn't sure, and he retched when she forced her fingers into his mouth, but he didn't bite. She pulled the saliva-sodden ball from his mouth and threw it on the floor.

'No, Sanj, naughty boy. Chloe and Alison have other things to put in your mouth. Alison, I think he deserves to be whipped. What d'you say, Sanj, do you think you should be punished?'

Rather than translate what she'd said into Spanish, Chloe brandished the whip in front of his face.

'*Sí, maestra*,' Sanj whimpered.

'Yeah, well Little Miss McStrict, you can whip him,' she said, tossing me the whip.

I flicked it once across each of his shoulders and Sanj convulsed.

'Hey, take it easy. Don't kill him,' said Chloe, giggling.

'Shut up!' I laughed. 'I hardly touched him. This whip is cheap rubbish.'

Although the box said it was leather, the whip was light and thin as cardboard.

'That's it, let him have it,' said Chloe in a redneck accent, 'punish that dirty boy good.'

I gave up with the half-hearted whipping when Chloe stepped out of her skirt and pants and knelt on the bed.

She thrust her crotch into Sanj's bemused face and he started wriggling again.

Just as he'd done with the gag, he moved his head so fast and sharp I thought he'd do himself an injury. Chloe turned to me, rolling her eyes again, and pushed him down on the bed.

'Chloe, all his weight'll be on his arms, that'll be painful.'

'Hello? He's a masochist, it's what he wants, isn't it?'

She climbed on to his chest and sat astride him. Sanj's head was squeezed between her thighs and her knees pressed into his shoulders.

'Look,' I said pointing, 'he's hard now.'

Sanj's cock was now stiff and poking out the top of his lattice pants.

Chloe was sitting on him like a jockey on a horse. She pulled on his ears and rocked back and forth, galloping towards climax.

'Sonofabitch! Open your goddamn mouth!'

Sanj wouldn't open his mouth. I did what I could to assist by offering her my hand but it was no use. She couldn't come.

With a dissatisfied grunt Chloe finally gave up and flopped forward on top of him.

I stood at the side of the bed over the entwined bodies and lifted Chloe's damp hair off Sanj's face. His expression was blank but I could see from his PVC pants that he was still erect. Slowly and heavily, Chloe heaved herself across him and rolled off the bed.

'Well that was a complete waste of time,' she moaned as she pulled on her pants. 'Let's find the coke.'

She walked to the kitchenette and started opening and raking through the cupboards.

She found the shaving mirror with the chopped-up coke line and called me over. She stuck her head round the kitchen units and beckoned me with a nod. I felt a bit awkward leaving Sanj there like that.

'Oh leave him and come and talk to me, he's not going anywhere.'

Chloe was greedy with the coke. As I walked from the bedroom to the kitchen area she was sniffing up the last of it.

'So, we got sidetracked, you were telling me ...'

Chloe looked at me expectantly.

'Sorry, what?'

'Your dad! For Chrissakes, Alison, you said you killed him!' she said, opening more cupboards.

'Oh right, yeah. Oh I can't be bothered talking about that now. It winds me up. I get angry if I even think about it. Let's go home.'

'Are you kidding me? I want the whole story.'

'Och Chloe, can we not just leave it for tonight? I'm tired.'

'The whole story. I need to know. I might have to report you to the police. They're looking for you all over Raval, did you know that?'

'Ha ha.'

'So: your dad was taking you to the youth club and he crashed the car and . . .'

She wasn't going to give up. Earlier I had been in the mood to tell her, but now I was just fed up and frustrated.

'What was all that stuff today about us being a team, huh?' she huffed. 'I can rely on you one hundred per cent.'

It was easier just to tell her. Then there would be no more secrets between us, just as I'd promised today.

'OK. Right: He didn't crash when he was taking me to the youth club—'

'When he was sending the texts.'

'No, he didn't crash then,' I said in a flat matter-of-fact voice. 'We made it to the youth club, miraculously. I went in and he said he'd pick me up at nine when it closed. But the club closed early. The heating system broke down. When I came out I was surprised to see the car still there. I thought he was going to go home and come back for me. I walked back to the car. He wasn't there but I could hear his voice in the woods and I followed it. I saw him in the woods, with a woman. They were doing it up against a tree. They were grunting like pigs.'

Sanj called out to me.

'Esmeralda, *ven aquí por favor*,' he asked.

'*¡Cállate!*' Chloe barked at him. 'Your dad was doing it?'

'Yeah.'

'Who was the woman?'

'It was Isabelle.'

'No!'

I somehow felt that this wasn't as shocking to Chloe as she was making out, but at least she was kind enough to empathize.

'Isabelle, our childminder. My mum's best friend.'

'Yeah, I know who Isabelle is,' Chloe assured me. 'Bitch.'

'*¡Venga!*' Sanj called.

'In a minute, you pervert!' Chloe yelled.

'I shouted at them. I told them I was going to tell Mum. Isabelle begged me not to but Dad told her to go home. He practically threw me in the car.'

'Bastard.'

'He was driving and shouting at me and then he had another heart attack. That's when he crashed. He wouldn't have had that heart attack if I hadn't threatened to tell Mum.'

'Oh Alison,' Chloe said, opening her arms and enfolding me, 'you didn't kill him, none of that was your fault. He almost killed you. Then he lay dead on you with his fucking eyeball dripping. And you never did tell your mom, did you?'

I shook my head.

'You were only a kid. It's not your fault if he got caught with his dick where it shouldn't have been.'

'I know.'

'That's what men are, that's the way it is, even that scuzzball over there, they're all the same.'

'I know.'

We went quiet and I stayed in her arms a while.

'Come on,' she said eventually, 'don't let it get to you, it's all in the past now. Your dad is dead and he got what he deserved, huh?'

'Absolutely,' I agreed, sniffing.

'*¡Por favor!*' wailed Sanj.

'Let's get outta here,' said Chloe. 'Let's get some *churros* and go home, OK?'

'Yeah.'

I went back to the bed to find my shoes. Sanj was speaking to me but I ignored him. He was a scuzzball. As I sat on the bed looking for my shoes I became aware of a warm wetness beneath me.

'Och jeezo,' I said, disgusted, 'he's pissed the bed. That must have been what he was shouting about.'

'Well he shouldn't have been so quick to tie himself up then, huh? Stupid sicko.'

'Eeeuw,' I screeched, 'look, he's hard! I didn't think guys could do that.'

'Oh, guys can do lots of weird things. Probably gets off on soiling himself. Watch out, he'll take a dump in a minute. Filthy pig,' said Chloe. 'There's gotta be some more coke around here. Hey, Sanj!' she yelled. '*¿Dónde esta la cocaína?*'

Sanj yelled something back at her and began wriggling around again. As he moved a warm fizzy smell of urine rose up.

Chloe came out of the kitchenette and stood over Sanj.

'*Digame,*' she said softly.

Sanj wouldn't tell her.

'¡*Digame!*' she demanded.

She walked back to the kitchen and began again searching the drawers. I'd found my right shoe but when I looked under the bed the left shoe had rolled to the other side. I walked around the bed to get it.

'Pay dirt!' I heard Chloe shout.

Sanj was yelling and wriggling around, looking like he'd break an arm to get out of the restraint.

'Yippee! Look what I found,' Chloe squealed.

I turned and smiled. She held up a bag of coke the size of a brick. Sanj was going crazy. From the kitchenette Chloe waved the bag at him, teasing him. I bent down to dig out my shoe from under the bed and as I came up Sanj headbutted me in the face.

My nose exploded. I couldn't do anything. Sanj was screaming. I wanted to call for Chloe but I had forgotten how. There was a stinging behind my eyes. A buzzing in my head. I couldn't see anything. My hands were in front of my face. I touched my nose and cheeks but there was no sensation. My face was numb. Sanj was screaming and screaming. I didn't want him to scream. The neighbours might hear him. Someone might call the police. Slowly I took my hands away from my face but this only made Sanj scream more. The white sheet and his brown skin were spotted with my red blood. I tried to call for Chloe but all that came out of me was a grunt. Chloe stuck her head out of the kitchenette and when she saw me came rushing over.

'Oh my God, Alison, are you OK? What happened?'

I still couldn't speak. I was too confused to form words, but I made another noise.

'He hit you?' Chloe sounded like she wasn't sure. I knew she must be wondering how someone so restrained could inflict such damage. 'You hit her?'

Sanj was still screaming. I nodded yes. Yes he hit me. I wanted her to stop him screaming.

She punched him in the face. That quietened him. My breath came back. Now I found I could talk.

'He headbutted me.'

I could talk but my mouth was full of blood.

'Honey, let's get you cleaned up,' said Chloe, putting her arm around me.

I wanted to explain how unfair this was. I hadn't done anything to him. I hadn't taken his coke. I'd only done what he'd asked of us. Chloe put a cloth to my face to help mop up the blood.

She sat on the dry side of the bed and spoke to Sanj softly, as though she were reading a child a bedtime story.

'Hey, you little shit,' she murmured, 'it's all about you, isn't it? You want us to tie you up and play your sick little games, huh? You have kilos of coke in that drawer and you're too fucking mean to give a girl an orgasm or a little line.'

Sanj, with a wide-eyed stare, didn't take his eyes off her.

'But you crossed the line, buddy. You see what you did to her?'

Chloe turned to look at me and Sanj followed her stare. I took the cloth away from my face. It was Sanj's T-shirt. I could smell him off it. I retched and threw it on the floor.

'You hurt her, and you're gonna have to pay,' said Chloe. She jabbed Sanj under the chin with the handle

311

end of the whip. He choked, and when she did it a second time he started screaming again.

I didn't want him to scream.

'Shut up!' I hissed in his face, spraying blood.

Up this close I felt his breath on my skin and smelled the piss.

'He's making me sick,' I told Chloe.

'Yeah, I can't look at his perverted face any more,' she said.

She pulled the pillowcase off the pillow and put it over his head. With the bag over his head it was easier. Blood soaked through the pillowcase from the inside. He wriggled, the sack head moving from side to side like a scarecrow in a fairground House of Horrors.

'Go on,' said Chloe, 'hit him.'

The screaming was quieter now, muffled by the pillowcase, but still he wouldn't stop making noise. I had my hand balled into a fist, I didn't even know I did until his head connected with it and sent a painful shock up my arm.

'Uuh,' I groaned, and cradled my throbbing hand. Now he'd hurt my face and my hand.

He pulled his head as far away from me as he could. He arched his back, thrusting his pathetic pants at us with his fat cock straining through the plastic.

'Oh yeah, you like that, don't you? You sick fuck!' said Chloe, delivering an uppercut to the punchbag.

I punched once more, with the heel of my other hand, into the pillowcase. He sighed and expelled a moan.

'Look, he's come!' Chloe said, her voice a disbelieving squeak. 'Eeuuw!'

It was true, oozing out of the spaces in his pants and dripping on to the piss-wet bed was the slimy evidence.

312

The cock went limp, closely followed by the body, which slid, satisfied, down the bed.

I'm not sure what happened after that. We hit him. I remember punching into the punchbag, punching and punching, my arms feeling heavy and tired, my face and hands throbbing, my heart pounding. I remember the still body on the bed, Chloe and me breathing hard in the quiet, the bloody pillowcase, the spurt of dark red across the vanilla wall. I remember us both hurrying and crying and running down the stairs and Chloe saying, 'Don't stop, don't stop.'

Chapter 46

We ran, crying and puffing, through Raval. In a narrow street we passed two Asian guys, beer vendors with four-pack bracelets on their wrists.

'¡Hola, guapas!' one of them said, laughing.

Chloe ran straight past them, too fast for them, but they spread their arms wide as if they were going to scoop me up.

'¡Dejala! ¡Dejala, cabrones!' Chloe screamed.

Their smiles faded. They parted and let me pass.

When we got home I could do nothing but cry. Chloe pulled my clothes off. I let her tug my arms out my sleeves and shove me under the shower. The water was hot but I felt cold. She scrubbed me. After the shower she gave me pills and held brandy to my lips and poured it into me. She put me to bed and pulled blankets out of the wardrobe and threw them over me. I was crying and still cold. She tugged the blankets tight round me and cuddled into me.

'I hate him,' I sobbed, 'I hate my dad, I fucking hate him.'

'I know,' said Chloe, holding me, 'so do I.'

A strong smell of burning woke me. I hauled myself

out of bed, groggy from the pills, and dragged myself as fast as I could towards the smell. It was raining outside and there was black smoke. Out on the terrace Chloe was burning something in the bin, poking it with a stick.

'What are you burning?' I asked.

'Clothes,' she said without looking at me.

I went back inside and sat on the couch, crouching forward with my arms folded, my legs crossed.

'Oh for Chrissake, Alison, stop crying,' Chloe said when she came in.

I didn't know I was crying but I wiped my face and made an effort to stop.

'Where are the dogs?' I asked her.

'With Josep, don't you remember? I told you last night. Jeez, Alison, you have to try to hold it together.'

'What happened?' I sobbed, crying again.

'You know what happened.'

'We hit him, didn't we?'

'Yes we did.'

'We hit him too much. We . . .'

I wept quietly but Chloe didn't shout at me again. She sat with her mosaic box, fiddling with the small bits of tile, arranging a design for her chimney. After a while, I went to the bathroom and washed my face.

She was right. I did have to hold it together, but I had to shrug off this wooziness first. I threw cold water on my face and took deep breaths. I looked in the bathroom mirror and nearly started crying again. My nose was twice its normal size. I had black swollen bags under my eyes.

'We have to go back,' I said when I returned to the living room.

'What?'

'We have to go back to Sanj's, he's tied up. He could choke or anything. We have to help him.'

'Alison, stop. Stop right there. You know we . . .'

I didn't want to hear what she was going to say. I ran out to the terrace and pulled the door closed behind me. I ran to the edge and tried to draw oxygen out of the heavy humid air. She followed me out.

'Alison, come away from the edge.'

She said this in a calm soothing voice, like she was talking me down off the ledge.

'Are you scared I'll jump?'

'No. But it's slippy and the rain has gotten into the crack on the wall. It might not be safe.'

'We have to go back, help him, make things right. I just want everything to be right again, please, Chloe, we have to.'

'We can't help him now.'

I clamped my hand over my mouth.

'We can't go back there,' she said simply. 'They'll be looking for us.'

'I told you we shouldn't go to Raval!' I cried. 'Every time I go there something bad happens. Didn't I tell you we shouldn't go to Raval?'

'Yes,' said Chloe, 'you told me.'

'Well, what are we going to do, Chloe?'

'We're gonna stay here, lie low. Unless you still wanna move out?'

'No!'

'Well then, we're gonna hold it together.'

'Hold it together,' I repeated.

'That's all we can do.'

'I'll make coffee,' I whispered.

'Good idea,' said Chloe.

It rained on and off all day as she continued working on her chimney. I brought out coffee and watched her, but she ignored me. After sunset she ran an extension cable out and plugged in a lamp and carried on working from the top rung of the ladders.

The chimney looked misshapen. Before she began it had been a normal straight-sided chimney, but she had cemented a pregnant bulge on to one side, giving it a lop-sided appearance. It didn't look right to me, but she'd started grouting the tiles now so this must be how she wanted it.

Even though she wouldn't talk to me I stayed near her. Being out on the terrace in the rain with Chloe ignoring me was better than being inside on my own.

'We should eat,' she said finally, hands on hips, her face smeared with grout.

'I'm not hungry.'

'Well maybe not, but we have to eat. I'll go down and get kebabs.'

'No! Chloe, no, please don't go out.'

'You have to stop this. I'm only going down to the kebab shop. I'll be gone five minutes.'

She went out and slammed the door.

I heard shouting on the street and looked down. Chloe was gone a long time. I was in the bedroom crying when I heard the front door bang open.

'Alison?' Chloe came into the bedroom. 'I got you a kebab, come and eat.'

I followed her out to the living room. I'd thought I wasn't hungry, but when I opened the kebab I realized I was starving and gobbled it down like a dog. The brandy bottle was still on the table and I took a huge swig.

'Feel better?' said Chloe, smiling.

'Yeah, a bit. Want coffee?'

'Not right now, thanks.'

The brandy gave me courage to talk about it.

'Those two guys.'

'What two guys?' Chloe snapped.

'They saw me. They could identify me.'

'They saw nothing! They saw two girls in the street going home after a night out, so what?'

'They saw my face, how beat-up I am. They saw my green eyes.'

'Honey, your eyes are bruised black and blue.'

'No, but I'm telling you, Chloe, it's the green eyes. Esmeralda, that's what Sanj called me. He noticed. They all do, I see it in their faces, they're surprised I have green eyes.'

'So you have green eyes, so they noticed! Big deal.'

'Yeah, but those other men noticed them too, the men who were there when I found Bashed-Head Boy. They got a good look at me. Now they'll be looking for the same person for both.'

'Esmeralda.'

'Exactly.'

'Think I'll get back to the chimney,' said Chloe, standing up. 'I wanna finish it before my dad gets into town.'

'There was a lot of blood, wasn't there?'

She didn't answer me.

'Chloe, this is important, we need to talk about this. There was a lot of blood, wasn't there?'

'Yes.' She sighed. 'Yes, there was a lot of blood. Mostly yours.'

'But was there any on the floor? Did I get any on my shoe?'

'What the hell are you talking about?'

'Did I leave a footprint?'

'I don't fucking know!'

'I left a footprint the first time.'

'OK, enough. Stop talking crazy, what the fuck is this? What first time? A minute ago it was Esmeralda, now it's a footprint?'

'But Chloe . . .'

'Yeah, I remember,' she interrupted me, 'your shoe left a print outside the guy's flat, you told me.'

'You know I had nothing to do with Bashed-Head Boy. I didn't even know him, I swear to you. I only walked up the stairs, that's all!'

'You're not Esmeralda, and you're not Cinderella, OK? You're Alison, and you're sooo losing the plot.'

Chapter 47

I couldn't eat, I couldn't sleep. When I closed my eyes I saw the body on the bed, the bloodstained hood. So I didn't close them. I sat on the sofa watching Chloe out on the terrace. Hours would go by and I wouldn't remember them passing, there would just be more mosaic on the chimney. At night Chloe insisted I get into bed, but I didn't sleep.

We were dealing with it in different ways, I recognized that. Chloe became obsessed with her chimney. The rain never let up for more than about an hour but it didn't put her off. She set up a tent of clear thick plastic around the ladders to protect the tiling and worked under it.

'It has to be finished by the time Aged P gets here,' she said. 'He says I never finish anything.'

'But why d'you even care what your dad thinks of it?'

Chloe laughed. 'I don't know.'

For the next three days she did nothing but work on the chimney, stopping only to slurp at the coffee and biscuits I brought her or, after it got dark, to run down to the street to buy kebabs. I stayed in the bedroom while she was gone.

It was September now, winter was coming. I had never

320

seen rain like this in Barcelona. I should be working by now but I couldn't leave the flat. I missed my mum and brothers. I missed Scotland, I even missed Lisa and Lauren, but how could I tell them what had happened? I missed them and yet I dreaded having to explain. It was just as well my phone was lost. I didn't want to have to tell them, I just needed someone to understand.

Juegita. I missed her the most. She forgave me when poor Fanny got drowned, she wouldn't judge me. I asked Chloe three times a day, I begged her to pick up Juegita and the pups from Josep, but she refused.

'I miss 'em too, but I need to get the chimney finished. I can't have the pups running around under my feet.'

'But if I keep them inside, Chloe, please. I'll make sure they don't come near the chimney.'

'No. Anyhow, there's something else. There are vendors everywhere. Walking around with eight dogs, that's gonna attract attention.'

'Mahmood!' I groaned. 'I told you Sanj was connected. Mahmood is his uncle. He'll have every vendor in Barcelona looking for us. Looking for me.'

'Don't start with that again. I told you, we just have to hold it together until my dad gets here tomorrow. He'll fix it. He knows people. Everything is gonna be fine. You just need to get some sleep.'

I wanted to believe her. She was right, I had to hold it together, it was all I could do.

'D'you promise?'

'I promise. Can you hand me the trowel please?'

I sat on the terrace and watched her work, and watched the rain drip between the cracks in the walls.

Chloe's dad called the next morning from the airport, asking for directions.

'Fuck! I didn't know he was getting here so early!' Chloe wailed. 'The grout isn't even dry on this section yet!'

She made me take a bath and get dressed. She wouldn't take a bath or even shower; she threw a blanket over the maria and kept on with the chimney, cementing on the fancy crowns even though she hadn't finished tiling all the way round.

'If he sees it from this angle he won't know it's not finished.'

'It looks amazing, Chloe.'

Despite having other things on my mind I had to acknowledge that Chloe had done a fantastic job on the chimney, it was totally transformed. Until now I had always seen chimneys as warm, welcoming symbols of home, gently puffing on the skyline. Chloe's chimney, with its undulating shape and iridescent greens, yellows and blues, was more of a shimmering reptile. It was like a giant snake whose head had burst through the roof of the building, a beautiful toxic serpent.

Even though we were expecting him, we were both freaked out when we heard Aged P's loud knock at the door. The knocking continued for a few minutes before Chloe plucked up the courage to go to the hallway.

'Daddy?'

'Hey, honey, are you going to let me in?'

Chloe ran at the door and pulled it open. I couldn't see him at first. She had barely let him over the threshold before she threw her arms around him and buried her head in his chest.

'Oh Daddy,' she sobbed, 'I'm so glad to see you!'

'Hey, hey, hey! It's OK, Daddy's here.'

Chloe dragged him into the living room and on to

the sofa where she pinned him with a fierce cuddle. I followed, shouldering the bag he had dropped, and sat down. Philip was just as I had imagined him: tall, tanned, urbane, white teeth, greying temples. He shot me an embarrassed nod by way of introduction. He looked momentarily shocked by my battered face, but he was polite enough to try to hide it and turned back to Chloe, who was howling without restraint. I'd never seen her lose it like this. Things had obviously got to her much more than I'd imagined.

'Hey now. What's happened to my little girl?'

Chloe continued clinging to her dad and howling. Philip now switched to a sterner tone, as though he was speaking to a naughty child.

'Chloe. What is it? What have you done?'

This got an immediate reaction. Chloe pulled away from him and wiped her face.

'Why do you always assume I'm in trouble, Daddy? Can't I just be pleased to see you?'

'Sure you can.' Philip laughed. 'It's just that you're not usually this pleased to see me.'

He wasn't stupid. I could see he was humouring her. He thought she was unhinged; her behaviour certainly was. She'd gone from sobbing infant to snarling teenager in seconds.

'Come on, I want to show you something.'

She grabbed his arm and dragged him to the terrace door. I moved to follow, but this time it was me that Chloe snarled at.

'D'you think I could have a minute alone with my dad, please?'

'Sure,' I said politely, keeping up appearances in front of Philip, but I was taken aback.

It had always been just me and Chloe: me and Chloe against the world, against the dads. Now she was siding with him against me. She wanted to show him her chimney, I understood that, but she also wanted to get him alone, to tell him the Sanj thing was my fault. What could I do? Now, with her dad here to 'fix' things, they could call the police or turf me out on the street to face Mahmood's informers.

Chloe opened the patio door on to the terrace, led her dad out and closed it firmly against me. I waited in the living room, trying to hear what they were saying, but it was impossible: they kept their voices to a low murmur. After five minutes they came back inside, smiling.

'My dad is taking me out for lunch,' Chloe announced. She walked to the bedroom; I followed her and closed the door.

'You told him, didn't you?'

She was pulling clothes out of the wardrobe and wouldn't answer me.

'Chloe, what's going on?'

'Will you chill the fuck out!' she whispered viciously, buttoning a smart blouse. 'You're going to ruin everything. I have to go out with him. It's the only way he's gonna help us. I'm doing this for both of us.'

'Tell him it was self-defence. He can see the state my face is in, we can use that.'

'OK, self-defence.'

'And Bashed-Head Boy . . .'

'Yeah yeah, that was an accident. He fell over the banister.'

'It was nothing to do with me. I got there after he was dead.'

'OK, I'll tell him.'

She was rummaging in her make-up bag. She produced a lipstick and the mirror she usually chopped the coke lines on. The lipstick was a soft pearly pink shade I'd never seen her wear before. It made her look very young, very innocent.

'Chloe, you don't have to go out. Please, don't leave me here on my own!'

'Look, the man has come a long way, OK? He wants quality time with his daughter. I'll be back in a few hours, we'll tell him then, OK? I have to work on him a little more first.'

There was nothing I could do about it, nothing I could say.

Chapter 48

As soon as they left the flat I went and stood out on the terrace, listening to the tourists drag their suitcases along the cobbled street. How I wished it was me.

I should pack now. I could pack for both of us. It would save time when Chloe came back.

If she came back.

I'd have to hope she would, that her dad would fix things and we'd soon be on a plane to the States to start college.

I went into the bedroom and pulled my rucksack out from under the bed. There was no point in sorting Chloe's clothes from mine, we'd be taking everything anyway, but I didn't want to mix clean clothes with dirty ones. Chloe's clothes were strewn everywhere, the clean stuff in the laundry pile on the chair, the dirty stuff on the floor. I lifted the dirty clothes off the floor and piled them into the pillowcase I kept for my own dirty laundry. A vision of Sanj's battered head inside the blood-soaked pillowcase jumped into my mind. I didn't want to think about pillowcases. I shoved it forcefully to the bottom of the rucksack. Then I started on the drawers.

Chloe's underwear drawer had no system; bras, pants

and bikinis were flung in any old way. I tipped the lot out on to the bed and was amazed to find, rolled inside a hot pink swimming suit, my mobile phone.

Chloe searched that drawer for the phone, I saw her. There was no way she could have missed it. I remember she rifled through that pink swimsuit, it wasn't there then. This could only mean that she'd put the phone there since. Which meant that she'd found it again, or never lost it at all.

Maybe she thought she was doing me a favour keeping me away from Ewan. She was always jealous of him, Chloe needed to be the most important person in my life. She told me she'd called him and told him I was in hospital, but that he didn't want to see me. Maybe she hadn't called him at all.

There was one way to find out. The phone battery was dead so I found the charger and plugged it in while I weighed up phoning Ewan. If I contacted him he might turn me in. Even if he didn't, it might be dangerous for him to get involved. Ewan and Sanj's uncle Mahmood were known to each other. Mahmood might be watching, waiting for Ewan to lead him straight to me. But this sounded, even in my paranoid state, too far-fetched. I needed to speak to someone I could trust right now; more than anything I needed to hear a familiar Scottish voice.

'Ewan?'

I could hear him breathing but he didn't speak.

'It's me, Alison.'

'Yes, I know,' he said coldly.

'Can you speak? Is it safe?'

'What d'you want?'

So it was true, he didn't want to see me.

327

'I'm sorry, Ewan. I just wanted to talk to you, that's all.'

'Haven't got time. OK, bye now,' he said casually and hung up.

I went back to sitting on the sofa, my packing forgotten. I couldn't even cry any more.

So Chloe hadn't lied about Ewan, but why had she hidden my phone from me? And there was something else. Something she said before she left. She said that Bashed-Head Boy was an accident. That he fell over the banister.

I'd looked at lots of flats in lots of buildings before I got to Bashed-Head Boy's building. It was the only one that had a banister. All the other flats had a lift in the centre of the stairwell. How did Chloe know his had a banister?

I'd often wondered about Chloe's boyfriend, the one she and her dad were supposed to go to Vietnam with. She never talked about him. All I knew was she broke up with him because he wanted to party with his friends.

I went to see the flat in Raval because the Internet advert mentioned parties. I'd wanted to get invited. I had no proof that Bashed-Head Boy had placed the advert, no proof that he'd been Chloe's boyfriend. But I had my suspicions. If anyone was going to get the blame for Bashed-Head Boy, it wasn't going to be me.

I searched the flat, pulling out drawers, looking under the rugs and in behind furniture. I was looking for evidence: a photograph of Chloe with her boyfriend. There was nothing. Chloe didn't even have a camera on her phone. Apart from all the photos of her mum she had around the place, there were no other pictures. I thought this was suspicious.

Chloe had said they were going out for lunch, but

they'd been gone for hours. She was probably with her dad right now on a plane back to America, where the sun always shone and powerful people got away with murder and left their naive accomplices to take the flak.

And then someone knocked on the door.

I didn't freeze. I sat quietly awaiting my fate. I hoped it was the police rather than Mahmood's people.

A voice out on the landing shouted, 'Alison!'

It was Ewan.

I went to the hallway and crept behind the door and listened.

'Alison, are you there?'

Ewan waited for me to open the door. Had he brought anyone with him? I couldn't hear anyone else. I heard him sigh and begin to move downstairs. I opened the door.

'Ewan?' I whispered.

He stopped on the stairs and came back up again. He was alone. When he saw me he made no move to hug or kiss me on both cheeks. He made no mention of my black and blue face. I couldn't look at him, I felt so ashamed.

'It's good to see you Ewan, take a seat.'

'I'm not staying.'

'Oh, OK.'

We stood awkwardly in the living room.

'Were you just passing by?'

'No, I was at my work,' he growled.

'No, I mean, is that why you're here?'

'I'm here because you phoned me.'

'Right.'

'What is it you want from me, Alison?'

'Nothing. I don't want anything, I just want to . . . Could you pick up the dogs from Josep's?'

'Alison, I don't have time for this. I didn't come round here to run bloody errands.'

'Well, why did you come?'

'I'm wondering that myself.'

'Did Chloe tell you I was in hospital?'

'Yes,' he said and turned to walk out.

'Don't go, Ewan, please.'

'D'you want me to get your dogs or don't you?'

'Eh, yes. Yes please.'

He was back with the dogs within ten minutes. Juegita and the pups ran around madly, delighted to be home again.

'Thanks very much, that was good of you.'

'I don't know why you couldn't have gone for them yourself; it's only at the bottom of the street.'

'I can't, Ewan, I can't . . .'

'You can't what? Can't be arsed?'

He looked at me with such an expression of disgust I had to hide my face when I asked, 'Please, I need to know, have you heard about Sanj? What's happening?'

He lunged forward and peeled my hand off my face.

'So you're mixed up in this Sanj thing, are you? I might've known. The American bird, she got you into it, didn't she? That'll be why you've got a sore face. Well, you have no idea the trouble you're in. This is serious shit. Mahmood doesn't like people messing in his business. It's a lot of charlie. I've told you before, he's fucking dangerous. He doesn't piss about, d'you understand?'

When Ewan started shouting the dogs barked and jumped at him, trying to protect me.

'I'm sorry, but I warned you. You're just a stupid wee lassie from Cumbernauld. You're way out of your depth here, with people you can't begin to understand. I'd thought maybe you and me . . .' he tailed off. 'Och, I can't do this. I'm sorry, Alison, cheerio.'

He walked out and banged the door behind him.

I tried to calm the dogs. I got their food bowls out and filled them. They were gobbling the food as quickly as I could put it out, Josep obviously hadn't fed them properly, and as I was refilling the bowls there was another knock at the door.

I listened.

'Alison!'

Ewan again, he'd come back. He'd said some horrible things, but at least he'd realized how much I needed him. He would help me get out of this mess, he was a good guy after all, I always knew he was. This time as I opened the door he rushed at me, but it wasn't Ewan.

Chapter 49

Before I knew what was happening there was a knife at my throat and I was being dragged by the hair around the flat. Juegita growled and barked. Whoever it was kicked Juegita when she tried to jump on him; the pups yelped but stayed at a distance. He seemed to be checking that there was no one else in the flat and led me into every room, Juegita and pups following as we went. In the kitchen he closed the door and trapped the dogs there before shoving me into the living room. At the front door I'd only got a brief glance, but once I was thrown back on the sofa I knew him, no doubt about it.

It was Sanj.

He was alive, his face was ugly and swollen like a Halloween lantern but he was very much alive and threatening to slit my throat. I didn't know whether to laugh or cry.

'Oh Sanj, I'm so glad you're OK. I'm sorry for what we did; it all got out of hand. Sorry, *muchas* sorry.'

'¡*Dame la coca!*' he screamed.

And now it all became clear to me: *coca*, cocaine. Charlie, Ewan had said. I'd thought he'd meant my brother Charlie. He'd been talking about cocaine, of course, Sanj's cocaine, or more specifically, Mahmood's. The bag of coke in Sanj's kitchen cupboard, Chloe must have taken it. She must have stuffed it in her bag while I was punching seven shades of shite out of Sanj. But he was alive. This changed everything.

I wasn't a murderer after all, the police weren't after me. I didn't have to stay in the flat, except that now, with the point of Sanj's knife pressing on my throat, I kind of did.

'¿Dónde están las drogas? ¡Dame las! ¡Yo voy a matarte!'

I couldn't be a hundred per cent certain, but I was pretty sure that what he was saying was something along the lines of: where are the drugs, give me the drugs, I'm going to kill you.

'I don't know. Honestly, I don't.' I held my hands out in an I-wish-I-could-be-more-helpful gesture, but this did not help. Sanj pressed the knife closer.

'Chloe took it, mi amiga Chloe took your coca!'

Sanj's rage turned to despair. He looked dumbfounded, like he didn't know what to do now. Maybe Uncle Mahmood was going to kill him if he didn't get the coke back. Sanj was desperate, maybe capable of desperate things.

'¿Dónde está Chloe?'

'She left, she went out with her dad, they went for lunch but that was hours ago, I don't know if they're coming back.'

I could see that he didn't understand but I didn't know the Spanish words, so I kept saying the same thing.

'She's gone, I don't know if she's coming back.'

'¡Dame la coca, buscala!' he shouted at me, pulling me off the couch on to my knees. He pushed my head under the coffee table and then I understood that he wanted me to search for it.

I'd already searched the flat earlier, I hadn't found any cocaine, but I was in no position to argue. I went through the motions of looking everywhere I could think of. The knife was hampering the search. It was hard to get Sanj to understand I wasn't trying to escape, that I was trying to lead him to the next place to look. Leaning into the back of the bedroom cupboard was tricky and required trust on both sides, Sanj trusting me that I wasn't reaching for a weapon and me trusting him that he wouldn't panic and push the blade into my neck.

At the same moment we both heard it. Sanj pulled me in front of him. There was someone at the front door. Keys jangled in the lock.

Chapter 50

Sanj held me tight from behind, the knife blade resting on my throat, a warning not to cry out as we both listened to someone enter and move around the flat. In the kitchen the dogs were still barking, making it difficult to hear. It sounded like only one person, a light-footed person who knew their way around. If it was Chloe, where was her dad?

'Alison?'

Chloe walked into the bedroom.

Despite the strange scenario, her best friend held prisoner by a reputed dead man, Chloe showed no surprise.

'Hi, Sanj, you're looking well.'

She must have known he wasn't dead and yet she'd let me torture myself.

'¿Dónde está mi coca?' yelled Sanj, his battered face distorted with rage.

'I'm sorry, I have no idea what you're talking about.'

Sanj responded to this by swirling the weapon in front of my face before putting it back on my neck.

'Go ahead,' Chloe said, waving her arm to signify that if Sanj wished to sink it into my windpipe he should go for it.

'Chloe, don't wind him up. He's losing it, he could stab me, he's come close already, don't try to bluff him.'

'I'm not.'

There were a few issues I wanted to raise with Chloe, but right at that moment what was most pressing was that she didn't encourage Sanj to slit my throat.

'Chloe, please, talk to him in Spanish, calm him down. And for God's sake give him back his coke.'

Sanj was pushing me forward towards Chloe and screaming a torrent of Spanish, his voice high-pitched and hysterical.

'OK, OK. I'll give him it,' said Chloe, holding her hands up.

'Tell him! In Spanish!' I yelled.

'¡Vale, vale! ¡Venga, yo la tengo! Mira.'

This calmed him and she turned and walked out the bedroom. Sanj pushed me forward and we shuffled out into the hall, where Chloe was waiting.

She lunged at him, punching his already well-pummelled face and catching him under the chin. This winded him momentarily, but not long enough for him to let go of me. She grabbed his knife arm and did manage to pull it back six or seven inches from my neck, but as he shook her off his arm sprang back and the knife sliced through my skin. Suddenly I was watching my blood pour on to the floor and trying to catch my breath. The fighting ceased.

Nothing made sense. I was covered in blood, but when I tried to staunch the flow my neck felt intact.

'It's your ear, he's cut your ear,' Chloe said, pointing to a piece of pink flesh on the floor.

As we all looked down Sanj released his grip on me and grabbed Chloe in a headlock.

'*¿Dónde está mi coca?*' he screamed.

'OK, OK, I'm getting it!'

I picked up my piece of ear. They'd be able to sew it back on at the hospital, but I'd have to freeze it or something. Lucky the dogs were still in the kitchen, or one of them would have gobbled it up by now. Sanj and Chloe were shouting at each other. Maybe if I put it in milk. I had to do that right now.

They were screaming at each other and Sanj was shouting my name as he dragged Chloe through the living room, out the patio doors on to the terrace. He was shouting and gesturing and I had to go out there too. Reluctantly I followed and brought my ear.

When we got out there Sanj went on shouting at me, but I didn't understand what he wanted.

'The coke's in the chimney. He wants you to get it out.'

'Or what?' I asked.

'Or he'll cut my throat.'

I caught Sanj's eye and waved my arm magnanimously. 'Go ahead, Sanj, be my guest.'

'He won't do it. I've already invited him to kill me, he's chicken,' Chloe said sadly.

She was full of surprises. In a fast manoeuvre she grabbed Sanj's arm with both of hers. But she didn't push it away. Instead she lunged at it, trying to impale herself on the knife. I realized then what a mad bitch she truly was. I'd always known she was crazy, but I never thought she'd commit suicide just to get her own way. And she would have, if Sanj hadn't been stronger.

They tussled over the knife until eventually he managed to pull it out of her hands. He sprang away from her as if she was diseased.

Sanj rushed up the ladders to the chimney. Chloe

337

screamed as one by one he threw her four ceramic crowns on the terrace floor. She shrieked and sank her teeth into her own hand and danced short stomping steps.

'You filthy fucking bastard fucker!' she shrieked.

Sanj had torn off a poly bag that had been taped to the inside of the chimney. Still ten feet off the ground up the ladders, he checked the contents of the bag. At the same moment Chloe and I rushed to the bottom of the ladders, Chloe in an attempt to topple him, and me to stop her.

While I tried to pull her away Chloe heaved and kicked. I weighed more, I should have been stronger, but I wasn't a foam-mouthed lunatic like she was. We struggled and she managed to break loose from me. She rushed at the ladders and gave them a fierce push. I ran after her but it was too late. The ladders rocked from foot to foot and then shifted, sliding down the wall. We watched as Sanj plummeted through the air. As he fell he brought lots of mosaic pieces, a windfall of yellows and blues and greens all around us. His face hit the ground first, bursting his nose like a peach.

His right hip landed next, smashing into the terrace. Sanj lay twisted and groaning. Sobbing and howling, Chloe walked across the terrace to her toolbag and got out her hammer. She moved towards him and tried to bring it down on his head. I put my hands on her hips and pushed, throwing her off balance, and she missed her target. Still sobbing, she turned to come back. I was ready to run, to leave Sanj to his fate if she turned on me, but it was as if she didn't even see me. She was only interested in battering Sanj.

He was dragging himself along the terrace with his arms, but he wasn't moving fast enough. He wouldn't be able to get away from her. Screaming in pain, he rolled on to his side and pulled himself on to his feet. To give him a chance of escape I stood in Chloe's path, but she had lost interest in him. Sanj hobbled out the flat with his bag of cocaine as quickly as his smashed hip would carry him.

Chloe sat weeping, her legs splayed out in front of her like a rag doll, amongst the rubble. Without its fancy crowns the chimney looked like a ruined fairy-tale castle.

'He tried to hurt my chimney!' she wailed.

I waited until she'd stopped crying, which was quite a few minutes, before I spoke. I wanted her full attention.

'You're seriously bonkers, Chloe,' I said, 'you need locking up.'

'No I don't,' she smiled.

'I'm deadly serious, you're mentally ill, you need help. You would have killed him.'

'I knew you'd stop me,' she shrugged.

'Why is it my responsibility? I wasn't there to stop you when you murdered Bashed-Head Boy!'

Chloe giggled. 'You think I killed the boy in Raval?'

'I know you did. And not only did you murder him but you tried to set me up for it!'

'You're crazy,' she laughed.

'No, you're crazy, but you think you're very clever. You dragged me away from the scene and cleaned me up, trying to make me look guilty. You told me not to go to the police. Now I understand why: me covered in blood in front of all those witnesses and then running away. The police were bound to think it was me.'

Chloe held her hands up. 'Whoa, whoa, whoa. OK, first off I didn't murder anybody. And second: if I'd murdered him and framed you, why would I have you move in here with me?'

'I don't know. Guilty conscience?'

'But if I was a murderer I'd be kinda stupid to get involved with the chief suspect, wouldn't I? That might lead the police straight to me. Think about it, Alison, it doesn't make sense.'

'But nothing makes sense with you, Chloe. You let me think we'd murdered Sanj!'

'Did I *say* we'd murdered Sanj?'

'No, but you let me think it. I was going out of my mind. Did you think that was funny?'

'Come on, it was a little bit funny.'

'No, Chloe, it wasn't. It was really cruel.'

'You knew I did stuff like that. You knew from the start.'

'I knew you were cruel to Lisa and Lauren, but why me?'

Chloe didn't answer; instead she asked me a question.

'How did you get the dogs back from Josep?'

'What? Ewan picked them up.'

'Ah,' she said. 'See? I told you not to pick up the dogs. I knew Mahmood's people would be looking for us. That must be how Sanj found us, *Esmeralda*.'

She said the word Esmeralda in a teasing playful tone.

'And you hid my phone! You told me you lost it, you lied and I can prove it!'

'Honey, we've all lied. You stole my underwear, you even stole my money. Did I give you a hard time?'

'Chloe, this isn't a game. I can't take this any more. It's dangerous for me.'

'Oh yeah, that's right. Your heart attack,' she sneered.

'What about my heart attack?'

She smirked.

'Are you saying you made that up? I saw the report from the hospital. It said a heart attack.'

'Whatever.'

340

'Chloe, please. Stop fucking with me. This is important. Please just tell me the truth now. I won't mind if you lied, but it's really important that I know the truth. Did I have a heart attack?'

'And you won't be mad with me?'

'No,' I said, tasting the bile in my throat, 'I won't be mad with you.'

'You didn't have a heart attack. It seemed like you wanted to have a heart attack. I made 'em do all the tests, but no, you didn't.'

I kept my voice calm.

'And college? We were going to go to Berkeley, weren't we?'

'That was why you stayed with me, wasn't it? That was what you wanted.'

'Just tell the truth, Chloe.'

'No, *you* tell the truth! That was why you stayed with me, wasn't it?'

Without hesitation I replied.

'Yes.'

She didn't answer my question immediately. She didn't have to. I knew now that going to college in the States was never going to happen. It had just been another hook in my mouth.

'Probably not,' she said wistfully. 'Maybe sometime, but I wasn't sure. I didn't know if I could trust you.'

'So you were testing me.'

'Yeah, I suppose.'

'Telling me I'd had a heart attack and letting me think I'd murdered Sanj; that was your way of testing our friendship?'

'Hey, it's not my bad if you're paranoid. You're free to think whatever you want. We have fun, don't we?'

'No, Chloe, we don't,' I said.

'Now who's not telling the truth?'

'You call this fun? You're dangerous, Chloe! You've used me; you've made me fucking miserable. Can you not see what you've done?'

'But it's fine now, isn't it? Your heart's a-pumping. Sanj is alive and well and, thanks to you, he's got his coke back. Juegita and the pups are home. No harm no foul, huh?'

She was right. Everything was back to normal, but when she mentioned my heart a-pumping it began to pump faster and faster.

'You don't even care what you've done to me, what you've put me through. The only thing you care about is that fucking chimney.'

Adrenalin flooded my system and tingled in my spine. With every breath I took I felt my body fill up with rage. I was a balloon filled to bursting point.

'Give me that,' said Chloe, taking the piece of my ear from me. 'I'll put it in the freezer. We'll need to put antiseptic on the wound.'

When she came back she stood with the TCP in her hand, open-mouthed at what I'd done.

'Now do you get it, Chloe?' I yelled. 'Now d'you see how much you've hurt me? This is the only way to get through to you!'

I bashed the hammer again into the crack I'd made in the chimney. The tiles had come off and I was through the plaster to the bare bricks.

Chloe ran at me and delivered a flying kick. She missed completely and fell back. I hit into the chimney again, the force of the hammer-blow making the muscles in my arm quiver.

'See? It's not funny now, is it?' I screamed as she scrambled to her feet.

She jumped on my back and put her arm around my neck, trying to choke me. She couldn't stop my arm without releasing her chokehold, and I managed to land another two blows to her precious chimney before she pulled me over and threw me to the ground. My arm was weak with hitting the chimney, and it was easy for her to take the hammer from me. She lifted it out of my hand and held it above me.

Everything went dark. The event I had spent my life waiting for, the sensation I had anticipated so many times, was here. I was dying. It was dark and there was pain, but inside the pain, at the very root, there was bliss. In the dark, the pain and the bliss were so intense they merged and made a euphoric excruciating high-pitched buzz. A flatline. A flatline that stretched on and on without end.

It didn't last.

The bliss was the first to go.

My head hurt, my arms and legs too. I couldn't move. I was weighed down by something soft and something hard. The soft thing was Chloe's body, which lay motionless on top of me. The hard thing, that held us both down, was the crushing weight of the collapsed chimney.

Epilogue

It's not that I'm scared of going to hospital. It's pain and sickness and knives slicing through my skin that worry me. You of all people must be able to understand that.

It's not just the surgery, it's the shape I'm going to be in afterwards: swelling, scarring, bits popping out or dropping off. OK, maybe not dropping off exactly, but you know what I mean. It's gonna do ugly things to my body, that's for damn sure. My legs are already getting criss-crossed with blue veins. I look like one of those three-dimensional road maps of California they sell in truck stops.

Of course Aged P is delighted, you know what he's like. This is exactly where he'd like to have me: flat on my back, under his control. D'you know he even had the gynaecologists gang up on me? They told me I'm 'elderly *prima gravida*'. Elderly! How can thirty-four be elderly?

I'm still a kid. I'm more of a kid than you are. Sure, I have Botox, but think about it: I get a lot more exercise than you do and my diet is way healthier. But even though I'm fresh and lovely on the outside, my insides are officially elderly. It's not fair.

P wants to hire a team of nannies to look after 'the

little man', as he's calling it. I said knock yourself out. The fewer diapers I have to deal with the better. Oh, and wait till you hear this: he asked when the baby comes if I could please stop calling him Aged P. He doesn't want the kid to grow up hearing it. OK, he's kept in shape, he still looks pretty good naked and, sorry, I know this is a bit gross but it has to be said, he's no slouch in the sack either, but he's sixty-six with a serious heart condition, I mean, that seems pretty damn aged to me. If I'm elderly, he's gotta be aged. But it gets worse: he started on again about me giving up work. I told him no deal. I didn't spend four shitty years at college to give up everything because a kid comes along.

Remember how excited we used to get talking about college? What a let-down that was. I wasn't cut out for medicine. One sick person in my life is plenty for me. If P hadn't got me switched to corporate accountancy I would've dropped out. And we never did do that frat-party stuff, did we? The other students didn't get my Scottish accent and they were just so cliquey. The social life was juvenile anyway, sad little cheese and wine parties hosted by the Phrenology Society or the Klingon Language Institute. Duh, no thanks. That was when I first got a therapist, d'you remember? She still goes on about my trust issues. It's probably true; I think I do have trust issues but I've got you to thank for that. Actually, having trust issues hasn't done me any harm. It was probably due to not making friends that I graduated top of my year. So thanks for that, Chloe.

If I hadn't done so well at college P might not have taken me into the company and I wouldn't be on the board right now. I know he said that he just needed someone on the board he could actually trust, but don't you think I'm the best person for the job? Believe me, I work hard, you know I do, but I don't think the other board members will ever accept me. Of course it's awkward, but I love my job so fuck them.

Oh, I knew there was something else I had to tell you! This morning I had a meeting with a private detective. When I say private detective you think 'gumshoe', don't you? But she was nothing like that. This detective is a woman, Miss Elizabeth Small. Apparently she's the best in the business. If it's done nothing else, accountancy has helped me appreciate attention to detail, and Miss Small left no stone unturned. Honestly, you'd have been impressed. Oh yeah, her report was very interesting. Very interesteeng, Meester Bond.

There was a copy of a twelve-year-old newspaper article, with a translation from Catalan to English. It was an account of an incident in an apartment block at 15 Calle Hierba, Raval, in Barcelona. Ring any bells, Chloe? Fifteen Calle Hierba was the apartment block I'd just run out of when you first met me, remember?

A young man, William Fenton, age nineteen, a US citizen, fell to his death over a banister. William Fenton, was he the one you were going to Vietnam with? Was he your boyfriend, Chloe? He was, wasn't he? The report said William Fenton was a student visiting Europe for the summer before returning to California to continue his studies. Everything was in the file: the police report, medical records, the autopsy. It was very detailed.

There was a pretty gory account of the location and severity of William Fenton's wounds, an analysis of the alcohol and drug levels in his blood, and a list of the contents of his stomach. There was a lot of boring technical data I didn't understand so I skimmed through to the summary and conclusions, which I'm sure you're as keen to know as I was.

Well, apparently William Fenton's wounds were consistent with a fall of twenty metres. There was no evidence in the form of contusions or otherwise to suggest that he had been coerced or pushed. He had drugs in his bloodstream but these were found to be prescribed medication. On further investigation his medical records showed that he'd been diagnosed with labyrinthitis, a condition of the inner ear affecting balance, the chief symptom of which is dizziness. The autopsy report concluded that William Fenton had most probably suffered a dizzy spell and fallen over the banister.

Most probably, that's what it said, but we know different, don't we, Chloe? Don't we, Chloe? Did you know he had labyrinthitis? Oh, you're a slippery one. Miss Small, the finest detective money can buy, and even she can't catch you out. It's OK. I don't mind if you pushed him, really I don't. It's just that I'd like to know. I wasn't trying to get you into trouble; I only wanted to close the book on Bashed-Head Boy, but you're never going to crack, are you?

The company is giving Philip a dinner, a Goodbye, Good luck and Thanks for everything, as he calls it. He's promised that this'll be the last of the retirement parties, thank God. I don't mind this one so much; he's going to announce his successor. That'll be fun, seeing all their wrinkly old faces.

I've come a long way. Who would have thought that a wee heifer like me from Cumbernauld would end up running one of the top US companies? I know I'm lucky, more than lucky, I suppose: blessed. Just think of all the crazy dangerous things that have happened and yet I've always come out OK. Spooky, isn't it? It's as though I've had an angel watching over me.

The very first time I saw you I thought you were an angel. In those first weeks in Barcelona, when you shared your apartment with me, brushed my hair and looked after me; when you lay softly snoring on the pillow beside me, you were like a beautiful angel.

But let's face it, Chloe, you were out of control. That childish nihilism couldn't last; you wouldn't have got away with it for ever. You'd have ended up on a murder charge. Your inheritance couldn't have bought you out of that. You'd have spent years in some Catalan prison, or worse, back in the US on death row with only Philip to visit you, pitying you through the bars.

When the chimney fell on us I thought I was dying. I thought we were going to die together. I didn't mind, it meant we'd be together in the afterlife and when we met my dad, you'd kick his balls.

It was a weird thing to happen, the chimney falling on us, but I guess it was to be expected: all that rain and all, all that unbalanced weight. The first thing I remember was the weight shifting above me, bricks and rubble, and your weight on top of me. When I dug out to the light there was blood pouring from between your legs and your body was twisted like a broken Barbie doll or something. 'Flail chest' they said it was. The top half of your body was facing the opposite direction from your bottom half, it was totally gross.

I suppose your body saved me from the worst of the damage. But that's only fair, isn't it? After all, you started it. You tried to smash my head in with a hammer. If the chimney hadn't fallen on us you might have killed me, d'you ever think of that?

Oh yeah, and who got us out of it? Who clawed us both out of the rubble with her bare hands? Who crawled across the terrace and called the ambulance? That would be me. *De nada*. My pleasure. Alison Donaldson at your service.

You don't know this, but as soon as they'd plastered my wrist and strapped up my shoulder, I asked to be allowed to see you. I sat all night with P. We watched over you in the private room on the top floor of the hospital, sitting together in silence, the only noise the swish and bleep of your life-support machines. You were pretty messed up. It was horrible when they told us they had to amputate your arm. We both cried. For the next four weeks we took shifts sitting by your bed, talking to you, waiting for you to wake up. P called your mom dozens of times. She was busy with a new art installation down in Mexico. She sent flowers. I know you don't like hearing this, Chloe, but she's a fucking bitch.

While we were in Barcelona, P and I shared the apartment. He could have stayed at a hotel but he wanted to be near your things, he said it made him feel closer to you. Isn't that sweet? I didn't mind, we were rarely in the apartment at the same time. One of us was always at the hospital. A few times, when the doctors took you away to do more tests, P and I would eat together in the hospital restaurant. My wrist was still in plaster and P cut up my food for me. Four weeks later, when you were well enough to travel, we transferred to St Bartholomew's in Los Angeles, where, again, we sat by you while the doctors went through all the neurological tests.

It took for ever but eventually they let us take you home. We rub along all right, don't we, Chloe? I know you miss P and me when we're at work, but the nurses keep you company. Come on, be fair, even when I'm rushed off my feet I make time to pop your aspirator in your mouth and tell you about my day, don't I? What am I doing right now? I know that crying is part of your condition but it's pretty upsetting for us, Chloe. Things were better before they changed your medication, when you dozed all the time. My dozy little Bashed-Head Girl. I'm going to ask the doctor to change it back. I can't bear to see you crying like this.

Cheer up, we still have fun, don't we? What about last week when Phil went to London? I knew you'd like that new night nurse, James. He's pretty tasty, isn't he? He's a great kisser. Although I think it freaked him out when I held your hand. He thought it was just going to be me and him. James said what we were doing was sick, but I could see he got pretty excited when I opened your nightie. You've still got great tits.

I saw James at the case meeting after that. I winked at him and that freaked him out too, so I don't think we've anything to worry about, he's not going to tell. Maybe James and I'll put on another show for you next time P is out of town. You'd like that, wouldn't you? You dirrrty girl.

These case meetings annoy me, they always put P on a downer for weeks and you know how boring he is when he's like that. As usual, the doctors had no good news. I don't know why we bother. It's always the same story: core brain damage is irreparable, unresponsive to functional neuromuscular stimulation, locked-in syndrome, blah blah blah. And when we ask they always say that most probably you'll stay locked in for the rest of your life.

Most probably.

They suggested, again, a resolution: a muscle relaxant. You'll be so relaxed you'll stop breathing. You won't suffer. Don't worry, we told them it's not an option. P said he'll fire every one of them if they ever suggest it again. You're part of this family, Chloe, and we want you with us.

Old Aged P is almost as stubborn as you. Look how long it took for him to name me executor of your estate. P knows as well as I do the tax benefits of doing it this way. I don't know why he resisted so long, he's just mean I guess. But now that I'm carrying his baby – your little brother – he can't deny me anything.

When we found out I was pregnant P was keen to tell you right away. I think he thought the shock of it might snap you out of your locked-in syndrome, that you might suddenly come to your senses and throw a hissy fit like in the good old days, but of course you cried. It's the only thing you can do.

I don't think you'll ever have a hissy fit again, but I suppose we've both changed. I'm not the fat stupid Scottish girl I was. Haven't you noticed? I don't even have a Scottish accent any more. Sometimes I wish the chimney had never fallen on us, that we had gone to college together like we were supposed to. You'd probably be a famous artist by now. But you wouldn't have wanted P and me getting together, and you absolutely hate that I'm the executor of your estate. I know you do, I can see it in your eyes. But lighten up, eh? We're family now, as well as being best friends. We've been through so much together. I have you to thank for all the good things in my life. It kills me to see you like this. We have to face the facts: aged P is sixty-six, he's old and ill, he won't be around for ever. But we'll still have each other. I'll never leave you, Chloe, I promise. And I know you'll never leave me. Pretty much the only good thing about your locked-in condition is that, whatever else might happen, I'll always have you with me, my Chloe, my angel.

THE END